THEN COMES A DRIFTER

The Drifter Duology
Book One

C. M. Banschbach

Uncommon Universes Press LLC
1052 Cherry St.
Danville, PA 17821
www.uncommonuniverses.com

This is a work of fiction. Names, characters, businesses, places, events, and incidents are either the products of the author's imagination or used in a fictitious manner. Any resemblance to actual persons, living or dead, or actual events is purely coincidental.

Editing: Katie Phillips and A. C. Williams
Proofreading: Hannah Wilson
Formatting: Sarah Delena White

Cover Design: E. A. H. Creative Design

ISBN-13: 978-1-948896-40-5

To Monica

For loving Dayo first, and not being afraid to walk your own path.

CHAPTER ONE

Another day, another town.

Laramie brushed dirt from her olive-green jacket and loosened the dust scarf around her neck. The sun beat down mercilessly, reflected back up from the asphalt in endless dancing waves. She adjusted the sunglasses on her nose—those scarcely doing an adequate job of cutting the glare from the tired whitewashed buildings lining the main street.

A weather-beaten man, barely of middle years, but aged more by the sun, appraised her motorcycle from his seat outside the gas station.

"Nice bike." He tipped his head in a quick greeting.

She swallowed to clear the grit from the back corners of her mouth where even the dust scarf hadn't kept it out. "Thanks." She swung her leg over the seat and stood, arching her back ever so slightly to stretch out the cramped muscles after having ridden for three straight hours along the lonely desert highway.

"Fill her up?"

Laramie nodded, peeling away leather gloves from sweaty fingers. She liked the people in small towns like these, different from the bigger cities back east. They never wasted time on excess words.

She dug out a water bottle from the left saddlebag and took a long drink of warm water. The price listed above the pump made her frown. It had increased from the last town.

"Passing through?" The man leaned on the pump. His steady gaze took in the entire length of her tall frame from her calf-high boots and canvas trousers, the twin knives strapped to her thighs, the jacket, and finally the long, blonde braid coated in dust. She tapped a finger against the bottle, waiting for him to make it back around to her face.

"Might stay a few days. Looking for some work to get me to the next town," she said.

He squinted into the sun and spat carefully away from both their boots. "What kind of work?"

"Anything that needs fixing."

"Mechanic?"

She nodded.

"Any good?"

She lifted a shoulder. "I worked my way all the way over from Caldwell."

His jaw worked a moment before he spit again. He nodded slowly. "That's a fair ways away."

It was. Three hundred miles, four towns, and lots of empty desert to be exact.

"Any good with generators? I've got a cranky one out back."

"I can take a look in exchange for that gas."

The pump clicked and the man returned it to its holder, nodding his acceptance of the deal. Laramie took the handlebars and wheeled the bike after her new employer.

He gestured at the few feet of shade alongside the building, and she left her bike there. The generator rested a few feet away, a block of machinery sputtering and grumbling from its place along the wall.

Laramie flipped open the saddlebag hanging off the right side of the motorcycle. Her leather toolkit lay on top, embossed with her name. She smiled every time she saw it. A gift from Kayin before she'd left weeks ago. Something to help her remember him out on the road. Like she really needed any help.

She unzipped her jacket and shrugged out of it, leaving it across the bike's seat, and rolled up the sleeves of her thin green shirt. A slight breeze curled around the gas station's corner, wicking away sweat from her neck and kicking up more of the never-ending sandy dirt to skitter around her boots.

She squatted by the generator and opened the paneling. The man stood back, arms across his chest, watching as she poked around the machine's workings.

"Looks like your carburetor is clogged up, and you've got a couple of fried coils here in the back. Had a big surge recently?"

Another stream of spit left a swiftly evaporating mark on the concrete. "Lightning strike a few days ago. I've got a couple spares, I think. Or might have to go down to Jackson's place to get some."

She sat back on her heels as he went inside. Bits and pieces of junk littered the concrete behind the station, all hemmed in by a rusty chain link fence. A water tower was visible from her vantage point, faded black lettering declaring Talbott "The friendliest town this side of the Anthis Valley."

It's probably the only town this side of the Anthis Valley. She used her dust scarf to wipe sweat from her forehead.

Scuffing announced a dog meandering its way from the station over to her, panting in a good-natured way. She ruffled its gray-streaked ears, earning a lick.

"Here you are." The man came back, holding two new coils.

It was the work of a few minutes to install them, and then she started in on the carburetor. The man settled back against the wall to watch, turning his head periodically to spit away from her.

Laramie propped her sunglasses up on her head and ditched the dust scarf.

"Been drifting long?" he asked.

"A few years." She took the grease rag he handed down and wiped her fingers before reaching back into the machine.

He pondered this in silence. She waited for the follow-up most people seemed surprised to announce.

"Seem a bit young to be drifting the lower country."

Laramie lifted a shoulder. "Most people just want something fixed."

He nodded. "And I guess those help with all that."

She tilted her head up in confusion, until he tipped his chin at her. Understanding flashed. Her eyes. Gray with small drops of blue scattered in the iris—bits of magic still clinging to her blood, telling the world she still had a knack for her people's old skill with building and mechanical things.

"Itan, aren't you?"

"Last I checked." She smiled, though the real answer was more complicated than that. Her eyes and hair said yes, but her heart and mind hadn't really been for a long time.

A few more minutes' uninterrupted work finished off the carburetor. She closed the paneling and flipped the generator on. It started up with a steady hum.

"You know you'd do better with a harnesser." She pushed back up to her feet.

The man shrugged. "I've got the gas, so I don't concern myself much with the lightning. Some other folks round here use it on the rare occasion we get some strikes."

Laramie wiped her hands on the rag and shoved it in her back pocket as she put away the tools. Maybe she'd be able to find some more work around. Dust always gunked up the harnessers and most folks didn't know the best way to clean them out.

Though to be fair, no one really knew how the harnessers even worked. They were remnants from the days when magic and science collided to gather and transform lightning for use. She'd been lucky enough to figure out how to open one up and poke around inside to get it running again on its mystery power source.

The man frowned down at the generator. "All right. Guess you earned yourself that gas. I'll spread the word around. You might head up the road and drop word yourself at the store if you're looking to stay a few days. Always something around here that needs fixin'."

Laramie nodded and stuck out her hand. Calloused palm met calloused palm and they parted ways. She wheeled her bike back around to the station lot and settled onto the leather seat. The engine came to life with the comforting roar that always managed to still the itch in her feet for a little while.

The station manager pointed her up the road with a last wave and she waited for a truck to rattle past before pulling out.

Worn speed signs warned of radar enforcement, but towns that size rarely had more than two officers. A cross street later, long stretches of connected buildings stood tall on either side of the road. Wooden awnings stretched over the sidewalks, providing some shelter from the sun.

Pharmacy, salon, two bars, clothing store, post office, then general market store. She guessed at the faded parking lines and idled to a stop, tucking keys into her pocket. More signs of life stirred in the stores, hurrying along sidewalks to get out of the heat, driving along the road behind her in dust-beaten trucks and cars.

Some looked curiously back, others ignored her, intent on their own business. But the whole town would know she'd been there in the next hour. That part was just good for business.

She propped her sunglasses up onto her head as she pushed open the door and stepped into the artificial coolness of the store.

Ordered aisles, a flickering light in the back corner, never-ending dust clinging to the baseboards by the door. It looked like every other store west of the crumbling towers where the green hills gave way to ragged brush and dried riverbeds.

"Help you, stranger?" a cheery voice called.

An older woman who'd earned her age in spite of the sun made her way over from the baked goods display. Her nametag introduced her as Mollie.

Laramie returned her smile. "Yeah, need some travel packs, and wouldn't turn down a recommendation for the best place to get a meal around here."

Mollie laughed. "Travel packs back this way." She gestured over her shoulder.

Laramie followed, grabbing a chocolate bar from a shelf as she passed. She'd have to eat it before leaving town, or else it'd melt all over her saddlebag. She'd learned that the hard way when she'd first started crisscrossing the lower country three years ago.

"How many you need?"

"How far to Danton?" Laramie countered.

"On your bike? About two days. But you'll hit Arrow and Ceasefire between here and there."

9

"Five, just to be on the safe side, then."

Mollie grabbed five packs from the shelf, the thick brown paper crinkling under her hands. Neat type spelled out the different items in each pack—dried meat, hydration packs, thin cans of vegetables, and an extra nutrient bar.

They made for boring meals on the road, but lasted longer than anything else she could buy. One of these days she'd figure out how to rig a cooling system in one of her bags.

She trailed Mollie back to the register, snagging a few more items on her way. Mollie rang her up and Laramie handed over the neatly pressed bills that resided deep in her wallet.

"You the one that's looking for work around here?"

Laramie arched an eyebrow. It had taken maybe five minutes to drive down from the gas station.

"Yeah. Need anything?"

"Not right now, but I know the Dunstans were needing some help out at their place. They probably have some extra space for you if you need."

"Thanks." Laramie flashed a smile. She gathered up her purchases and stepped back outside, nudging her glasses back down.

She held a short debate with herself as she stored the packs in her saddlebags. The post office was next door. They usually doubled as record keepers and courthouses when circuit judges drove through. Best just ask before she got too busy.

The office clerk popped his boots down off the counter when she walked in.

"Help you?" He leaned on the counter.

"Looking for some records on a family." She carefully dug out the photo from the inside jacket pocket. She'd put it in a protective covering a long time ago to preserve the edges worn from sleepless, tearful nights.

"Name's on the back." Hesitation slowed her hand. She always hated handing it over, even for a few minutes. Like somehow it would vanish in the wind and the dust for the short time it spent in someone else's hands.

The clerk turned it over. "Sol ... Solfee..." He drew his head back, brow scrunching in effort.

"Solfeggietto," she supplied.

"That's a mouthful. What is that? Upper country tribe?"

"Itan." The word rolled from her mouth with a little bit of pride. Even after all these years.

His mouth pursed at the corners as he nodded. "Solfeggietto," he murmured softly under his breath, at least closer this time with the pronunciation.

"Doesn't sound familiar. Relations of yours?"

"Yeah. Folks in the picture passed away years ago, but I always check for any other relatives when I pass through towns. Just to see, you know?" She shifted, anxious to have the picture back.

He set it on the counter, face up. "I'll go check the records. Be back in a sec."

"Sure." Laramie pressed her fingers on the edge of the photo. A young couple stared up at her, laughter spilling out of every line on their faces as they wrapped arms around a young boy of about seven, and a girl of about five. The pigment had faded to a light brown at the edges, but all four of them had blond hair, the same gray eyes spotted with blue, and the anticipation that life was never going to be anything more than the clapboard house with roses under the windows and each other.

Hard to believe it had been sixteen years ago. She didn't remember the day the picture was taken, didn't remember the

softer sun of the upper country above the Rift, and barely remembered the sweetness of the summer roses and the melons
growing on trailing vines in the garden boxes out back.

"Sorry. Nothing on that name, or even on any other Itans in
the area." The clerk returned, his mouth still twisted down, this
time in regret.

Laramie tucked the photo away. "It's okay."

There were never any records. And all of the Itan settlements
on either side of the Rift had been wiped out a long time ago by
Tlengin raiders. In the three hundred years since the Itan had
migrated to Natux to build the river bridges across the Rift, they'd
still not ventured far from their own people. It had been a long
time since she'd run into another Itan.

"Though." He leaned on the counter again, tapping his chin
as if debating his next words. "I did see a passing note about a
small group of Itan heading west to the Christan Mountains a
few years back.

Her heart leaped at the first solid lead she'd gotten in years.

"But those are the far border of Rosche's territory." He shook
his head as if giving up on the possibility of her finding a way
there. "They might not have even made it through."

Laramie caught the corner of her bottom lip under her teeth.
She'd heard rumors of Rosche, even back east. His name became
more common in the desert as she'd kept traveling west. A self-
styled baron—more like warlord—who'd carved out a massive
territory for himself ten years ago.

He controlled most of the oil in the western territories of the
lower country. Not even the current governor-general bothered
with him. Just adjusted the map borders to exclude him from
the more civilized areas, and tried to negotiate a price slightly less

than exorbitant on the oil and gas exported from his territories.

"Got a map?" she asked.

The clerk raised his eyebrow again, but headed to the back wall and pulled a neatly folded square from a drawer. He spread it out on the counter.

"Here's us." He pointed to a dot near the middle of the desert. The Anthis Valley cut a wide swath to the east. She could walk her fingers from the valley to the Christan Mountains in two steps, cutting her way west across Rosche's territory without a problem. She leaned on the counter.

"I'd planned to cut up north to Danton." The town settled closer to the Rift—a gaping chasm torn across the width of the continent between the upper and lower countries. On the way around back home.

"Mountains are out of your way then."

Laramie nodded. She'd be heading straight west, instead of north and a little east. But if there was a chance of finding more Itan, that meant maybe finding some blood relatives. It might be worth the risk.

She smoothed a crease to better study the territory on the other side of the mountains. More desert turned to canyons that eventually emptied rivers into fertile lands. She'd never been that far. No one she knew had.

"That a traveler band?" the clerk asked, nodding to her wrist.

She followed his look down to the braided leather cord wrapping three times around her left wrist. Red, brown, and blue. The colors of her traveler family.

"Yeah."

"Bit light for a traveler, aren't you?" This time both eyebrows raised.

She forced a smile through the ire that flickered. True, she stood out against the black-skinned Aclar travelers with her lighter Itan skin. But it didn't make them any less a family together.

"Adopted in. Lost my birth family to Tlengin raiders when I was a kid. Travelers took me in." They were the family she remembered the most.

"Sorry. That's a bad business." The clerk shook his head. "About the only good thing about Rosche is he wiped most of the Tlengin out a few years back."

"Can't be too upset about that." Laramie nudged the map back toward him.

He began to fold it back up. "Really thinking about heading that way?"

She shrugged. Rosche's territory expanded north where the desert heaved itself up into a caprock and rugged hills before they tumbled off into the Rift. And too far south where unrest still simmered between Natux and Cricea. The only way to the mountains would be across.

"I don't know. I've got a few other places I'm planning to go around here. Maybe they'll turn up something."

Although once she finished her circuit up to Danton, the mountains would be the last place in the lower country she hadn't yet looked. Her last chance to find some Itan.

The clerk's face melded into something serious and intense. "Please be careful. I'd hate to think of you disappearing into that territory. Those stories don't even get told around campfires at night."

Her hand fell to the knife on her left thigh. "Thanks for the warning. And thanks for checking."

His face immediately lightened. "Sorry I couldn't turn anything up for you."

"No worries. You gave me a lead though. I appreciate it." She rapped her knuckles against the counter as she pushed away.

"Safe travels. And I mean it about Rosche's territory!" he called after her.

Laramie half turned to give a wave of acknowledgement and pushed back out into the sunshine. She stood a minute on the sidewalk, hands on hips, debating.

She had supplies. There were at least three more towns along the western highway she could work through to get the supplies she needed to cut west.

Leave now?

Her fingers fell to the braided cord around her wrist, twisting it around and around. She'd promised she'd meet back up with the family by autumn. They'd be up at the eastern river bridges by then, ready to camp out for the winter among the more forgiving hills.

Summer was on the wane, though the days still burned hot under the unforgiving sun. It'd be a tight run, if she could make it into the territory without being found. And then hunting down more rumors of an Itan settlement, if it even existed.

Maybe she'd send a message to Ade and let her know what she'd found. That she'd probably be late to the winter camp-grounds. Ade would understand. The woman had raised her since they'd found her in the burnt husk of a building after the raiders swept through her town.

Her motorcycle rumbled to life. She kicked the stand up and settled her scarf more securely around her neck. She pushed back-ward onto the road and propped boots up on the pegs. Dusty wind stirred the loose bits of blonde hair long fallen from her braid.

Ade always laughed and said not even the travelers had given Laramie the itch to roam. She'd had that all along. Drifter was in her blood. She was born to ride the wilds, searching for something that she never could explain.

She left town in a roar of dust, headed west.

Maybe this time, she might find it.

CHAPTER TWO

Forget the cooler system. I'm going to invent better travel packs.
Laramie peeled off a strip of meat and attempted to chew it into submission. For the number of times she vowed that while sitting on a tarp somewhere on the side of the road, she still hadn't done it.

Maybe because she couldn't figure out how to bottle the taste of chicken roasted over an open flame. The scent of corn and potatoes steaming in their wrappings among the coals. The sweet and spicy tang of the seasoning the Aclar travelers rubbed over anything they ate. The spice brought life to everything except travel packs.

She sighed, brushing dirt from her trousers. The red dirt was everywhere, underlying the finer top layer of grittier sand. It peeked out from the roots of the mesquite bushes and cacti littering either side of the highway. It brazenly draped itself along exposed hillsides, competing with the rough red and gray rock thrusting from the earth to create miniature hills and gorges that broke up the deceptively flat landscape.

The gorges were empty of water, but come a sporadic rainstorm, they'd be filled with life-giving runoff to turn the red and gray and brown into a lush green landscape teeming with the life that usually hid away from the sun.

She leaned against the rough wall of the derelict tower perched atop one of the rocky hillsides overlooking the highway. The smooth, keyless door hadn't yielded to her touch. They never did, though she always like to try. They were sealed by the magic that had fled over three hundred years ago when the Rifts mysteriously opened up across every continent. Maybe she didn't have the right kind of magic.

With magic draining from the land and the people, the towers had been left to ruin. They stood like silent sentinels, slowly crumbling in on themselves as if in despair that only hints of magic remained, lurking as spots of colors in someone's eyes. Reminders of the civilization which had fallen to ruin when the magic left.

Laramie pushed her sunglasses up to the top of her head. The bits of blue in her gray eyes were only enough to instill in her a knack for machinery and building—a gift left over from her Itan ancestors who were once the greatest architects and inventors before the Rifts.

Thunderclouds loomed to the northwest—lumbering gray giants huddled over the distant hills. They likely wouldn't make it as far as her little campsite, but she'd still cover everything with the waterproof tarp.

Lightning flickered, illuminating the edges of the clouds piling atop each other. Another strike spiked the ground. If anyone was lucky enough to live over there with a harnesser, they'd have a good harvest. If the machines were calibrated correctly, they could get a month's worth of energy off one or two strikes.

She'd read once the towers had been fueled by lightning, powering telescopes or boosting the magic of the Natuxian tower workers who once held mastery over the elements. Now, generations later, all that was left was the memory of how to catch the lightning as an additional power supply to oil and gasoline.

She shoved the rest of the bland meal back into the wrapper and stuffed it back into the saddlebags, exchanging it for a stiff leather tube. She carefully slid out a canister the length of her forearm. The contents flickered with bright white light—contained lightning she'd been able to siphon off from a harnesser.

Enough charge to last for a long ride. She returned it to the tube. It would attach to the engine in a specially modified space she'd made for it. The lightning could take over powering the engine, giving her an extra boost of speed without sacrificing the fuel that was already running low. She'd attach it and then refill the tank and spare gas can in town tomorrow before making her first big push west.

Rosche's borders lay half a day's ride away. His territory was big enough she might be able to sneak her way through. The town she'd passed through that morning said his gangs were always riding around, through the gas station attendant had put the numbers in the thousands.

She didn't care who Rosche was, there was no way he was supporting thousands of men. His territory wasn't that big.

Hundreds maybe, and even those numbers still gave her good enough odds of avoiding them on empty roads. She returned the canister to its place and laid out her knives and pistol on the tarp to clean.

Am I really going to do this? It was a risky move, going straight through known gang territory. And if he'd taken out the Tlengin, running into any of his riders would be bad news. Her knife scraped over the whetstone with a comforting rasp. The twin blades had seen her through plenty of trouble. And her pistol had gotten her through the rest.

She paused a moment, tapping the blade against her boot. It would be a long day's ride to the other side. One long day, or a week going around. She blamed the itch in her feet for the whispers saying she should risk it. That it had been too long since she'd ridden on pure adrenaline.

Ade would kill me. The traveler woman had raised her, taught her to ride. Lekan had taught her to fight, and Temi how to coax machines to do her will. And Kayin? Kayin had stolen her heart from the moment he'd backed her in a race without question.

Kayin would be right beside me. A smile toyed at her mouth. It had been too many weeks since she'd seen him. Kissed him under the wide sky. Wrapped her arms around him as they swayed to the music of the guitars around the open campfires.

The only reason he wasn't there was the traveler family needed him. *I don't deserve how he waits for me to come back over and over.* She always swore that one of these days she'd settle back in with the travelers, but the drifter itch couldn't be stilled even with their migratory lifestyle.

But—her gaze fell to the west where the setting sun had flung purples, flaming reds, and yellows against the sky and turned the storm clouds a deeper gray—she had a feeling that whatever she was looking for might be across those mountains. She sheathed the knife with a snap. Her heart whispered that every time, and she'd yet to find it. *Maybe I'm just doomed to wander forever, searching for … whatever it is I'm looking for.*

"Or maybe, I'm just being melodramatic," she told the scrub brush huddled close to the ground.

It didn't answer, but a deep coughing roar came from somewhere over the hills already covered in deep shadow. Her hand fell to her pistol. It sounded like a jacklion, and knives wouldn't do much good against the large tawny beasts.

Laramie pushed to her feet, turning a slow sweep around her campsite, looking for any telltale shadow of a stalking predator. The solitary creatures were common enough out in the wilds between towns. She'd scared more than one off with a shot at their paws. For all their claws and teeth, they were skittish and easily intimidated.

Nothing stirred. Keeping the gun in one hand, she dug into her saddlebag again, pulling out a slender canister she hung off the handlebars. A flip of the switch sent a fluorescent light popping and snapping before it steadied. The near-soundless frequency it emitted would keep any neighboring jacklion away.

Still, she stayed standing, gun at the ready for another ten minutes, making sure the creature hadn't decided to make its way over. Finally satisfied, she knelt back down, flipping out her bedroll. Her weapons stayed close as always. She'd woken up face to face with a red-scaled viper one time too many to make that mistake again.

Stars stretched out for miles above her, unhindered by artificial lights like some of the larger cities around whose outskirts the travelers would sometimes camp. She always got restless if she couldn't see the full sky.

Sleep took a little longer to claim her due to the possibility of a jacklion still out beyond the hills. But the coughing grumble never came again, and the gentle noises of the nocturnal scavengers and the overhead rustle of the occasional nighthawk continued uninterrupted. Eventually she shut her eyes and tucked deeper into her bedroll to drown out even those noises and fell asleep.

CHAPTER THREE

This is it. Laramie pulled to a stop, setting one boot down on the hot asphalt. The only thing marking a change in the swirling dust and sun was the metal sign on the side of the highway, probably put up by some townsperson warning good folk not to go any further. She shifted her seat on the leather, already hot under the morning sun.

Nothing stirred ahead of her. Nothing moved behind her. No dust clouds, no shimmers of the sun on motorcycles. She swallowed a sudden dryness in her mouth. From what she'd been able to piece together from maps lingering in back drawers showing the territory from before Rosche's takeover and borders closing, the road cut straight through to the mountains.

Best estimates put it running right past the citadel he'd thrown up to house his gangs. There were a few smaller roads that would take her safely away and around from there. She could even cut cross country if she needed to. Her wide tires had held up to her minute inspection that morning, and she'd put her patching kit on the top of her saddlebags just in case she needed a quick stop.

She pulled the dust scarf up over her nose and mouth. The wind blustered stronger, kicking up more dust in swirling clouds that skittered over the ground. She checked her pistol in its holster in front of her right knee. But still she hesitated.

Last chance to turn around. Backtrack a few miles and take the highway up north and east instead.

But the empty highway and shimmering heat waves beckoned her in. Dared her to try to make it across.

Is it worth it to go across?

Maybe, the wind whispered back. The chance to find someone on the other side. The travelers were family, but Itan were her blood. It was a chance to maybe find a relative. Maybe find someone, *someone,* who could remember her parents for her.

She revved the engine, pushing off with her foot, moving forward before she could talk herself out of it.

No one jumped out from behind the closest hill. No motorcycles roared from the yawning gorge to her right. Only a few buzzards lazily turning on wind currents in the distance.

Her hands relaxed a fraction on the handlebars.

One hour passed.

Two hours.

She made a turnoff on the first highway intersection she came to, heading a little more south and west.

Midday came and went with a brief stop to refill the tank from the spare gas can tied on the back of the bike.

Then she saw it.

A stirring of dust in her left side mirror.

She swallowed hard and half turned, catching the glint of sunlight on something metal. Not a dustdevil.

Maybe devils riding the dust clouds toward her.

She shifted gears and coaxed another burst of speed. The dust fell behind, but only for a moment. It picked up speed. She did the same, but figures became visible through the dust, shadowed silhouettes in featureless helmets.

Laramie flipped a switch. A tremble ran through the bike as the booster took over, feeding converted lightning to the engine to push her faster, the yellow stripes on the road blurring together in one continuous streak.

The figures fell behind. But the flare of relief smothered itself.

Dust stirred to her right. Dread tightened deep in her stomach. Riders wove expertly across the rough terrain, angling toward her and the highway. She didn't dare shift again. One wrong move, one wrong breath, and she'd be a smear on the asphalt.

Closer and closer until the roar of their engines cut over hers as they kept making headway. The leaner build of their motorcycles boasted a more powerful engine than hers. Quick glances gave her a count of ten riders. Dark leather jackets, except for one in dull red. The glint of handguns in thigh holsters. Red helmets with a black stripe and some sort of emblem painted on the left side. The red-jacketed rider had a rifle strapped in front of the handlebars.

He wouldn't be able to use it at his current speed, but she didn't want to see what his range could be if he decided to stop.

Three riders cut behind her in a blur of movement. Flanked on all sides by faceless riders, she recklessly pushed for a bit more speed. The red-jacketed rider matched her speed, pulling up in front of her. She caught a brief glimpse of the front of his helmet as he checked his mirror. A dark plastic visor removed even the hint of a face.

Dust crept in under her scarf, choking her. Or maybe it was the sudden fear and gasoline fumes swirling around her.

Show you're just as tough as any rider out there, Ade's words echoed in. She began to slow down. The riders around her mimicked her.

Don't back down.

Slower and slower until she rumbled to a stop. The leader set a boot down, revving to turn his bike to block the road. Before she could even think to move, he had a handgun out and pointed at her head.

Engines idled around her, matching the throaty grumble of her bike. Gloved hands settled on weapons. She kept hers on the handles a moment longer, still trying to pick out some features behind the leader's helmet. Then, she unlatched her hands and sat straighter, lifting them in surrender.

He kicked his stand down and stood from the bike in a fluid motion. Keeping the gun raised and centered at her forehead, he stalked forward, as graceful as a desert cat. Pausing four steps away, he undid his helmet and pulled it off.

Sunglasses still obscured his eyes, but his jaw clenched in an unforgiving manner. Dark hair was cut close in a military style.

Rosche or a minion?

"What's your business here?" His voice came gruff and a little hoarse, like the helmet hadn't spared him the mouthfuls of grit clinging to her teeth.

She swallowed to dampen her mouth. "Just passing through."

A faint quirk disturbed the iron set of his features. Amusement or irritation, she wasn't sure.

"You miss the signs?" The long barrel of the gun didn't waver, but something shifted in his voice, like he was raising an eyebrow behind those glasses.

Laramie allowed a quick smirk. "No, I saw them. Still decided to take the shortcut."

This time, she did catch the eyebrow raising above the sunglasses. Movement rustled through the other riders, like they couldn't believe her answer either.

"Shortcut to where?"

"Other side of the Christan Mountains. Any chance you'd give me an escort?"

A quick humorless exhale broke from him, and he shook his head. The rider closest to him lifted his visor.

"Incoming." The rider jerked his head back toward the growing cloud of dust.

Obvious irritation broke over the leader's face. "Circle up. Zelig might still try and fight for her."

The riders behind her maneuvered their bikes in a closer circle, hemming her further in. The leader stepped back toward his bike, hanging his helmet on the handlebars. He sat sideways on the seat, arms crossed over his chest, gun still out in hand, trigger finger slowly tapping the pistol's silver slide. Not fast enough to be anxious, more like irritation at whoever was coming.

The second troop swirled around them. Laramie pressed the dust scarf to her mouth, taking shallower breaths as the dirt finally settled.

The new riders were outfitted similarly to her captors. Another man in a red leather jacket stood from his bike, ripping a scarlet helmet with blue stripes from his head. He sported dark hair in the same cut as the other troop leader who still reclined with deceptive carelessness against his bike.

"Gered!" the newcomer she assumed was Zelig snarled as he pushed his way through, into their circle.

Gered tipped his head up in greeting, though his arms stayed crossed and his gun remained resting against the crook of his elbow. None of his troop moved hands from weapons either.

"We saw her first. She's ours." Zelig leaned in close.

Gered's eyebrow raised again as he barely shifted to look Zelig in the eye.

"Seems like we got here first." His voice maintained the same even meter. "And she's now in our route."

Zelig's face flushed and he clenched his fists. "Rules are rules. We spotted her, she's ours!" He yelled like that would make it any more true.

"Rules also say that you have to make the catch to keep the catch." Gered lifted one shoulder, his finger tapping once against the pistol.

"Conveniently remembering the rules now, are we?" Zelig sneered.

"I always remember them." Gered's voice softened into something even more deadly. "We caught her, so you can shift off or try and take me right here."

That seemed to catch Zelig's attention. Laramie caught a slight bob in his throat above the collar of his jacket before he masked it with a sneer.

"We'll take her in together and let Rosche decide."

Gered stood, matching Zelig even for height even though the second troop leader still seemed to look up at him.

"All right then." Gered shrugged. "But my unit is taking lead. Deal with that, or like I said, shift off."

Zelig subsided, jerking his head in quick acceptance, but the look he shot Gered was pure venom. Gered came toward her again, gun settled loosely by his side. Laramie didn't move as he took her pistol from its holster and slid it into his belt. He took her knives next.

"Follow us. You make a run for it, you're fair game for them." He jerked his head to where Zelig now sat astride his bike, still glaring at Gered. "Or for this." He wiggled his handgun. "You decide."

Laramie shifted on her seat. She'd been warned. She'd done it anyway. Time to accept the consequences and start planning her way out. It seemed that chance was better with the more restrained Gered than with Zelig.

She jerked her chin in a nod. "Where are we going?"

His expression never wavered. "Home."

CHAPTER FOUR

Four riders rode in tight formation around her. Laramie didn't know if she should be honored that the remaining sixteen riders also accompanied them. Zelig apparently didn't trust Gered, and the other troop leader hadn't hesitated to bring the rest of his men.

The afternoon sun beat down, blinding in its intensity as they made the turn back onto the main highway and kept heading west.

Eventually something solid appeared among the shimmering heat waves ahead. From his place at the front, Gered began to slow. The rest of the riders followed suit, the throbbing of engines cutting down to a less throaty roar as they pulled over onto a small dirt track running toward a refueling station.

No attendant came out to greet them. Instead, two riders climbed off and went to the shaded pumps, pulling off helmets and gloves. One punched a series of numbers into a keypad and locks disengaged around the pump handles.

Gered wheeled his motorcycle forward first and killed the engine. Zelig did the same at the other pump. As soon as he was done, Gered pushed his bike away and the rest of his troop fell into an orderly line to wait their turn.

Laramie sat on her bike, wondering where she was in the

process as her four escorts hadn't left her yet. Gered came over, helmet once again off, and gun drawn. He gestured to her. She kicked the stand down and killed the motor, intending to slip the keys into her pocket until he held out his hand.

She scowled at his blank face still hidden behind sunglasses and handed them over.

"Over here." He flicked the gun to the shaded side of the outbuilding. "Hands where I can see them."

She made an exaggerated show of holding her hands out from her sides as she slid down to sit against the wall.

"Dayo!" he called.

The rider at the pump pushed his motorcycle away and parked it beside Gered's. He pulled off his helmet revealing the black skin of the Aclar. His curly hair was cropped close in the same military style as Gered and Zelig.

"Take care of her bike."

Dayo nodded, turning a sharp glance at her open scrutiny.

What traveler family is he from? And what is he doing here?

"Listen to me." Gered's low voice jerked her attention back to where he now crouched in front of her. "We're headed to the Barracks. Rosche looks at everything we bring in. You have one chance when you meet him."

"A chance for what?" Laramie tipped her head back.

A humorless smile crooked the corner of his mouth. "The only thing Rosche likes better than whiskey and women is a challenge. If you want to stay out of his bed, impress him and you might get a chance to prove yourself in one of the units."

She swallowed hard. "Why are you telling me this?" A quick glance around confirmed they were out of sight of Zelig and most of his men.

"Because I've seen plenty of women get brought back. He uses them up and then kills them or throws them to the wolves." He inclined his head in Zelig's direction. "You seem like you have more of a chance than most."

She leaned her head back against the wall. She almost wished she didn't know exactly what she was riding into now.

"So what happens if I make it into these units?" She flicked a hand around.

"You're looking at it." He tilted a glance over his shoulder at his unit moving through the refueling line. "And you ride until you die."

Horror settled in her gut. *I should have ridden harder.*

"You could have just let me go," she said.

Again, that humorless smile flickered. "I don't have a choice either." He pushed to his feet and left her alone.

Not alone.

Another rider came and stood a few paces away, hand casually braced on a holstered gun. Laramie squinted at the young man. *Something's off.*

His skin stood out too pale against his short dark hair. And the dusty freckles scattered across his cheeks and nose were out of place. She looked to the others. Helmets were off all around the troops as they drank water and refilled gas tanks. Most had the coppery brown skin of the lower country, probably had the same brown eyes faded from bright silver over the years, and the rest, like Gered, had the paler skin more common in the upper country.

Unease built in her stomach. They all had the same exact shade of black hair despite different skin tones. The same haircut. The same style jackets and thick tan canvas trousers. Like someone had tried to force them all through the same mold.

Why?

The only thing that differed were small personalizations to motorcycles, but even those seemed stifled, like tiny acts of rebellion etched into seats and engine covers. Each rider had at least one long barreled handgun in a thigh holster. Some had knives strapped to their other leg or in an arm sheath.

Except for Gered. The sun caught the white handles of his twin guns with a mesmerizing glint—oddly bright among the darker hardware sported among the rest of the troop. His rifle didn't quite look uniformly military either, not like the long-range rifles she'd seen occasionally among the governor-general's soldiers.

His men all had patches on their left sleeves matching the red wolf emblem on their helmets. Zelig's men, a ridgeback hog. It seemed to suit their differences.

"Gioia." He beckoned to another member of his gang—a shorter, more slender figure than the others, with an almost boyish face. It took a second for Laramie to realize it was a young lower country woman hidden behind the haircut and loose jacket and trousers. Maybe around her own age.

She came over, water bottle in hand, and extended it down to Laramie.

"Thanks." Laramie nodded.

"Take however much you want. We'll be at the Barracks in about two hours," she said. She didn't school her features nearly as well as Gered did, and plenty of emotion leaked out from behind her sunglasses, spilling across the darker freckles spotting her copper skin. Laramie wondered if she was one of the ones Gered had mentioned.

Laramie drained half the bottle. "Any advice?" She capped it slowly.

The woman looked down at her for a long moment before extending her hand for the bottle.

"Fight hard. I hope you're as tough as you look."

Not exactly reassuring. Laramie watched her walk back to her bike and shove the bottle into the small pack on the side. *But this isn't anyone's fault but my own.*

The guard stepped closer, beckoning her up with a gloved hand. "Time to go." His voice lacked the deepness of maturity, but his green eyes didn't falter. Laramie pushed to her feet and stepped out of the shelter of the building, right into Zelig.

He pushed up his glasses, leering down into her face. "Once we get back, Gered boy's not going to be able to protect you. Don't worry, I will."

Laramie forced a careless smile. "I can take care of myself just fine, don't you worry." She stepped around him and headed to her motorcycle.

She settled onto the leather, some sense of security falling back over her at the feel of the bike. Like she could still control something in the mess.

She reached for the keys, then remembered Gered still had them.

"Drifter," he called.

He already sat on his bike. Something closer to a real smile quirked the corner of his mouth as Zelig stomped his way back to his troop. Gered tossed her the keys and pulled his helmet back on.

All around bikes came back to life, idling as riders donned helmets, and adjusted jackets and gloves.

Laramie shifted into gear. *Two hours to go. Let's see if I can out-tough a psycho.*

Two hours passed quicker than she wanted. Mountains appeared, ragged black shapes thrusting up against the western sky, any defining features obscured by the sun setting behind them. They grew incrementally with each mile, and eventually another squat shape appeared.

The Barracks.

Dark gray walls topped with razor wire surrounded a tower. Broad squares of light peppered around its sides. More lights appeared to the north, sprawled across the low hills a safe distance away, forming into the shapes of houses the closer they rode.

The gangs didn't deviate toward the town, heading directly up to the fortress. Gered lifted a hand, waving in two short bursts. A figure on the walls waved back and gates opened on the southern side as they exited off the highway.

Laramie whispered a prayer for luck to Jaan, the patron of the travelers, as they rode into a vast compound. The main tower loomed in the center of the compound itself, surrounded by at least ten other long, low buildings.

A strip of asphalt stretched from the gates up to the tower, with more pavement in front meant for parking motorcycles. The rest of the compound was brown dirt that looked like someone might have once tried to put grass down, but winds, sun, and the constant passing of tires and feet had destroyed that dream. Only tenacious patches remained around buildings or as dried sticks poking up in clusters through the dirt.

Gered rolled to a stop and Zelig pushed up beside him. Laramie's escort nudged her up behind them. The rest of the riders fell back into a wide semicircle as another barrier from which she couldn't escape. The guards patrolling the walls halted long enough to stare down at her before continuing their circuit with rifles slung over shoulders.

Laramie reluctantly killed the engine as the units did. One of the wide doors opened and a figure appeared. *This has to be Rosche.* He had the same dark hair cut in the military style. Short sleeves rolled up around bulky arms. A snake tattoo wrapped itself twice around his left wrist, the head resting on the back of his hand by his thumb.

Gered and Zelig pulled off their helmets, and Gered tucked his sunglasses away as he stood from the bike. From his tall and muscular frame, Laramie half expected Rosche to punch holes in the cement steps with every bootstrike, but he approached her with the same stalking grace as a red-scaled viper tracking its prey.

"What do we have here?"

CHAPTER FIVE

This could be interesting. Gered watched the drifter's posture stiffen as Rosche approached her.

"Caught her trying to cut across the territory, sir." His even statement came moments before Zelig's protests. Rosche held up a hand, silencing Zelig and stepped closer to the drifter.

Rosche loomed tall over the woman where she still sat on her bike, but she didn't flinch or draw back. Flat brown eyes studied her, and the unsettling flicker of madness gave way to appraisal.

"Just thought you could ride through?" His mouth turned up in a smirk.

The drifter stood slowly, but with a sureness declaring she'd maybe done this a time or two.

With the same deliberateness with which she'd done everything around the riders, she pulled her dust scarf down and propped her sunglasses on top of her head.

"That was the idea."

Rosche's grin widened and he sidled closer. Beside Gered, Gioia stiffened and stared at a point on the ground. The drifter loosened her hands by her sides, side of her mouth quirking in irritation.

A faint flare of interest sparked, a thought that maybe she'd actually remember his words and take her chance.

Rosche reached out and brushed a hand over her dusty braid. She swatted his hand away. His eyebrow raised in what was likely supposed to be flirtatious anticipation.

A faint scuff betrayed her setting her feet more securely on the ground. Gered curled his fingers into fists. *She's going for it.*

She threw herself forward, plunging her shoulder into Rosche's gut.

"Oh, dust!" Dayo muttered in surprise beside him. Gioia's head flew up.

Rosche stumbled back a step before his arms wrapped around the drifter's waist. He fell to the ground, smashing her into the dust. She gasped, but threw herself into a roll out of the way of his punch.

Back up onto her feet, hands ready in front of her. She blocked two quick strikes and kicked out at his knee. He caught it with his foot, slamming their feet back down to the ground. She danced away, hands weaving in front of her as she waited for the next strike.

He feinted forward and she dodged backward again. Gered tapped fingers against his bicep. Rosche had the advantage of height, weight, and experience in wars and enforcing his own rules. But the drifter moved on sure feet, quick like a desert wind.

Rosche's grin slipped a little as she batted away another punch. She blocked a roundhouse kick, redirecting it and throwing him a little off balance. His slight stagger gave her enough time to sneak in a few of her own punches. His returning punch to her side knocked her back a few stumbling steps, eyes wide in shock at the force behind it.

She wheezed a little, but still stood ready. Rosche straightened and made no move toward her.

Interest sparked his look at her. "Not bad," he allowed, brushing dirt from his shirt. "You might make a good addition to the gangs."

"I get a say in that?" She lowered her hands a fraction, still tensed for a fight.

Gered flinched at the raw dissent in her voice.

Rosche lifted his eyebrow again. "I can come up with a better alternative if you'd rather?"

She spat toward his boots, and straightened, squaring her shoulders.

He laughed. "Gered, you always bring in the minimum, but this time you might have brought something worthwhile. You and your unit can help yourselves to a reward."

Gered kept his face schooled in the emotionless mask that served him well. "Thank you, sir."

Zelig fumed beside him. "Sir, I'd like to point out my unit saw her first and gave chase. He stole our catch from us."

"This time he was a better rider. That's the rules, Zelig," Rosche snarled, leaning closer to the surly leader. Zelig frowned but didn't argue.

Gered didn't move, his arms still across his chest, but a faint twitch of triumph along his jaw threatened to give him away.

"Gered." Rosche turned to him. "You brought her in, so she's your responsibility. Make sure she knows the rules and meets with the other recruits."

"Sir." Gered gave a nod and pushed away from his motorcycle.

Rosche leaned close over the drifter for a long moment. "Good luck, newbie." He winked and sauntered back inside.

The woman scowled at his back as he went.

"I'm not going to forget this, Gered boy," Zelig hissed in his ear.

Gered didn't flinch from the venom in Zelig's voice.

"Sure you have enough brain space to hold onto it for longer than five minutes?" Dayo taunted as he shoved hands in his jacket pockets. Gered's jaw twitched again.

"Shift off." Zelig spat at Dayo's feet.

Gered loomed closer to the unit leader. "You heard Rosche. We got the catch, so shift off."

Zelig worked his jaw like he was going to spit at Gered, thought better about it, and turned away. He grabbed his bike and wheeled it away, cursing his troop to do the same.

More than a few sneers from Gered's unit followed their retreat.

"Drifter." Gered turned to her.

"Laramie," she snapped.

He lifted an eyebrow. "*Laramie.* Bring your bike."

He began to wheel his bike across the dirt. She followed suit with the rest of the unit. Tires ground across the dirt as they headed around the main tower where more long buildings spread out. The large four painted on the side of their home barrack even looked vaguely welcoming.

Double garage doors took up the bottom floor. A staircase ran from the ground up to a broad door off a long porch.

Dayo punched in the lock combination and the left garage door raised. The unit began to wheel their bikes in. The right side of the garage stood empty, enough room for the thirteen bikes from Unit Five not back from route yet.

"Did you know that would happen?" Gioia's soft question held him back a moment.

He regarded her from the corner of his eye. She stared at

Laramie, her barely-masked nausea since the moment they'd picked up the drifter finally fading with the threat of Rosche gone.

He shrugged. "Good thing it did."

Gioia tipped a look at him, the faint smile on her lips that almost made him soften. But he couldn't. Not out in the open. Not around anyone else. Not with Rosche likely watching them from one of the upper levels of the tower. The warlord liked to keep an eye on things.

He pushed his motorcycle into the garage, past the drifter who hung back at the entrance, a first hint of unsurety around her.

"Put your bike over here." Gered pointed to the back corner of the garage. "We'll get you a better one later."

"What's wrong with mine?" Laramie lifted an eyebrow.

"Too bulky."

Her shoulders stiffened and ire flushed her face. He matched her glare, daring her to make an argument. She raised her chin and pushed her bike over where he'd indicated.

"Gioia, show her where she goes." Gered turned away. Gioia would take care of the drifter and make sure no one would try to mess with her.

Gioia flashed a tight-lipped smile at him and stepped over to Laramie. She knew what he was doing. "Grab whatever you need to from your bags and follow me."

Laramie detached the right saddlebag from the bike, tucked it under her arm, and followed Gioia toward the far end of the garage where more steps led up to another door and disappeared inside.

"What's this, the third time you've pissed Zelig off this

month?" Dayo's laugh jerked his attention back.

He shrugged. Zelig blustered and sneered, but there was no real threat behind him. "Am I supposed to be scared?"

Dayo scoffed. "No. But he's got a look like he might do something stupid one of these days."

Gered arched an eyebrow. "Didn't know you cared so much."

"Yeah." Dayo shrugged carelessly. "But if you're gone, that means I might have to take over Four and that sounds like too much work."

A grin twitched as he pulled his gloves off and tossed them into the helmet. "I'm gonna go for the official debrief with Rosche. Save me a drink," he called over his shoulder as he headed out of the garage, missing Dayo's return gesture.

Out in the dusky twilight, the air had cooled marginally. Gered rolled his shoulders to loosen them up as he stuck hands in his jacket pockets. A few riders from other units gave him a wider berth, nods of respect which he ignored.

Once he'd made the report, he'd go make sure the drifter was settled in and try to figure out what it was about her that unsettled him so much.

CHAPTER SIX

Laramie followed Gioia into a wide room filled with couches and chairs. A bar divided it from what was supposed to be a kitchen, but looked more like storage space for as much alcohol as the inhabitants could cram in. Several hallways opened off the main room, and Gioia headed for the furthest to the left.

"You'll bunk up with me." She halted at the second door on the right. A rusty keypad sat to the left of the door. "Code's eight-three-five." She punched in the numbers and the door swung open.

"I'm assuming I don't share that around?" Laramie asked wryly.

A bitter smile twisted Gioia's face. "Not unless you want some unwelcome visitors."

She flipped on the light revealing a narrow room with two beds against opposite walls, a closet missing a door, and a dresser listing to the side.

"Charming." Laramie stepped inside.

"Yeah." Gioia ditched her jacket and gloves. A tattoo wound around her left wrist, but she tucked her hands in her back pockets, obscuring it from view. "But better than the alternative." Her jaw hardened for a moment. "Hope you don't mind. The other roommate option is Corinne, and there's a reason we don't share.

Girl's certifiable."

Laramie didn't remember seeing another woman in either unit. "How many women are there in the gangs?"

"If you make it in? Three." Gioia pointed to the bunk against the opposite wall. "You can take that one. I'll dig up some blankets from somewhere."

"I can use my bedroll for right now." She rubbed her side. Punching Rosche was like hitting a brick wall. But his hits had been like the brick wall punching back. *I'm going to have some bruises.*

Gioia nodded. "That'll work. Showers are downstairs. We have our separate one from the rest of the unit. Meals are in the tower's mess hall. We have our own table down there as well."

"You share with another unit?" Laramie asked. The riders hadn't taken up any space on the empty side of the garage.

"Yeah, we're Unit Four, and we split with Five. They're out on route right now. We usually don't cross paths too often since we're on alternating rotations."

"What's my role in all this?" Laramie set her pack on the bed. It creaked in response.

"Training. There's a few other recruits right now, so you'll join in with them. Though you seem a step above them already."

"Conscripts?" Laramie bit back.

Gioia leaned against the wall. "Some really are volunteers. Poor boys from some of the towns who think it's a better life up here. Which it might be since they'll get three meals a day and don't have to live under our boots anymore."

"Sounds like you're not really a fan." Laramie decided against sitting on the bed. It looked like it might collapse out of spite.

Gioia shrugged a shoulder. "You might say that. Come on,

got a few more things to show you around here. Training starts at five hundred hours, so you should probably turn in early tonight."

"Can't wait." Laramie tossed her sunglasses on the bed and loosened her dust scarf.

Gioia gave something a little closer to a real smile. "I know it sucks, but I'm glad you made it here instead of the command tower." Her throat bobbed. "But I think you'll be all right. You shouldn't have a problem with most of Four, but when Five comes around, you might have to be more careful."

She tilted her head to the door and led the way back out. The main room had been overtaken by most of the unit. They'd shucked jackets and lounged about the couches and chairs, beers in hand. The steady buzz of conversation didn't halt as Gioia and Laramie entered.

A movement in Laramie's periphery announced Gered. Without the jacket and gloves, a snake tattoo wrapped itself around his left wrist, mouth parted wide as it stretched toward his thumb.

A twinge of alarm prodded Laramie as she noted dark spirals on left wrists around the room, just like Rosche.

"He really takes the whole imitation thing seriously, doesn't he?" Laramie nodded toward the tattoo.

"Unity in identity makes us stronger," Gered intoned.

"Sounds completely sane." Laramie tucked her hands into her jacket pockets.

Gered scoffed a humorless laugh. "I wouldn't repeat that outside. Here." He extended her gun.

She took it, sliding the magazine free and checking the bullets inside. All there. A tug at the slide revealed the last bullet still chambered. It clicked back in place, and she holstered it in the back of her belt.

"Knives?" She raised an eyebrow at him.

He held them out, snatching his hand back as she took them as if glad to be free of their touch.

"Don't go anywhere without those. Don't hesitate to pull the trigger. Only the tough survive here."

She'd begun to think his facial muscles were broken with the lack of emotion he showed, but his eyes made up for it now that she could see them. Gray with speckles of blue around the iris, they burned into her as if trying to extract a promise. Her heart rammed into her chest. It had been a long time since she'd seen scraps of blue in someone's eyes.

Gray and blue eyes. He probably had blond hair under the dye. All the marks of the Itan. Once her people. Now wiped out except for the one in front of her, hidden under the shadow of the Barracks.

She didn't have to tip her head back very much to meet those gray eyes. "Don't worry about me. I can take care of myself."

"I'm counting on it. Remember, if you dust anything up, it's on me." It didn't sound like a threat so much as a promise that he would come after her if anything happened.

She slid her knives into the sheaths with a satisfying hiss of steel on leather. "Well then, guess I better learn the rules."

CHAPTER SEVEN

You'd think if he's going to keep us here, he might spring for some decent beer." Gered crushed the can and threw it at the garbage.

"You going to bring that up at the next meeting?" Dayo tipped a drink.

Gered leaned forward on the table and rubbed his eyes before reaching for another can. "Sure."

Dayo chuckled as he propped his boots up on the table. They had the back common room to themselves. The riders in there had cleared out as soon as he and Dayo entered with their beer.

"Still, it's not that bad." He regarded the beer in his hand. "Once you get to the fourth or fifth one."

Gered rubbed his eyes again. "That many? We're behind." The can opened with a hiss of releasing pressure. Dayo laughed.

The bitter taste of another drink cascaded over his tongue. He scraped a hand over his dyed hair and sighed.

"All right over there?"

Gered threw himself back into the chair. It creaked against his sudden weight.

"Just this dusting place." Same as it always was.

Five years of fighting, and scrapping, and killing all to maintain some sort of hierarchy Rosche didn't care about, and got too much amusement out of watching between keeping the gangs in line with motivational words or harsh punishments.

Gered did enough to keep Four solidly above the middle of the pack of thirty units. But not too much so Rosche started to care and remember what exactly he could do. Too low, and his unit would get next to nothing. But he'd give anything to be anywhere else.

"Regrets about our catch today?" Dayo lifted an eyebrow.

Gered slowly shook his head. He'd warned her. That's all he could do. She'd surprised him with the rest, and the hits she'd landed on Rosche hadn't exactly been love taps either.

"You did what you could, *kamé*."

"Yeah, well, go enjoy a night out on the town on me then." Gered slammed his beer down harder than he meant to.

"Maybe I will instead of getting drunk in here with your morbid ass." Dayo took out his knife and began to spin it on the table.

Gered's shoulders tensed. He hated knives. Even holding the drifter's had been bad enough. Dayo knew better. He must be getting drunk.

"Holding you back again, am I?" He forced himself to relax. He wasn't thirteen and bleeding all over his shirt anymore.

"Always." Dayo smirked. He spun the knife again. It rattled against the uneven boards. Gered swallowed hard.

"Dust! Sorry." Dayo slammed his hand down on the knife and yanked it away.

Gered forced a smile and a shrug, not trusting his voice to say it didn't bother him. "So what's your bet?"

Dayo wiped beer from the corner of his mouth after he drank. "What?" He squinted a little.

"On if the drifter will make it. I know everyone else has made theirs." Gered eased back further into the chair.

"I don't need to bet. She'll make it. You?"

Gered drank again. Not too much. Never too much. It left a body helpless to fight. Just enough to blur the world comfortably around the edges.

There was something about her that set him on edge. And it might be the dusky blonde hair, and gray-blue eyes.

But he didn't doubt she could make it. She'd somehow survived the Tlengin's war on the Itan, and he already knew Rosche wasn't any worse than the raiders.

"Same," he finally said. "You see her band?"

The Aclar travelers roved in tight knit groups, never really leaving their caravans, or associating with those outside their societies. How the drifter claimed ties was anyone's guess.

Dayo's face hardened and his can crinkled under sudden pressure. "Yeah."

"That going to bother you?"

Dayo drained half his can in one draft. "No. I've no idea how or why she has a traveler band, but maybe her family cares more than to sell her off to a gang."

An apology hovered on Gered's tongue. There was an unspoken rule between them to not bring up lives before the gangs. But he knew it had bothered Dayo to see the band. Like it unsettled him to see Itan features for the first time in years. He just didn't feel like dealing with any difficulty between his lieutenant and the drifter.

He tossed back the last few gulps of beer, swallowing the apology with it. "Think I'm done. Harlan tracked me down at dinner to give a lesson to the trainees tomorrow since we'll still be in."

"Better you than me. Go do Unit Four proud."

Gered tossed the can at Dayo's head. Dayo snickered as it sailed harmlessly past.

"Don't wake me up when you come in," Gered warned.

"What if I'm feeling cuddly?"

Gered flipped him off and stood. Dayo's laugh followed him down to their shared room. The keypad blurred momentarily before steadying.

The door clicked shut behind him and he leaned against the frame, checking every corner of the bare room out of instinct. *Never turn your back on an unchecked room.* The rule echoed every time he stepped through a door.

He pushed away from the wall and undid his holsters, setting one handgun on the bed, the other went on the pile of his jacket. Boots went next. The room was one of the few with a built-in sink. He splashed water over his face and arms, not feeling like staggering downstairs for a shower right then.

Never-ending dust flaked off his skin, even though he'd washed since they'd been back. He wished the snake tattoo rinsed off as easily. Balling the towel in his hands, he sighed again. *Forget about the dusting girl already. There's nothing else I can do to help. There's never anything else I can do.*

Crawling wearily into bed, he slid the pistol under his pillow and rolled on his side, back to the wall. Maybe he'd even drunk enough to sleep through the night.

⌣

Gered woke to Dayo's raucous snores. The lieutenant had made it far enough to take off his boots, sprawling across the blankets on his bed against the opposite wall. Shaking his head, Gered gathered up clean clothes and headed out to the showers.

Dayo still hadn't moved by the time he got back. Gered didn't bother with his jacket, buckling on his guns and grabbing his sunglasses before heading out. His long sleeve shirt covered down to his wrists, but still couldn't cover the entire tattoo. He'd hate it until the day he died.

A few of his unit were still in the mess hall. Gioia met his gaze and offered a small smile. He ignored it with an effort and picked up a water bottle and nutrient bar and headed back outside. Harlan had asked him to be out at the range at ten hundred hours. He had about five minutes to get there.

He made his way to the smaller gates on the northern side where the ranges were set up a half mile from the walls. The sharp crack of handguns announced he was already late, so he slowed his pace and started on the nutrient bar.

Harlan stood behind the line of seven recruits, hands braced on hips, watching target practice. Gered strolled up beside him, adjusting his sunglasses on his nose. He took a long drink of water and assessed the line.

"Looks like you got one or two decent ones out here."

"Yeah, one or two is right." Harlan shook his head and crossed meaty arms over his broad chest. "What am I supposed to do with these scrawny kids?" He half turned to Gered as if he had the magic solution.

Scrawny. An apt enough description for three of the younger recruits. They must have come from some of the townships. Another had been caught slumming along the border, and the other two in the group had come in looking for the gangs. And then there was the drifter.

Laramie, as she'd informed him last night. She stood relaxed, hitting her target with impressive accuracy.

"Heard you brought that one in yesterday." Harlan jerked his chin at her.

"How's she doing?" Gered kept his voice disinterested.

"Not bad." That from Harlan was practically a recommendation to join the nearest unit. "Better than this shrimp is. Hey! How many times have I told you to fix those feet?" Harlan yelled at a young boy of no more than sixteen, whose arms looked barely strong enough to hold up the handgun.

"You're right. I can't watch this anymore." Gered set the water bottle on the ground and strode over to the young boy.

"You trying to hit yourself with the recoil?" he snapped.

The boy bolted to attention, eyes wide as he looked up at Gered. His throat bobbed in a nervous gulp. Gered rolled his eyes behind the glasses. Doing the bare minimum still didn't diminish his reputation among the gangs. That was something he was fine with. Meant less work all around.

"Eyes front." He snapped fingers in front of the boy's nose. "Arms out. Fix those feet." He nudged the boy's feet wider with a boot. "Now try." He stepped behind the boy watching him line up the sights at ... "For dust's sake, what are you aiming at, kid?"

"All yours, Gered!" Harlan called with a mocking laugh.

Gered waved and turned back to making sure the kid didn't accidentally shoot his own foot off.

He spent the next half hour going down the line, spending time with each recruit. He actually didn't mind teaching. Guns and shooting were what he knew. They were survival skills. Which made him a dusting expert.

He finally got to Laramie. She arched an eyebrow and turned

back to the target, snapping off four shots into the double rings of the bullseye.

"Anything to work on?" she asked, face blank, but voice full of smugness.

He crossed his arms over his chest. "You bobble it a bit between shots. You need to absorb your recoil better."

She visibly bristled. In truth, it was the slightest of movements, but he wanted to see how well she could hold her temper.

"You gonna show me by putting your arms around me?"

His lip twitched against his will. "That's a good way to get someone shot."

She huffed a bit of a laugh. "All right."

He shifted to move back to the head of the line where the scrawny kid leaned too far back on his heels again.

"Hey. Gered, right?"

He tipped a nod.

She tapped her finger on the side of her gun where it dangled comfortably by her side. "Thanks for the advice yesterday."

Gered gave a slight shrug. "You did good. You look like you've got some talent. I'd hate to see it wasted."

"Even if I bobble the recoil?" She smirked.

His mouth twitched again. "Even if."

"Hey." She halted him again. "How long does it usually take before a recruit's inducted into the clone show?"

"Why? Got somewhere to be?"

"Yeah, actually. Supposed to meet up with my family in a few months."

The word stabbed at him. "You don't have a family anymore. Once the gang gets you, that's your family."

Her jaw set in a stubborn jut. "Not if I have anything to say about it."

A chill cut through him. She actually looked determined enough to try to run.

He stepped forward, and she blinked at his sudden closeness. She was almost tall enough to look him in the eye.

"Listen to me." He kept his voice low. "Don't even think about running. It can't be done. You'll just end up back here, or worse."

"Know this from experience?" Her shoulders squared in challenge.

He dug his fingers deep into his upper arm to distract from memories.

"Yeah," he said softly. Her eyebrows rose and she rocked back slightly to better regard him. "If you run, I'm going to be the one putting a bullet in your skull from seven hundred yards away because that's going to be the kindest thing I can do for you."

"And how many times have you done that?" she asked undeterred.

"Five." He gradually relaxed the pressure of his fingers. "So take my word for it, and accept that in a few weeks you're going to lose the braid and get a dusting tattoo and be one of us for the rest of your life."

"Sure. I'll get right on that." She tossed her braid over her shoulder, stubbornness still filling her jaw.

He turned away before he could find himself admiring her resolve and wishing he wasn't such a dusting coward.

CHAPTER EIGHT

Come on, Lare! Everyone goes." Axel wove back and forth in front of her. She resisted the urge to smack him for using the ridiculous nickname he'd given her, unasked.

"What if I don't want to go?" She kept walking. He kept backing up in front of her.

The lanky teen was persistent, she had to give him that. He kept trying even when Harlan inevitably yelled at him for every little thing. His shooting even improved after a few minutes with stone-faced Gered.

"You should go. That way you can scope out the other units and see where you might want to end up. When the choosing comes, you can at least put your bid in."

Laramie swallowed the retort that she wasn't going to be around that long. Gered's face, and she imagined his eyes too, had been full of knowing warning about running two days ago at the range. They hadn't crossed paths since. The recruits' training schedule and—whatever the units did on their time off—didn't really overlap.

She only really saw Gioia in the room before and after the day's training. The trainees had their own table in the mess hall. She'd gotten to know them over the past few days. The two who'd come looking for the gangs, she stayed away from. They had violence in their veins.

Axel was a bundle of bright energy. She hated to think he was trying his hardest to be part of the gangs where it looked like anything remotely good or wholesome was beaten out of a person. The other two teens were more subdued, but just as eager to prove themselves as Axel.

But if everyone really goes, then I might get a better count of numbers.

"Okay, you convinced me."

Axel's face melted into a bright grin. "Knew I could."

She couldn't help a returning smile and eye-roll. "When do these fights happen?"

"Right after dinner tonight. Honestly, don't you listen?" Axel shook his head in remonstrance.

"I've only been here three days." She lightly punched his shoulder. He mocked an injury, limping a few steps for good measure.

"True, but you've already caught up with the rest of us who've been here for months." For the first time, Axel's cheer faded. Laramie hoped there wasn't some sort of permanent solution for anyone who failed out of training or didn't get chosen by a unit.

"Hey." She jogged a step to catch up with him and slung an arm around his shoulders. "Your marksmanship improved the other day. I'd say you have a pretty good chance of getting into whatever unit you want."

"Nah." He shook his head. "Gered probably wouldn't want me in his unit."

Her heart stuttered for a second. *Someone wants to be in his gang?* Although he seemed vaguely like a decent person, she still hadn't quite forgiven him for bringing her in, then insulting her bike *and* her shooting.

"No one else?"

Axel shrugged lightly so as not to disturb her arm. "He helped me out of a jam when I first got here. Taught me how to stand up for myself without getting beat up in the process."

Laramie quirked an eyebrow. "Gered did?"

She didn't know why that surprised her. He'd done the same thing for her.

"And Dayo and the rest aren't so bad either. Most of the other units are assholes."

"Guess I really do need to go to these fights since I obviously don't know anything." Laramie shook her head. Tension was obvious between some of the units, such as Gered's and Zelig's. But then it seemed Zelig's meatheads didn't really get along with anyone.

"You've only been here for three days," Axel offered.

She laughed and nudged him away. "True. All right, let's get food and then you can show me where we're headed."

He jogged up the steps into the tower, but her steps slowed as they had every time she'd walked through the wide doorway.

The mess hall took up most of the bottom floor. Upstairs was Rosche's domain. Twin staircases curved up on either side of the wide anteroom. Two large banners draped from the banister— red with coiled black vipers.

Pretentious.

She'd yet to see more than glimpses of Rosche since her initial encounter, which was fine by her. But every time she stepped inside, the feeling of being watched nudged at her back like an itch that couldn't quite be reached. A shiver cut down her spine as she walked under the trailing banners. Her hand fell to her knife out of instinct and it gave her a little reassurance.

The feeling faded as she entered the cavernous dining hall. Axel was already heading for the recruits' table wedged in the very back corner. Almost half of the thirty tables were filled, raucous conversations echoing off the stone ceiling and pillars.

Numbers painted on the long wooden tables marked each unit's territory even within the hall. As far as she'd been able to tell, they were ranked by skill level. Or by Rosche's determination of their worth.

She collected her tray from the counter and headed back to their table, ignoring some cat calls and staring down a few leering riders. Gioia was the only one who looked up from table four and acknowledged her. Dayo laughed over something, but a smile never cracked Gered's face.

Laramie returned Gioia's slight nod and kept walking, neatly avoiding one of Zelig's men attempting to trip her. She reached the dimly lit corner without incident and slid in opposite Axel.

"There's some new faces around." She nodded to tables one and two.

Axel barely looked up from shoveling the unappetizing chicken and rice mash into his mouth.

"Oh, yeah, those are Barns and Moshe's units. They just got back from patrol. They're not bad." He paused to drink. "Moshe's probably the best shot in the whole gang behind Gered. You don't want to mess with either of them."

Laramie scraped up a forkful of rice. Moshe sat tall at Unit Two's table. But unlike Gered, he smiled and laughed with his men.

Barns nearly bowed the bench under his bulk. There wasn't much spare fat on his frame—muscles bulged from under his long sleeve shirt and even his snake tattoo looked beefier than everyone else's. A sly smile permanently lurked in the corner of his mouth, his eyes always watching something as he talked.

Laramie tapped her fork against the plate. The units were never all in the mess hall at the same time. Some had more than the ten riders that made up Gered and Zelig's gangs. Only the patches on left sleeves helped her sort riders into their respective units.

How many riders am I going to have to outrun?

Axel pushed his plate away and eyed hers. Laramie rolled her eyes and handed him the roll. He beamed at her and ate it like he hadn't just eaten an entire oversized helping of food. Though she remembered being that way as a teenager and Ade complaining she couldn't keep her fed.

It might help to get someone on my side.

She dismissed Axel. The boy had a wide-eyed look around any rider. And she didn't want to get him in trouble. Her gaze fell to table four. Gered had warned her against running. It sounded like he'd tried. *Would he be interested in trying again?* Maybe she'd sound out Gioia later if they happened to be in the room at the same time.

She forced down another bite. She'd have to get more comfortable around everyone to see what kind of allies she could find.

After the meal finished, Axel led her to the second-largest building in the compound sheltered in the northwest corner, just outside the outer ring of barracks buildings.

"Come on!" He beckoned over his shoulder, pushing his way through the crowded riders.

Shouts and cheers reverberated off the wood, pounding through her chest as she pushed and shoved her way through, trying not to lose sight of Axel. He made for another thick ring of riders, clustered around an inset dirt arena.

He scored a position right at the top railing, looking directly down. She tried to catch her breath as she slammed into the rail beside him, scowling at the rider who'd crashed against her. The rider flashed a drunk grin and she swatted his hand away. He stumbled off and she turned back to the arena.

Barns and some other rider bare-knuckle fought in the arena. The impact of punches and their grunts were audible even over the noise.

Those not watching drank heavily at benches or tables pushed up around the outer edges of the building. The thick smell of beer and sweat and dirt permeated the air, and she took a few shallow breaths to accustom herself to it before turning her attention to the fight.

For all his bulk, Barns redirected his opponent's attacks with ease. The rider began to get frustrated and his attacks came more open and aggressive. Laramie shook her head. *He's toast.*

Sure enough, Barns finished him off with two well-placed punches. He collapsed into the dirt, breathing heavily, before taking Barns's hand to regain his feet. Barns sent him limping off with a grin before raising his arms above his head and shouting victory. Riders leaned over the edge of the railing, pounding the boards with tattooed hands.

"Who's next?" Barns turned in a slow circle.

Laramie ignored him and pushed up on her toes trying to get a better view of the back corners to count riders. Axel tugged her arm, bringing her attention back to the arena. She frowned at him, but his grin melted some of her frustration.

"Gered!" Barns shouted. "Come on! I need a challenge tonight!"

Laramie perked up in interest despite herself.

"Gered!" A rider somewhere along the rail shouted and more and more voices picked it up, chanting frenetically.

She found him, leaning on the rail across from her. His expression didn't change, maybe a bit of annoyance creasing around his eyes. Dayo pounded his shoulder and shouted something in his ear. Gered rolled his eyes and shrugged out of his red jacket, shoving it into Dayo's chest with something closer to a smile.

Dayo whooped and held the jacket above his head as the cheers reached a new pitch. Gered placed a hand on the rail and jumped down into the arena.

Barns grinned and pulled his shirt off. Gered rolled his eyes as "Oohs" spread around. The rider tossed his shirt up to a man from his unit. Gered raised an eyebrow, and his lips moved.

Barns tossed his head back with a laugh and replied. Gered shook his head, his jaw shifting as if trying to hide a smile. He pulled his shirt off and handed it up to Dayo.

The rattle of hands on boards picked up again, along with shouts as betting started.

"Who do you think will win?" she yelled into Axel's ear.

He half turned his face toward her. "Gered!" Money changed hands with a rider on his left. Laramie resisted the urge to roll her eyes. The kid's man-crush on Gered was something else.

But she leaned a little closer on the railing to watch. Gered and Barns circled each other, mouths moving as if they'd done this a hundred times before. Though from Barns's challenge, maybe they had.

Unlike the rider previous, Gered didn't take Barns's baiting moves. He kept his hands low and ready, feet testing the ground with every step.

Scars traced all over his muscled torso. Two lines of script ran lengthwise down his right forearm, but she was too far away to make out what they said. A spotted jackal leaped from his back up the right side of his ribs, its teeth dripping blood on his chest.

She swallowed hard. Tlengin raider sigil. For a second the air filled with smoke and screams. Laramie drove her fingernails into her palms, bringing her back to dust and betting.

Barns had made his first attack. Punches were thrown and blocked with dizzying speed. Gered dodged a kick. A strike caught him on the ribs, right on the jackal's nose and he staggered back a step. Barns lunged forward to follow up his advantage and got a kick to his knee.

Okay, I understand Axel's hype. Laramie shook her head. Barns was skilled to be sure—his attacks followed more of a military martial arts form. But Gered? He'd barely broken a sweat. Laramie recognized at least three different fighting styles, two of which were not being taught to the recruits. Lekan had taught her some of the Benshin style from the upper territory, but mainly she stuck with the travelers' school.

Then it was over. Gered grabbed Barns's arm, twisting it and throwing the bulkier man to the ground.

I bet he could even take Rosche.

Barns accepted his defeat with a good-natured grin. Gered clapped his shoulder and moved off. Calls followed, trying to coax him to keep his place as the new challenger in the ring. He shook his head.

Someone shouted a slur at his back. He didn't pause, raising his middle finger high. Laughs broke out.

Dayo reached over the railing to help him climb back over. But movement on the other side of the arena distracted Laramie. Another rider jumped down.

"I challenge Gered for Unit Four!" he shouted.

Gered paused, his shoulders tensing. Dayo jerked his head up to study the challenger as a hush spread around the arena, rushing to drown bits of laughter and conversation in the back corners.

Gered turned slowly and stalked back to the center of the arena. Barns watched, arms crossed. The rider stood, posture loose and confident, but Gered ignored him, scanning the rails for something else.

Laramie followed until she found Zelig leaning on the rail, jaw set in anger.

"Sure you want to do this?" Gered didn't move his gaze from Zelig.

The rider pounded his chest and bellowed something incoherent. Zelig didn't break eye contact as he gave a slight nod.

"Barns, you'll judge?" Gered asked.

Barns nodded and backed away from the center of the arena.

"What's happening?" Laramie whispered to Axel.

"Anyone can challenge for a leadership position. Some units are always fighting. This guy's an idiot if he thinks he can take over Four." Axel shook his head. "Gered never loses. And he brought his riders all the way up to Four after he killed the last unit leader years ago. Some Tlengin relative of his, I think."

A chill slithered over Laramie. This time there was no betting, only hushes of whispers rippling around the arena. Riders stood on tables in the back to get better views.

Barns waved them closer together, discussing something with

them in a low voice that didn't carry even in the silence. Gered and the other rider nodded once, then stepped back.

"All right!" Barns shouted. "Rules of the arena apply. Winner takes Four."

He dropped his hand. This time, there was no testing, no circling. Gered charged forward, getting two sharp strikes in before his opponent managed to get his hands up. He caught the returning punch in both hands, wrenching the wrist into a crunching angle.

The man doubled over to get Gered's knee slammed into his chest. Gered released him, shoving him away. The rider stumbled, face slack in shock and pain. Gered grabbed the rider's shoulders, pulling him down and smashing a knee into his face. He dropped without a sound.

A hush followed as Gered spat contemptuously.

"Anyone else?" he shouted as he spun in a slow circle, fury still leaking from his eyes.

Dusting hells. Laramie stared at him. *Seconds* to take down the man.

A few heads dared shake around the arena. Barns prodded the fallen rider with his boot.

"What do you want done with him, Gered?"

Gered locked eyes with Zelig again. "String him up for the rest of the night."

He turned his back on the arena, accepting Dayo's hand to climb back over the railing. The crowd stirred back to life, conversations returning as two more riders jumped in and hauled the fallen rider away through a door set into the arena's side. Zelig scowled as he watched and then pushed away.

Gered donned his shirt again, tugging the sleeves down to his wrists, covering all but the winding neck and head of the snake. Dayo passed his jacket back before turning to gleefully collect money from riders who pressed in around them. Gered leaned close to shout something in Dayo's ear before pushing out of the crowd.

Laramie wasn't the only one who tracked his path. Gioia pressed her lips in a tight line where she stood beside Dayo, hip braced against the railing. She didn't move, didn't change her even expression, but Laramie recognized the subtle way she leaned forward toward him, the look in her eyes.

Maybe Axel's not the only one with a crush.

Laramie pulled back from the rail and hit Axel's arm. "I'm gonna get some air!"

He shouted something back and pointed at the two new occupants of the arena. She shook her head, not wanting to stay.

She took one look over her shoulder. Gioia had turned her attention to the arena, trading words with Dayo now. Dayo leaned into her shoulder, eyebrows raised in a teasing, goading expression. She pursed her lips and pulled a few bills from her pocket with a roll of her eyes. Dayo laughed and leaned on the rail to shout at someone on her other side. It was the freckle-faced kid. The young rider listened for a second, watched the fighters in the ring, then nodded, taking whatever bet Dayo made.

Gioia raised a hand in annoyance, but kept watching the fight. Maybe she needed to have a conversation with Gioia anyway. Unit Four seemed like they were decent people, for the limited interactions she'd had with them. And if she approached Gered, she didn't want to mess anything up for them. The Barracks didn't seem like a place that forgave mistakes or oversteps easily.

When she finally broke free of the press of bodies and

sweltering atmosphere, Gered was nowhere to be seen. She took a deep breath of the cleaner desert air. With the sunset, it had begun to cool incrementally. The breeze wicked away the last stench of sweat and men. Nothing stirred in the compound other than the faint motion of sentries on the walls above.

She came up short as she rounded the bulk of the tower. A dark figure slumped between two wooden posts in the middle of the yard. She assumed it was the rider Gered had defeated. The cuffs holding him up were going to be hell on his injured wrist.

From what Axel had said, the fights seemed to be a weekly event where everyone but those on sentry duty went to relax and lose whatever money they'd stolen from people that week.

She tapped a hand against her knife. She didn't want to go back to the arena. *Might as well get some sleep.* It had taken a few nights to trust the lock on the outside of the door. The rules had been read out to her on her first day of training. Most didn't really apply to her as a woman given she was only the third in the gang.

Rosche got the women. Town was the place to go for that when leave was given. No romantic attachments allowed as a unit rider. Everything was brought to Rosche first, and then distributed as he saw fit. Keep fights clean. The arena was the place to settle deeper scores. The unit leaders were second to Rosche and their influence waned the higher the troop number. No one ran, no one disobeyed, or they got a bullet. The posts were for minor infractions that weren't enough for a bullet, but still enough a lesson needed to be taught.

The rules hadn't stopped the looks and comments. She'd ignored most and broken at least one nose. Gered hadn't been lying when he told her to keep her weapons on her at all times. Axel had been happy to inform her that word of her challenge to

Rosche had also spread around to those who hadn't witnessed it, giving her a little more protection.

She paused when she got to bunker four. The left garage door was halfway raised, faint light spilling out onto the dirt. She tapped her knife again. She'd seen all of Unit Four scattered around at the arena.

Which meant it could be Gered. Though she was seriously rethinking talking to him after the fight and the anger seeping from him. But she needed to make some sort of connection with a few riders to get some better information before trying to run.

Ever since the first day, he'd ignored her. But it seemed he just ignored everyone who wasn't in his unit. A conversation wouldn't hurt, right?

Deciding against just sliding under the door, she went up into the building first. She ran a hand over her braid. *Am I really going to try this?* Her traveler family's faces flashed in front of her eyes. Kayin's smile played in her mind. A rare bout of homesickness swept over her. If she got out, she was headed straight back to them. She'd try for the Itan settlement later.

I was a complete idiot to do this. She twisted the leather bands around her wrist. *I'm getting back to them. And preferably before I get a new haircut.*

Squaring her shoulders, she opened the door to the garage and stepped inside.

CHAPTER NINE

The light came from the back corner of the garage, over by the unit bikes. She stepped softly off the last stair onto the concrete floor. The comforting scent of gasoline and leather filled the space. Her fingers itched to hold a tool and tinker with her bike.

She crossed over to the light. Her bike still sat against the wall, lonely and shoved aside from the sleeker gang motorcycles.

"Looking for something?" Gered's voice startled her. He sat on a low stool, partially hidden by a motorcycle, wrench in hand.

"Just making sure you hadn't stripped my 'bulky' bike for parts." She ran a hand across the dusty seat of her bike, silently apologizing for having abandoned it for the last few days.

He snorted something like a laugh and turned back to the bike.

"That yours?" she asked.

"No." He grunted as he turned a bolt loose and pulled the engine cover off. "It's Dec's. But kid doesn't know anything about engines, so I make sure it stays running."

"He the one choking up on the clutch?" Laramie raised an eyebrow.

Gered nodded, tossing the wrench down in favor of another tool. "Never said he was a good rider either."

Laramie quirked a smile. Gered seemed more relaxed. This was already more conversation than they'd had so far. His jacket draped over another stool, and he'd pushed up his sleeves to his elbows to escape the inevitable grease and oil.

"Where'd you learn?" She flipped open her saddlebag, relief whooshing through her at the sight of her toolkit still intact on top.

He didn't answer for a second, and she snuck a look over her shoulder. His jaw had tightened again as he focused on the engine. Then finally, "I was raised by Tlengin." He practically spat the words. "They taught me everything I know."

Anger bubbled inside her. "Tlengin killed my entire family." Fury flowed through her words despite her attempt to control it.

His shoulders bunched together. "You want me to apologize for that?" he snapped.

"No, just wondering how many innocent families you slaughtered," she shot back. From the stories she'd heard, Tlengin didn't tattoo that sign on just anyone. He'd betrayed their people and taken up with murderers.

Gered's hands stilled. She took a deep breath. This was not the way to start a conversation with someone she potentially wanted to get on her side, never mind someone clearly capable of quick, sharp violence. Even if the spotted jackal came back periodically to haunt her dreams.

"Sorry," she said, but it still tasted a little bitter.

"Legitimate question." He resumed his work.

She bit back a "Well?" and buckled her saddlebag closed.

The wrench clinked against the concrete again. "I've never killed anyone I didn't have to." His soft words were heavy. She swallowed hard and squatted to check the engine.

"They took me from my family." His next words sent a stab through her gut along with the memory of his scars. There were too many to assume he'd gotten them at the Barracks. Besides, no one seemed to want to mess with him. And after the display in the arena, she didn't blame them.

Maybe she'd misjudged slightly with the tattoo.

"Sorry," she whispered, tilting another look back at him. He shrugged, still intent on his work.

"How'd you end up here?" The question jumped out before she could keep it in.

"Tlengin tried to make a move on Rosche's territory. They lost. But Rosche doesn't like to waste opportunities. I passed his tests and here I am."

Another burst of anger quelled her reply. "Who touched my bike?"

The lightning canister was gone, carefully removed. That was hers. Her invention she'd never shared with anyone. Only Kayin, who'd helped her with it until it worked.

Gered rose from the stool and went to the workbench against the back wall. He flipped back the lid on a toolbox and nudged aside some cloth before pulling the flickering canister out. He extended it to her, his face infuriatingly blank.

She snatched it, cradling it in her hands as she turned it over, looking for any signs of tampering. He sat back down with a slight exhale.

"That's smart. Carbon inlay and mercan routers? How many miles can you get off that?"

She bristled at the ease with which he'd apparently figured out how it worked.

He twisted on the stool to look up at her. "I'd hide that if I were you. If Rosche heard you had something like that, he'd have you making it for every bike in here, and then say goodbye to the rest of the lower country."

The canister suddenly felt hot in her hands. Bikes would be able to run on the electricity instead of gas, extending their speed and travel time and taking away their dependence on the resource. The gangs would be able to ride anywhere they wanted.

"You didn't tell anyone?"

He shook his head. "I took it off as soon as I had a chance to look at it. That's the sort of thing Rosche definitely doesn't need to know about."

"Thanks." She tapped it against her palm.

Nothing about him seemed to add up. Someone raised by the Tlengin should be utterly ruthless, not going around trying to keep secrets from his commander. No one who fought like he did should be giving out advice to the very people he caught to help them survive.

She slid the canister into its case, then buried it in the bottom of her bag, feeling for the slight give in a seam which hid another compartment anyone who wasn't Aclar would know to look for.

"Anything else I should know about your 'maintenance' on my bike?"

A snort came from him. "No. I didn't do anything else. You maintain it yourself?"

She scoffed. "What, you think I drift all over the lower country without knowing how to take care of my bike?"

He raised a shoulder. "Just curious. I'm the only mechanic in the unit. Be nice to have someone help out."

She softened a little. *Maybe this is my in with him.* "Sure. Anything you need help with now since we're both down here?"

He shifted more comfortably on the stool. "Dayo's almost worn out his rear brake pad again. You up for something like that?"

She grabbed her kit, a grease cloth, and the parts she needed from the tool bench before heading over to the bike lingering in the circle of light. It stood lurched to the side, the kickstand splayed awkwardly out.

"He seems like a better rider than that."

The huff that seemed to pass as Gered's laugh came from his direction. "He's a showboater."

Laramie nodded. That seemed to fit with what she'd seen. He rode fast and loose, daring the consequences of a wrong move. Gered rode like he moved—steady and controlled.

She resecured the kickstand first. Grabbing another stool, she settled in to work. He seemed content to remain in silence, but her mind buzzed with too many thoughts to keep them all to herself.

"Are challenges like that common?" she blurted.

Something like a sigh cut from him. But he answered. "If there's someone worth taking down. Winning can get you more respect, lift you higher in the ranks."

"What if you'd lost?"

A scornful huff sounded. "I wasn't going to lose."

She raised an eyebrow as she slid the first brake pad out. *Someone has a very high opinion of himself.*

"Did you have to accept it?"

"You can refuse, but you lose face. Maybe get people thinking you might be weak. And if you can't defend your position, you don't deserve to have it."

"Has anyone ever challenged Rosche?"

This time a bark of laughter came from him. "No one's that stupid."

Undoing another bolt, she carefully lifted the caliper off and brushed it clean of dirt. "Really? Years of running this area, and no one's tried to take him down?"

"I thought you would have noticed how tight he's got it all locked down." A bit of sarcasm laced his words.

This time she snorted as she rubbed cleaner over the metal. "To be fair, it took several hours before someone noticed me. So that's on you." A glance over her shoulder showed his head shaking as he worked.

"But really. I'm getting the sense not everyone is an avid supporter."

"Picked up on that, did you? Smarter than you look, drifter."

She could have cut through the sarcasm with a knife. "Maybe I'm just curious about my new overlord."

He sighed again. "Rosche got his start in the Cricean war years ago. Then decided to build up his own little army and take over the area. Technically he did solve some issues with crime runners out here, and everyone was so grateful they didn't notice him just absorbing the runs and building up his forces. He's been taking more and more land every year. He pays well, so that's one way he keeps riders around. And most everyone here would be in a jail outside the territory."

Even you?

"Follow orders, obey the rules, and life's not so bad as a rider."

"Just don't leave?"

Gered stayed quiet so long she didn't think she'd get another answer. "He keeps a tight watch on everything. Running disobeys his order of things and he doesn't like something he can't control."

Laramie replaced the caliper and reached for the new pads. Gered's voice had gained a new tension since she'd asked. She lapsed back into silence as she placed the new pads and tightened the bolts back up.

Wiping her hands off, she spun on the stool to face him.

Now with his sleeves rolled up, his other tattoo was visible. There was something naggingly familiar about the curling script, the looping dip and swell of the letters. She blinked as she realized it wasn't in the common tongue either.

"It's Itan," he said.

Heat rose to her cheeks.

He spoke some words and she closed her eyes, letting her native tongue rush over her.

How shall I fear that from which I'm protected by Heaven's wings?

She could speak Itan, but not read it. Her family had been killed before she learned her letters, and while the travelers were proficient in multiple languages, they often couldn't do more than speak them.

Gray and blue eyes. Was that the only bit of Itan left after the claims the Tlengin and the Barracks had laid on him?

"Been a while since I ran into another Itan," she said, hesitation almost making her stumble over the words, not sure what he might do with them though he'd just shared their native language.

He straightened, twisting his back to stretch it for a second before returning to work. "I was Tlengin longer than I was Itan. Another few years here, and I'll have been a viper longer than I was Itan."

He wasn't old enough to have been taken late by the Tlengin.

And the raiders had destroyed the rest of the Itan settlements along with hers sixteen years ago. Besides, the postal clerk had said the Tlengin raid on Rosche's territory had only been several years ago. He'd been taken as a kid. And the message was clear in his words. He didn't see himself as Itan anymore.

"So why get the tattoo then?"

He brushed the edge of his sleeve, adjusting it like he'd rather pull it down and hide the tattoo again.

"I knew it would piss a few people off." But his focus fell to the tattoo for a long moment before he rotated his arm down to shift it from sight. That didn't seem to be the reason. The old verse didn't seem like the type of tattoo a raider would get either.

"You haven't run into any Itan with the travelers?" He tipped a glance at her. There was curiosity there, not cruelty mocking what she'd lost.

She twisted the leather around her wrist. She'd been looking for years, but most had vanished when the Tlengin got it into their heads that killing Itan was holy business in honor of their nameless god they claimed lived in the Rift.

"No. I'd caught word there might be some settlements up in, or across, the mountains. That's where I was headed."

"Whoever told you that was probably lying."

Irritation sent her bristling. "Why, you know that for sure?"

His expression didn't change. "No, but Itan are too valuable for Rosche to have let by."

A bit of unease crept over her at the flat look in his Itan eyes. What might Rosche want from her then?

"And I do know there's not much past the mountains. You wouldn't find any even if you could get there."

"I'm looking forward to proving you wrong." She tossed her

braid over her shoulder.

"Thought I told you to forget that." He didn't look at her, but his voice reverted to the dangerous calm.

Laramie pushed to her feet. "Guess you thought wrong."

She wasn't staying there. No matter what he said, no matter what the stories said, she was getting out and she was going home.

His shoulders lifted in a short sigh, and he shook his head. "Don't be stupid. Stupid doesn't survive."

She looked down at him. He didn't return the glance, staying focused on his work.

"I'll keep that in mind." She replaced the kit in her saddlebag. "Let me know when you need help down here."

And she left.

CHAPTER TEN

Gered paused at the door back into the bunker, listening. Quiet lingered on the other side. He'd heard some of his unit return from the fights, their voices audible under the garage door he'd left open for some air while he worked.

He just hoped Laramie had disappeared into her room.

There'd been a moment where he felt almost comfortable around her, then she'd started staring at his tattoo. And like an idiot, he'd talked about it, bringing up memories he'd long ago hidden to save them from the brutality of the Tlengin. He so very rarely took them out, and never to share with anyone.

Only for himself when he desperately needed a reminder that maybe, somewhere out there, some good remained in the world.

Easing open the door, he stepped into an empty room. He felt a fool at the relief that washed over him. Admitting he'd once been Itan had only increased the unease he felt around her. Like he'd given up a part of himself he'd never meant anyone else to see, despite the gray and blue eyes he couldn't hide. And each glimpse he caught of her tugged at burned memories and ghosts.

Pain flashed through his hand as he shut the door. He flexed his fingers into a fist, breathing through the discomfort of swollen and bloodied knuckles. Barns never held back. His ribs already threatened bruising later.

Gered pulled a cold beer from the cooler and pressed it against his knuckles. Going immediately to work on the bikes hadn't helped the soreness in his hands. But he'd needed something familiar to calm the rage and the fight throbbing through his veins after the challenge.

The main entry door clicked open and shut. He didn't look up from his hand, recognizing the light tread coming over to him. Relief petered in.

"Get the bikes sorted?" Gioia leaned against the counter opposite him. She kept her voice light and casual, though they both tensed to see if someone would stir in the other rooms.

"Yeah. Didn't get to yours yet." He finally dared to look up.

She lifted a shoulder in a shrug. "It's okay." Her light brown eyes turned down to his hand. A breath hitched over her lips and she turned a quick glance over her shoulder. They were still alone.

Gered's breath froze in his chest as she gently reached for the beer and his hand and took over the task. It wasn't necessary and they both knew it.

"How's it feel?" She tilted a look up at him.

He cleared his throat. "Stings a little."

Her thumb brushed the back of his hand. They both stared down at where their skin met. With the gang rules, this was all it could ever be. Rosche liked controlling every bit of his riders' lives. If anyone found out about them, they'd be well and truly dusted. And Gioia would be worse off than him. She'd be lucky if all Rosche did was take her back to the tower.

So this was what it was. Small touches stolen when no one was there. Brief moments of time where they could imagine for a second what could be if they were free. Sometimes they didn't even talk, just stood together and dreamed in silence.

He shifted, tightening his fingers around hers. The blood and bruises covering his knuckles another mocking reason it could never be. Someone like him didn't deserve someone like her.

"How'd … how'd you do tonight?" He had to force his voice to work.

She turned a slight smile up at him, nearly stopping his heart. "Not as well as I did betting on you."

A quiver of a smile touched his lips. "Hope you didn't listen to Dayo again."

"I did learn from the last time."

A laugh teased his chest. She was the only one who could almost draw it out. Her and Dayo, who'd barged his way in and declared them friends. Something Gered had never really had. It'd taken some getting used to.

"You okay?" She kept tracing his hand with her thumb.

She'd always seen through his non-answers and avoidance. "Just been on edge recently. Needed to get away from the noise for a bit."

"Anything to do with the drifter?"

A quick sigh escaped. It had everything to do with the drifter. With the restlessness that came from riding the same routes, enforcing Rosche's rules day after day, forcing down the powerlessness at being unable make his own decisions. Unable to have anything he truly wanted.

"Maybe."

She arched an eyebrow at him. He conceded with a slight shift between his feet.

"How's she settling in?" he asked.

"Good, I guess." Gioia paused, her grip tightening. "I saw

you talking to her when we brought her in. I was glad she didn't have to go through the same thing I did."

For a moment, a pit yawned in his gut, remembering what had happened to her could happen again if they dusted this up. "Why do you think I warned her?"

A sad sort of smile turned up her lips. "You'd have done it anyway. I know you help the newbies who are lost around here."

Like he'd helped her.

He swallowed hard. It was always quick, always with an unspoken promise they wouldn't tell who'd helped them out.

"So?"

She shook her head in slight aggravation. "So I know that you really do care even though you pretend not to."

This time he shook his head. Caring meant trouble for a person. Caring meant weakness. He hadn't ever been able to afford that.

Gioia pushed forward, until only their linked hands separated them—a small bridge between their bodies. His heart pumped frantically. Still he held back. Fear overwhelming the desire to kiss her, to take her in his arms. Fear that if he started, he wouldn't be able to stop and wouldn't be able to figure out a way to keep living the way they had for the last year.

Her gaze lowered until she stared at his chest. He hated the black in her close-cropped hair. It was brown under the dye. He remembered that much. He'd give anything to see it again.

"Caring isn't weakness," she said.

"Caring is what trapped us like this."

He felt the nudge of her breath against his hand. He had to push her away so he could regain his balance, regain the unfeeling hollowness he wore like his jacket. His body wouldn't do it, so his words had to.

"Caring is something only fools believe in."

She took the hint and stepped away, leaving him free to breathe again. "Then I guess I'm a dusted idiot."

But there was no anger in her eyes. Just sad understanding. She knew as well as he did it could never be. But it didn't stop her wanting and hoping either. Slowly, she unlaced her fingers from his.

"See you tomorrow, sir."

And like that, they were back to the unfeeling unit leader and the simple rider. Nothing more. Except he watched her every step from the room, and she turned one last time to look at him with eyes full of sad longing before she vanished into her room.

CHAPTER ELEVEN

H ow's your hand?" Dayo yawned as they exited the bunker into the bright morning sunlight.

Gered zipped up his jacket, somehow feeling safer for the action. Flexing his fingers, he held up his hand for Dayo to see. Bruising and some swelling scattered over the knuckles, but: "It's fine."

"You need anything for it?" Dayo peered at it.

"Put something cold on it last night," he reassured.

"I didn't think Zelig was really stupid enough to challenge." Dayo scrubbed a hand over his head, bringing it down to rub his eyes.

"Are *you* okay this morning?" Gered raised an eyebrow.

Mid-morning more like, and Dayo had come in after he'd already gone to bed.

Dayo shrugged. "Found a card game after the fights."

And probably something stronger than a cigarette. Gered tucked his hands into his jacket pockets. What Dayo did on his own time was his business, and he never let it interfere with unit business.

"Save anything from the fights?"

Dayo scoffed. "Have some faith in me, why don't you?"

Gered lifted a shoulder with a doubtful expression. Dayo

shoved him and Gered stumbled a few steps with a smirk.

"I don't remember what I did with your share then."

Gered huffed a laugh. Even if that were true, there was nothing around worth spending money on.

They reached the tower and jogged up the steps inside. Breakfast had long been cleared. The kitchen didn't care about units oversleeping. They grabbed nutrient bars and water instead.

"Your brake pads are changed out, by the way." Gered pushed the bar into his pocket.

"How late did you stay in the garage?" Dayo asked before drinking half his water in a long gulp, not quite disguising his returning concern.

Dayo had his ways of keeping busy, and Gered had his.

Gered shifted a little as he slowly undid the cap. "The drifter did it actually. She came down to check her bike and ended up helping."

"Really?" Dayo lowered the bottle and looked at him in surprise. Everyone knew the garage was Gered's territory. Even Dayo rarely bothered him down there. "I guess she is Itan. Probably has the knack for it." Dayo finished off his water, tossed the bottle, and grabbed a new one.

Like me. "Yeah. She might even be able to keep up with all your maintenance requests."

Dayo rolled his eyes as they headed out of the mess hall.

"Gered." A voice halted them in the atrium.

Tension rushed through Gered and his hand twitched down toward the pistol on his left leg. He eased it into a fist instead as Rosche stepped down from the stairs.

"I was going to come looking for you."

"Sir." Gered nodded.

Dayo had gone still beside him.

"Dayo." Rosche flicked a glance over to him.

"Sir." Dayo added a salute.

"Both of you, walk with me." Rosche headed out the main doors and Gered and Dayo hurried to catch up. Gered slid on his sunglasses, another bit of armor in place, like maybe they could make Rosche forget the skills displayed openly in the blue in his eyes.

"I saw your challenge last night, Gered."

The words caught him off guard. Rosche had been there? But maybe it wasn't surprising. Rosche always knew everything, and there were nooks and crannies in every building where someone could lurk unnoticed.

He glanced over to the posts in the main courtyard. Empty. The rider had served the sentence set and was probably in the tower's med center getting taken care of.

"Efficient as always."

"Thank you, sir." The words dug their way from his mouth.

"Do you think Zelig will challenge you again?" Rosche asked, a bit of concerned curiosity in his eyes.

"He seemed to accept the defeat yesterday."

Zelig had still looked pissed as Gered left the fights, but within the rules of the arena, Gered was the clear winner. And Zelig would have to be extra stupid to keep challenging him if that rider was the strongest he could send after Gered.

Rosche hummed thoughtfully. "I've no doubt you can take care of it if he does. But come to me if something else happens."

Gered hated the almost paternal concern in Rosche's voice. Like he really cared. Severi would do the same thing, and then drag his knife through Gered's skin when he felt Gered hadn't done something good or fast enough. Or sometimes just because he felt like it.

"Yes, sir."

"Dayo, I heard you cleaned up last night, too." A bit of amusement came through Rosche's words.

"Always, sir." The cheer in Dayo's voice seemed painfully forced to Gered. But Rosche didn't appear to notice.

"Have you tried the new brew down at the *Roadhouse*?"

"Yes, sir. Last time we headed into town. I prefer the amber though."

"That is one of their better ones."

Gered had to allow the fact that Rosche did know something about every rider under his command. In most riders, it instilled a bit of pride and loyalty that Rosche could talk to them about something personal. Like he really cared. That way it was easier to forgive and forget when he killed or punished on a whim.

They passed around the rear of the tower, stopping at the garage door which housed Rosche's personal bikes. Rosche tapped in the code and the door raised.

"You run a good crew, Gered. Gioia continues to impress me." This time Rosche turned a sharper look at him.

Gered kept his features schooled in the mask he'd perfected a long time ago. His sunglasses hid his traitorous eyes. He hated the way Rosche said her name, caressing the syllables as if he still owned her.

"She might be able to beat Gered at the short range someday." Dayo kept a careless note in his voice.

Rosche smiled. "That I would pay to see."

Gered forced motion into his limbs, making some gesture indicating he wasn't concerned about his uncontested rule as the best shot in the garrison.

Rosche ducked into the garage and wheeled out his bike. It had an extra bulk the rest of the gang bikes didn't—a larger engine, heavier horsepower. It fit the man perfectly.

"How's the drifter settling in?" he asked.

"Seems to be doing just fine, sir," Gered said.

"Good. She seems like she has … potential." A slight smile quirked Rosche's mouth. "She bring anything interesting in?"

Gered's mind flitted back to a canister filled with harnessed lightning, shouting danger in its design and function.

"No, sir. But she does have the knack for machines."

Rosche wanted an answer and he might as well hear about the knack instead of something else.

"Good. Even more potential, then." Rosche gave a pleased smile. "It's been a while since you've seen someone with blue eyes, hasn't it?" A probing edge filled the question.

Gered approximated a shrug. It had been a long time. The Tlengin had made sure of that. He had no idea how she'd survived, and he really didn't care to know. Those things were better left buried. But he knew all too well Laramie's anger at the Tlengin for wiping out their people. Though he seemed to have had more opportunity to bury it deep.

Rosche smiled, a warning in the sight. "Just make sure she keeps performing, Gered. And I'm sure we can find a use for that knack of hers."

"Yes, sir." Gered took the underlying warning for himself as well. Rosche didn't tolerate mediocrity in a useful asset for very long.

"Good." Lightness filled Rosche's tone, the friendliness back. "I'm going to check the recruits myself today. You boys watch each other's backs."

"Yes, sir." They both saluted, stepping back to avoid the cloud of exhaust and dust as Rosche started his engine and drove off.

Dayo hissed something under his breath in the traveler language. "I need to go hit something."

He didn't have as many reasons to come face to face with Rosche as Gered did. But at least he'd gotten better at hiding the hate at Rosche's heavy tax on his traveler family when he did.

Gered's water bottle eased a crackle of relief as he loosened his grip. "Want company?"

Dayo flashed a bitter smile. "Let's go."

———

Gered's back hit the mat with a thump, Dayo pinning him with triumph beginning to light his eyes. Gered allowed a quick smile, kicking his legs up around Dayo's shoulders and twisting, redirecting Dayo off him and to the mat.

"Not fair!" Dayo growled, tugging his arm still in Gered's hold.

"You fall for it every time." Gered released him.

They lay on the mats, staring at the ceiling. An hour after the conversation with Rosche, Dayo seemed to have punched out his anger.

"Need to go again?" Gered asked.

"No. Think I'm good, *kamé*." Dayo tapped his fist against Gered's arm. He sat up with a groan, wiping a sleeve across his sweaty face. "You good?"

Gered held a breath for a moment. The anger and frustration swirling inside him had abated for a few moments.

"I'm good."

Dayo stood and leaned over, extending a hand to haul him to his feet.

"Sure?" He raised an eyebrow.

Gered began to pull the wraps from his hands. "I thought this was for you."

Dayo snorted and tugged his own wraps free. "Right. Because you didn't pull some of your punches."

Gered worked his hand against the swelling and bruising. He shouldn't have sparred so soon after a bare-knuckle fight. "Did I hurt you?"

A huff came from the traveler. "You think I can't take a punch after being here for three years?"

Gered stared at his hand. That wasn't the point. A nudge to his shoulder brought his focus up to Dayo.

"I know you won't hurt any of us."

Us. Unit Four.

Though some days the anger from being trapped for so long threatened to spill over, and only Dayo's laugh, Gioia's smiles, or the calm of the garage helped soothe it and the fear at the violence he could do if he let it unleash.

"Hey!" A voice from the doorway turned their attention.

And the rest of the anger vanished at the sight of Gioia standing there, hands laden with water bottles and paper-wrapped objects making a determined push to scent the room with something other than sweat.

"Heard you both came this way. Dec and I got food." She glanced at both of them. He noticed the way she stared longer at him, the way her cheeks darkened a little at the way his sweaty shirt clung to him. It made his fingers fumble at the wraps he still held.

"Gee, you are a treasure. A diamond in a barren wasteland.

Has anyone ever told you this?" Dayo scooped up his boots.

Gioia's smile flashed, and Gered's heart thudded oddly.

"No. You can keep talking though."

"A rainstorm in a drought. Brighter than the Lion's Mane in the northern sky." Dayo shoved his feet in boots and tossed the wraps into the dirty pile. "Out of curiosity, what did you get?"

"Beef wraps from that little hole-in-the-wall on Timber."

Dayo clutched a hand to his chest. "A queen among women."

Gered allowed a smile as he retrieved his own boots, listening to Dayo and his increasingly ridiculous platitudes. Gioia stuck her nose in the air, gesturing for Dayo to continue.

His feet settled a little firmer on the ground as he watched Dayo sling an arm around Gioia's shoulders and relieve her of the bottles, watching how she didn't flinch, just turned a smile to him as they waited for him to finish.

They all wore their masks well. Him, a stone void of emotion. Dayo, a little too loud and boisterous. And Gioia, a careful carelessness. And only like this were they okay with letting them slip.

Unlike Dayo who'd left his boots undone, he carefully tightened his laces. Holsters next, a routine check to his pistols before sliding them home.

Once done, Gioia ducked out from under Dayo's arm and led the way outside to a bench on the shaded side of the training building. They took a seat, and Gered eased down into the empty space beside her.

He took his wrap, the brush of her fingers against his grounding him again. The sweet and spicy scent of the meal grew stronger as he undid the waxy brown paper. A thin round of bread filled with shredded beef, spicy cabbage, and topped with cheese and roughly chopped cactus fruit barely held itself together in the confines of the paper.

They ate in silence. Gered leaned against the wall, the heat drying out his shirt. Somewhere voices raised in argument, escalating until they cut off as fists likely started flying. Keeping fights clean was a laughable rule. In the hour since they'd been in the training room, someone new had been put into the posts. Off duty riders wandered around in groups of at least two. Always safety in numbers, especially the lower one ranked in the pecking order of the Barracks.

"Find anything good at the library?" Dayo crumpled the paper up.

Gioia folded hers more neatly around her wrap as she took another bite. "Who said I went to the library?"

Gered allowed a small smile. "It is conveniently close to a certain hole-in-the-wall on Timber."

A gentle elbow into his side drew a huff of a laugh.

It had taken months after her choosing into the unit before she'd let slip that she missed reading. He'd seen the tiny library before in town and found a way to direct her to it. Then it took a few more months before she'd been comfortable enough to go without him or Dayo. He'd never gone in. And when Dec came along and confessed to being a reader, Gioia had started taking him along.

Gioia's mouth quirked. "Fine. The other smart one in the unit and I went to the library. And yes, I did find something good."

"'Other smart one'? But I didn't go with you," Dayo said.

She rolled her eyes.

"Just don't stay up too late reading again. We're leaving early." The paper, spotted with grease stains, folded into neat creases under Gered's fingers.

"You could change the time we leave, you know." Gioia grinned.

"That's not a bad idea," Dayo chimed in.

Gered shook his head against another smile. "Maybe I'll change it to earlier."

"You're gonna be missing half the unit if you do," Gioia warned. "Your lieutenant included."

"I've been thinking about replacing him anyway," Gered said offhandedly.

Dayo mock-laughed, reaching over Gioia's head as she ducked and shoving at Gered.

"You don't have to worry anyway. I'm sure Laramie isn't going to want lights to stay on." Gioia crumpled her paper and tossed it at Dayo. He caught it and placed it by his side.

"Gered let her into the garage," he informed Gioia.

She turned, eyes wide. "Really?"

Gered winced a little internally, feeling a small stab of guilt for consistently keeping them out of his small refuge but then opening up slightly to the drifter instead.

"She's got the knack."

Gioia nodded in understanding, the bit of betrayal disappearing. The law of the Barracks was to take advantage of anything that might be useful.

"Makes sense. Hey, maybe she can help you keep up with maintenance on Dayo's bike."

"Hey!" Dayo lightly tapped her thigh with a fist.

A quick laugh burst from her. Gered dared lean a little closer.

"That's what I said."

"Okay, I'm officially putting in for a transfer to another unit who will better appreciate me." Dayo tipped his head back in an aggrieved manner.

"I heard Branson was looking to add to his unit." Gioia couldn't make it through without snickering.

Dayo mimed a gag. "On second thought…"

"Well, well, having fun over here?" a sneering voice cut in.

Gioia stiffened beside him as Zelig shrugged into his red jacket, another of his riders pushing from the training building to come up behind him.

Dayo reclined a bit more against the wall. "Here looking for a rematch?"

Zelig glared the rider's way. "No one asked you, *kamé*." He intentionally butchered the traveler word.

Gered watched Dayo from the corner of his eye, ready to step in if Dayo acted on the tenseness taking over his limbs.

"Need anything, Zelig?" Gered asked, drawing the leader's attention back to him.

"Maybe some company tonight." He flicked a gaze to Gioia.

Rage began to coil again in his gut.

She curled a lip. "Shift off."

Gered pushed to his feet, hands hanging loose by his sides, ready to pull the comfortable weight of one of his twin guns into his hand.

"I'll ask one more time. Need something?"

Zelig's lip curled up. "Maybe I'm tired of seeing you flaunt the rules and step all over me and mine."

The anger simmered. A breeze wafted by, brushing his skin. No jacket. He could move easier without it.

"Then grow some stones and challenge me yourself." Gered allowed his scorn to come through. "Or keep sending men, and after I break their arms, I'll come for you."

Zelig crossed his arms. "Sure about that?"

Gered took a second glance, making sure he hadn't missed anything the last time he'd sized Zelig up. *Still just full of himself.*

"Maybe not. I don't see anything of value worth taking your unit for."

Red suffused Zelig's face. "I'd watch your back, Gered boy. Or maybe I'll pick your unit off one by one." He flicked a glance at Dayo and Gioia who'd risen to their feet, watchful and ready.

Gered allowed a small smile. The kind that didn't move anywhere but his mouth. He leaned closer to Zelig.

"Try."

Zelig tried to hold his stare. Narrowed his eyes as if that would continue to threaten Gered. He backed off, slowly turned away, and strode off followed by his rider.

A light touch on Gered's hand dissipated the storm. He eased his fingers out of the fists he'd formed. One short breath and a look at Gioia settled him back.

Dayo muttered a few words that held the cadence of Aclar. "Idiot." He sniffed and tilted a wry look to Gered. "Need to head back inside to the mats?"

Gered dared reach out and brush Gioia's hand where she still lingered close by his side. Her brown eyes asked the question.

"No. I'm good." His fingers twitched a little. The only other way to get rid of the urge to fight was to work.

"Think I'll head to the garage for a bit."

"Okay." Gioia stepped back. The offer was in both their faces, but he turned away.

"See you later." He grabbed his jacket from the bench and strode off alone.

CHAPTER TWELVE

Laramie frowned at the motorcycle in front of her. It stood a little taller than her bike, with a more slender body. It had been made to race across dirt and asphalt and up and down mountains, not to comfortably transport a rider and her life across the country in long haul runs.

"You gonna get on, or stand and pose?" Harlan barked at her.

She restrained her retort. The man would retaliate if he felt so inclined. Laramie huffed a sigh and mentally apologized to her bike still in hidden exile in Unit Four's garage. She felt like she was cheating on it with the gang bike. The feeling intensified as she swung her leg over the seat and settled in, pulling on a plain red helmet. The engine thrummed to life with a coy purr.

The other recruits started up their bikes, beginning on loose circuits of the yard with varying degrees of confidence. Surprisingly, Axel showed himself one of the best riders. Laramie kicked up the stand and pushed off. She settled her feet a little higher and further back than she would on her bike. The handlebars coaxed her into more of a forward lean, inviting her to feel the testiness of the steering.

Harlan glared at her. She scowled back behind the shelter of the helmet and started a circuit. The motorcycle had a quick response to it, ready to drift wherever she looked. She guided it through several gear changes, the clutch engaging flawlessly.

Imagine where I could go on this thing with the lightning boost. She tamped down the thought as if Rosche could hear it all the way in the garrison building. A horn cut over the sounds of motorcycles. Laramie glanced up to see the psycho himself standing beside Harlan.

She followed the others' lead and rumbled slowly toward them, coming to a stop at the end of a ragged line of bikes facing Rosche.

He crossed arms across his chest and surveyed them all one by one, his expression flat. It only wavered when it came to rest on her. A faint smirk played across his face. She stared back for a second through the open visor before turning her attention forward. She'd seen the look before. She didn't have to play the game.

"Head out to the track," Harlan ordered.

Laramie took up the rear again. Even after several days of training, there seemed to always be some other part of the Barracks she hadn't seen yet. Axel took the lead, heading out the side gate, and driving past the shooting range.

She took her time following, still getting used to the responsiveness of the bike compared to hers. Axel disappeared, and one by one the other recruits dipped over a large hill and sped down to a wide dirt oval sprawling over several hundred yards.

The mountains loomed a little closer, beckoning to her with their subtle shades of greens and brown and reds. An engine revved beside her, rear wheel kicking up dust to throw through the open visor of her helmet. Coughing, she turned to glare at one of the older trainees, who leered a grin at her.

She flipped him a gesture telling him exactly what he could

go do and pulled away. Axel pulled up on her left side, his normally cheerful face a blank mask as he stared down the other rider. The rider laughed and spat in their direction before riding off.

"He's an asshole." An unfamiliar vehemence stained Axel's voice.

"He is that." Laramie cleared dirt from her mouth. "What do we do here?"

"Harlan will let us know. This is the first time Rosche has come out to watch in a while." Axel's throat bobbed as he watched Harlan and Rosche ride down to join them.

"What happens when he comes to watch?" Laramie asked.

"Sometimes nothing, sometimes he'll reward a trainee for doing well. Or punish one for not doing as well." A faintly queasy look spread over his face.

How many times has he been punished? A shiver cut down her back despite the heat trapped under her leather jacket. She was fine with Rosche staying in the tower, far away from them.

"You seem pretty good on the bike." She turned back to Axel. His quick grin resurfaced.

"Yeah, I've been riding for years. My family has a busted up dirt bike me and my siblings all learned on. These are way better though." His expression darkened again. "It's about the only thing I'm good at here, so at least I got that going for me."

"Hey." Laramie shifted her boots on the ground as she adjusted her seat. "I'm not too bad at hand-to-hand. Want to practice later?"

A faint smile tugged at his lips. "Sure."

"Listen up!" Harlan bellowed again. "Take the track one at a time, fast as you can. Drifter, you go last. The rest of these losers have been doing this for weeks now. Keep an eye on what they're doing so you can do the same."

A little explanation would be nice. But Laramie nodded and pushed her bike back to allow room for the others to go first. One of the other teens took off first in response to Harlan's signal.

His bike sped around the twisting and turning track full of obstacles and raised hillocks, hitting air a few times at more disguised ridges and bumps in the dirt. The third turn sent him skidding a little in the curve.

Harlan shook his head as the teen came back in a spray of dirt. Laramie waved her hand in front of her face to clear the cloud, watching with grim satisfaction as the leering rider botched the third turn, skidding too far toward the edge of the track and losing precious seconds.

Axel rode it well, hugging the inside of the track, leaning into the turns and shaving his time down into the one to beat. He came back in, exchanging a grin with Laramie as he flipped his visor back up. She pushed off, revving the engine to pick up speed and heading down the slight incline into the first turn of the track.

The other bikes had correctly shown the texture of the track. A series of dips and ridges waited past the second turn. The bike absorbed the shock of each one better than hers, and once free, she gunned the engine. Like Axel, she timed her turn to hug the inside. The bike seemed eager enough to help her out on the turn, tempting her to push faster.

Straightening out of the third turn, she shifted again to head into the smoother section of the track and drift in and out between a line of poles. Then through shallow dips of water, and up and down higher hills before heading back up to the start where she sprayed to a halt by Harlan.

"Not bad for the first time, drifter." Harlan allowed. "You're fourth in this pack right now. Back in line."

She rejoined Axel, who held out a fist. She bumped it with her gloved hand. "What's next?"

"Races."

Harlan began calling out names and pairing them up. Rosche still said nothing, just sitting on his bike, lips pressed in a broad line as he studied them from behind his sunglasses. Laramie tried to shake off the cold feeling lingering between her shoulder blades and focus instead on beating her opponents while still trying to stay slightly behind Axel. The kid deserved to excel at something in training.

Half an hour later, a crackle sounded in her ear, sending her jerking in surprise.

"Listen up," Rosche's voice followed.

The trainees turned toward him. Laramie glanced down at her bike, feeling stupid for not noticing the shortwave radio connected to the bike's handlebars and feeding the receiver in the helmet.

"We're going for a bit of a ride. Something you all need to see."

Unease threatening, Laramie fell in with the other recruits as they followed Rosche and Harlan away from the track. He headed north, cutting across country. The rough terrain demanded her focus as she wove around holes, low hillocks of sharp-edged cacti, and grasping mesquite.

They hit pavement and the engine whined a little as she shifted, as if displeased to be back on level ground. They rode for an hour. Nothing else came over the radio to indicate where they were headed. Rosche and Harlan stayed at the head of the pack, content to ignore them.

Restlessness began to fill Laramie with every uneven bump of asphalt. Finally, a sign flashed by announcing four miles to the next town. Shimmering heat waves distorted the road ahead, smearing the buildings as they appeared.

Rosche slowed and they rumbled into town at a more sedate pace.

What are we doing here? And what is it he wants to show us?

She glanced to Axel on her right as if the helmets would reveal anything.

The road spilled into a roundabout, and another unit already waited in the square, a bulky transpo truck with them.

The riders looked up in surprise at their approach.

"Fan out and try to look like you know what you're doing," Harlan's voice broke over the radio.

Laramie obeyed, coming into a neat stop beside Axel. The line was a little more organized than it had been that morning, but still not very intimidating. She imitated the others, and opened her visor to hear better without straining through the helmet.

The few townsfolk loading crates into the transpo truck shoved their load in and began to back away, open fear in their faces as Rosche stood from his bike and pulled his helmet off.

He ignored them and went straight for the red-jacketed unit leader who stood a little apart from his men. A middle-aged woman in jeans and long-sleeved plaid overshirt, open against the heat, hurried over.

"Rosche, what an honor! What brings you here, sir?" she asked, voice trembling a little.

"Mayor." Rosche inclined his head, but didn't move his gaze from the unit leader, who shifted under the scrutiny.

"It has come to my attention that you've been skimming goods here, Callan."

The man's eyes widened. "Sir?"

Heaviness fell in Laramie's gut. The man wasn't a very good liar. The mayor edged away.

Rosche loomed closer to the rider. "You should have been more careful about reports you turned in, and who you talked to about this little scheme." He deliberately looked beyond the man to his unit.

Callan swallowed hard and kept his gaze forward. "I'm sorry, sir. I just…"

"You thought you could steal from me?" Rosche bellowed.

The rider flinched, desperation flickering in his eyes.

Laramie's heart pounded.

"Anything to say?" Rosche asked.

Callan's hand moved to his gun. "Sir, I'll do anything to make it up to you. Please…"

Rosche moved with the speed of a pouncing jacklion. Whipping his handgun out, he pointed it at the man's head, and pulled the trigger.

Laramie flinched despite herself at the resounding crack. Callan crumpled to the ground like a broken doll.

The mayor gaped in surprise at the cold-blooded murder, some blood dusting across her light gray undershirt.

"Sir, I didn't know about this!" she pleaded with hand outstretched.

Rosche turned to her, holstering the pistol.

"I know." He rested a hand on her shoulder, and she flinched under it. "I don't hold this town responsible. However, the trucks have been light because of this. I expect double next time."

"Yes, sir." She nodded.

He released her and turned to the unit who watched him cautiously.

For a moment Laramie hoped they'd draw weapons and fire on Rosche, but a glance at her companions showed the truth. Rosche had brought them, the trainees, out with him. He wasn't concerned at all.

"Pearce!" he called.

A rider jogged over, wariness still in his eyes. He gave the fallen unit leader a wide berth.

"You now command Unit Fifteen. Make sure you get a red jacket when you're back in. Load up this piece of trash's bike in the truck and bring it in."

Pearce saluted. "Yes, sir."

"Don't think to make his mistake. There's plenty who'd love your new position," Rosche warned.

Pearce snapped a salute. Rosche ignored it and turned back to the trainees.

"Fuel up!" he ordered.

Harlan waved them to the eastern rim of the roundabout that spat out another road leading to the refueling station.

An attendant rushed out to help, keeping his eyes down and staying just out of reach. But the trainees for the most part ignored him as they pulled off helmets and muttered amongst themselves. Only one of the older trainees who'd come in as a drifter looked back over his shoulder where Rosche and Harlan waited with admiration in his eyes.

Laramie shuddered. She made a point to thank the attendant after he filled up the tank. He scowled in return, no kindness in his eyes.

She settled back onto the seat, taking a moment to let the warm breeze tease at her sweaty face. Axel wheeled his bike away from the pump, his sun-darkened face pale and drawn.

"You okay?" She kept her voice low.

"Yeah." He jerked his helmet back on and left it at that.

Once refueled, Rosche drove back through the town. Laramie risked a glance at the unit. The body had been moved, and the riders moved in response to Pearce's directions. Returning to business as usual. Rosche didn't turn his head at all, leading the way back to the highway as if he had no concerns at all.

Even though she knew nothing about Unit Fifteen or their former commander, Laramie allowed anger to build up in her chest. No wonder everyone obeyed the man who thought nothing of rolling into town and executing someone.

Gered's words the night before made more sense. *"He keeps a tight watch on everything." The unit was willing to snitch on their own leader. And someone's going to notice anything out of the ordinary if I try to leave.*

A sigh fogged her visor. *I really dusted up coming here.*

She'd just have to be more careful, take her time when she planned to make her run. Otherwise she'd be answering directly to Rosche, a scenario that was becoming even more unappealing every minute.

CHAPTER THIRTEEN

Unit Four's bunkhouse was a madhouse by the time Laramie returned, covered in sweat and grime. Her new bike had been left in the training garage. Since she hadn't earned a place in a gang, she couldn't use the bunker's garage.

She stepped her careful way up the stairs to the main door. Voices she didn't recognize shouted and mingled with others she knew from Unit Four. Most sounded friendly. There was at least one argument. A brief laugh struck her imagining Gered arguing with someone.

Laramie decided to finally brave it and slipped in. The rec room teemed with bodies, and the salty scent of sweat and dust and gasoline overwhelmed her own. Leather-jacketed riders squeezed past each other, some heading back into the rooms, some cracking open cold beers and lounging on the couches with Four.

"Who's this?" A hand flicked her shoulder.

She turned and looked up into cool green eyes with a bit of copper by the left iris. By habit she brushed his hand away. His upper lip curled back in a faint smirk and he took another sip of beer.

"We weren't gone that long. You fight your way out of the

tower?" he asked.

"No, fought Rosche and won and here I am." She pushed her shoulders back, keeping her hands loose by her sides.

He snorted. "You won?"

"She came through the territory and we picked her up. Rosche decided to give her a shot in the gang."

To Laramie's surprise, Dayo had sidled up beside her. The lieutenant leaned a casual hip against the counter.

"Yeah? She in with Four?" The rider still studied her with unnerving interest. She held his gaze, letting her eyes narrow a bit at the corners.

"Trainee. Gered hasn't decided yet if he'll stake her. She's bunking here since we picked her up." Dayo flicked a look at her and then back to the hallway. She took the hint and mock saluted both of them, before backing away and retreating into the safety of the room.

Gioia lay on her bed, reading a worn paperback. "How'd the day go?"

Laramie sat on her bunk, easing out of her boots and trying not to gag at the stench her socks emitted. "Got on one of your subpar bikes."

Gioia smirked over her book. "Still salty about that one, are we?"

"You can't just insult someone's bike and expect me not to say something every chance I get." Laramie grinned and tossed her jacket aside. "I'm guessing that's the other unit outside?"

Gioia grimaced. "Yep. Stay away from Connor. I'm pretty sure he's crazy and he seems to collect other nutjobs."

"Let me guess. Tall, green eyes, same boring haircut."

Gioia snapped a finger at her. "Got it in one. You're a smart one over there, drifter."

Laramie set aside her knives. "I tend to keep an eye out for crazy guys who try and corner me in kitchens."

Gioia tensed a little.

"Dayo came over and ran interference."

She relaxed. "That's good or bad. Dayo and Connor don't play very nice with each other."

"Sounds like you just described the whole place."

Gioia snorted a laugh. "That's true. But welcome to bunker politics. Thankfully we'll be leaving in the morning. Rosche apparently learned early on not to leave two units in close proximity like this for any amount of time."

Laramie's stomach flopped. She felt like a spoiled kid, but … "Leaving?"

Gioia swung her feet over the side of the bed, giving her a sympathetic look. "Sorry. Back on patrol. We'll only be out for a few days. Three at the most."

"From what I just saw of my new bunker mates, I can honestly say I'm a little bit jealous I'm not in the unit." Laramie leaned over and pulled her bag out from under the bed.

Gioia chuckled. "Keep your head down, and time it right. Most of Connor's gang are partiers, so they'll be out drinking late at night either in town or over at the tower. Just make sure to lock the door."

"So I should definitely shower tonight since it doesn't sound like I'll have much of a chance?"

Gioia's smile came wry at the corners. "Yeah. You want to go now? I'll walk you down and stay with you. They don't mess with me anymore, but you're new. Might as well take advantage of safety in numbers."

Laramie dug out clean clothes. "Thanks."

Gioia nodded, folding the corner of her page and setting it down on the ragged table.

They took the back stairs down to the shower rooms. Someone had made sure there was a separate area for women. Water splashed and ran in the showers already. Laramie paused and raised an eyebrow at Gioia who grimaced.

"Looks like you're about to meet Corinne," she said the name like she'd gotten a mouthful of dust.

Gioia rapped twice, then three times, then once more on the door before pushing in. "She's dusting insane, but I still got her to agree to this so I knew who was coming in," Gioia explained. Laramie nodded, committing the sequence to memory.

The occupant of the room turned around as they came in. She stood taller than Gioia, with more curves to flaunt. Though Laramie had never seen Gioia without the baggier trousers and shirts that effectively hid everything about her.

Corinne apparently didn't suffer from the same shyness. Her fitted shirt hugged her body, allowing hints of skin to show just above her trousers, also skin-tight. Either makeup or engine grease smeared around her eyes, striking against her paler skin and highlighting the dark green.

"Fresh meat?" She pressed her tongue to her teeth, taking her time looking Laramie up and down. She sidled closer, peering down at Laramie, who wasn't used to other women being as tall, or taller than her. It irritated her.

"Decided to try out for these little gangs you've got out here. Heard it wasn't hard." Laramie returned the favor, keeping a slightly disdainful look on her face as she scanned Corinne. The other rider scoffed.

"Unit Four try and save you like they did this one?" She flicked fingers with long sharpened nails at Gioia.

"I can take care of myself."

Corinne pursed her lips in a mocking expression. "You should take notes, Gioia. I always said you could use some more attitude."

Gioia rolled her eyes. "You gonna shower or what, Corinne?"

Corinne sauntered away. "Maybe I will, maybe I won't. You gonna take a hot shower and wish Gered would come in here and shove you up against the tiles?" She flung a look over her shoulder.

Gioia tucked her hands in her back pockets and turned her face away, ignoring Corinne as she made several obscene noises. Laramie raised an eyebrow again.

"Charming," she mouthed.

Gioia gave a wry smile. "Yeah, she's not going to do much to watch your back."

Laramie turned away from where Corinne was undressing without a care in the world. "Noted."

True to her word, Gioia waited inside, close to the door while she showered. Laramie finished after Corinne did. The other woman dressed in clothes that probably technically met the uniform requirement and walked out, hips swaying side to side. She paused only to look down at Gioia again where the shorter woman leaned up against the wall, hands still in back pockets.

They exchanged a poisonous look, followed by some sort of almost acknowledgement they'd do the dance, but still stand up for each other when pressed. Laramie watched in interest as she dressed. Survival still didn't mean you had to be happy with your partner.

Laramie waited until Corinne slammed the door on her way out. "Who got here first?"

"I did. Though I took the long way getting into the gangs." Gioia shifted slightly between her feet. "Corinne impressed enough when fighting back against the unit who took out her travel crew that Rosche decided to put her right in with the trainees. She already came with some combat training and she's wicked with a knife..."

"Plus the crazy eyes," Laramie put in.

"Right." Gioia chuckled. "No one messes with her."

Laramie scooped up her dirty clothes, ducking them under the faucet to rinse them out. "About the rules that got read out my first day." She forced a swallow and the words to continue. She hadn't worried about it around Unit Four, but now with them leaving ... "Those actually get followed?"

Gioia sank back against the wall. "Mostly. There's a few that'll try and jump you in an alley. That's why you always keep a weapon. Rosche will punish those who decide to flaunt the rules outside of trips to town, but it doesn't stop some who think they could get away with it. Just out-tough these guys in Unit Five, and you should be good."

"Sounds like it's going to be a long three days for me," Laramie said.

Gioia chuckled. "You'll be fine. We'll be back soon."

I can take care of myself, she reminded herself. She'd just never been alone in the middle of a warlord's gang before. *Strange how priorities have shifted to trusting this particular unit.* She smiled wryly and followed Gioia from the bathroom.

The rec room had cleared out by the time they made it up. Most of Unit Five appeared to have gone to the showers or headed to get food. Laramie accepted Gioia's invitation to go to the tower together to eat. Might as well take full advantage before she was on her own again.

She almost hated how dependent she'd gotten on Gioia over the last few days after spending weeks out on the road by herself. The viper flags leered down at her as they entered the tower.

"Drifter." Rosche's chillingly deep voice halted her. Gioia went stiff beside her.

Laramie unwillingly pivoted to see Rosche sauntering down the stairs. He came over, hands in his trouser pockets.

"What did you think of the demonstration today?"

"It was ... effective, sir." Disgust roiled inside again.

He flashed a smile that only stoked the storm inside her.

"Good. You ride well." He swept a lingering look up and down her. She kept her chin up, feet braced a little wider.

"Thanks." She shifted to start walking again.

"Who taught you?" He now stood even with her, leaning against the railing.

Laramie gritted her teeth and turned again. "My traveler family."

Amusement lit his eyes. "You're a little light to be a traveler."

"Adopted in." Laramie said tightly. The last thing she wanted to discuss with Rosche was her family.

"They teach you to fight, too?"

She nodded. "In case I ran into any psychotic wannabe warlords."

Rosche curled a lip in a smile. "I like you."

"Wish it was mutual." Laramie tried to back away. Gioia had paled significantly, throwing her freckles in stark relief as she stared at her in something like horror.

Rosche only chuckled. "You have any other skills with that

tongue of yours?"

Gioia tugged on her sleeve as she turned again, ready to tempt fate. Her brain decided to listen to Gioia's warning.

"Are we dismissed?" Her tongue still couldn't manage to scrape all the sarcasm from the words.

Rosche pushed away from the railing and loomed over her. "For now. I hear you have some other skills and can be useful around here. Don't take a lesson from Gered on that."

Laramie's confusion escaped in a slight crease of her forehead. Rosche didn't explain, instead sliding his gaze over to Gioia.

"Isn't that right, Gioia?"

A flicker of irritation lit Gioia's eyes, chasing away the paleness. It faded just as fast as Rosche stepped closer. She went still, hands in her back pockets, staring at a point on the floor. Laramie tensed, ready to pull a knife.

"Enjoy your evening, Gioia," was all he said before he left them in the silent hall.

Laramie released her knife as Gioia shuddered a breath. She moved without a backward glance at Laramie, her strides fast and uneven as she entered the dining hall. Laramie followed slower, fighting the churning in her stomach.

When she got out of Rosche's territory, she was going to see if Gioia wanted to come too.

CHAPTER FOURTEEN

The garage door clicked open and shut. Gered paused, listening to the boot steps. A sliver of disappointment stung as he realized it wasn't Gioia. He wiped grease off his hand almost savagely. He didn't need to keep looking for her everywhere.

Laramie stepped into the light. A bit of tension tightened across his shoulders. He still didn't know what to do with her. Didn't know what to do with the way she kept coming into the garage, ready to work the engines like an Itan, when he'd been too afraid to acknowledge it for years.

She shoved hands into her pockets and glanced around the garage at the new bikes. "Need help with anything?"

"If you want." Unit Five treated their bikes like dust, but Connor paid up for him to do some maintenance if they happened to be in the Barracks at the same time.

Laramie grabbed the leather-bound tool set from her saddlebags, a stool, and settled next to the bike he pointed at.

He really should have expected she'd start a conversation.

"Gioia said you're headed out in the morning."

He grunted.

"Same place you kidnapped me?"

Gered rolled his eyes. "You were trespassing."

"Details." A bit of humor crept into her voice and an annoyingly small smile tugged his mouth in return. She might give Dayo a run for his money if her stupidity didn't get the best of her. Another reason not to get too comfortable.

"Yeah, that's our normal route. We'll be back in a few days." He didn't know why he hastened to reassure her.

"Gioia gave me some tips for the next few days." Laramie exchanged wrench for screwdriver.

This time he did smile down at the engine in front of him. Gioia was the kind of person who would keep looking out for someone.

"Any chance recruits are allowed to go out on a patrol as practice or anything?" she asked casually. Too casually.

The warmth nudging his heart vanished. "Thought I told you to drop that."

"Have you?" She tilted a wide-eyed innocent look over her shoulder. He rolled his eyes despite his irritation.

"Or have access to maps or anything?" A smirk built around her mouth.

He shook his head and ignored her. A faint laugh came from her direction.

"I told you that you won't make it."

"That's for me to find out, isn't it?" The challenge came back to her voice.

Irritation flared higher in his chest. He shoved to his feet and went to stand over her. She blinked up at him, tool dangling loose from her hand.

"It's only asking for trouble."

"You didn't seem like you cared."

"I don't." *Liar.*

She quirked an eyebrow. "Sure looks that way."

"It's not worth it."

Laramie draped her arms across her knees. "No one's ever left?"

"Not alive."

He'd put down the last few who'd tried. Only his skill with a gun had saved him the last time he'd pointed his bike toward the border. *I'll be fair. Three chances, Gered.* Rosche's words echoed in his mind. *You've used up two of them. Next time, I won't be as generous.* That had been right before he'd sunk a knife into Gered's skin, knowing full well what it did to him.

A chill froze his arms at the memory.

Laramie's face turned serious as he focused back on her.

"If I try, are you going to stop me?"

The chill reached up to choke his throat. "He'll make me."

"If I was to ride out of here right now, would you stop me?"

Half of him wondered if she really would grab her bike and leave right then. The other half knew he wouldn't turn her in if she did. His duty would come later when the units hunted her down, had her trapped, or slowed her down enough for him to find her in the crosshairs.

"No."

"All right then." She nodded and turned back to the engine.

That seemed to be the end of it. His boots scuffed the cement.

"Hey." Her soft voice halted him for a second. "You know I won't stop. But I won't bring you into this. I don't want to dust anything up for you and the unit. You seem like decent people."

"Damn straight you keep us out of your stupid decisions," Gered said harshly. "After you finish that, the bike next to you needs some work."

She tipped her head and returned to her work, staying silent. And for that, he was grateful.

~

Morning dawned in a haze of gray light. Storm clouds gathered over the mountains, faintly scenting the air of rain. Scant dampness tamped down the dust as Unit Four wheeled their bikes out of the garage. Gered tilted an eye up to the sky. Some bits of blue already peeked through. If it rained again, it would come hard and fast and be gone in minutes.

The engine thrummed awake, and he settled on the seat as more and more motorcycles came to life around him.

Gered pulled on his helmet and the world quieted a fraction. He flipped the comm switch and static crackled in his left ear.

"Check in," he said as the rest of his unit donned helmets.

"Dayo."

"Gioia."

He tried not to linger over her name.

The rest of his unit called out their names, tapping helmets and checking gloves and jackets. Gered gave a thumbs up and got nine returning gestures. He flipped the kickstand up and pulled out.

The main gates swung open in front of them and the guard tapped his chest twice with a closed fist before pointing it up in the air. Safe riding.

Gered raised his right hand in thanks. The dust trying to sneak its way up under his helmet lessened its advance once they hit asphalt. Dayo crept up just behind him on his right, enough to see in his periphery. Gered checked his mirrors. The rest of the unit staggered themselves out behind him in their preferred riding pattern.

Gioia rode on his left, one bike down, visible in his mirror. Always visible. Even if she didn't keep her bike in position, he moved to keep her there. Sometimes seeing her helmet and slender form hugging the bike was the only thing that kept him grounded in the world of sand and heat and violence.

Four hours of riding put them at their first stop on their route. The sun broke through as they rumbled past the town's population sign. A pumpjack creakily rose up and down in the field beyond it. Gered slowed a fraction to allow a tumbleweed to rattle across the road in front of him.

A young boy stood on the porch of a whitewashed house, face solemn and a little rebellious. Gered almost shook his head. He didn't like to think that maybe in a few years, if he was still alive, he'd be putting down the boy for something stupid.

They rumbled down the main street. Most of the people out and about glanced up, but didn't deviate from their routine. The units were a common sight in the towns. A way of life that hoping and wishing couldn't change.

Gered pulled into a space before a two-storied building. A weather-beaten sign marked the mayor's office. He killed his engine and pulled his helmet off. The sun hadn't driven off the faint humidity lingering in the wake of the rain, and his jacket clung to his back with the tenacious dampness.

He wiped sweat from the side of his face and hung the helmet from a handlebar. Dayo did the same, rolling his shoulders loose before standing and joining Gered on his way into the office.

A blast of recycled air hit them in a cool wave, chilling him for a moment before his body adjusted. He tucked his sunglasses away. Wooden benches lined the small lobby. An older woman looked up from the desk by the wall, a bit of fear lingering in her look.

"Gered, good to see you again." She wavered a smile.

Gered gave a tight nod. It was never a good day when the unit rolled into town, even if he was less heavy-handed than the previous unit leader.

"He in?"

The woman nodded and hurried from behind her desk down the hall and pushed open the door. Gered followed without pause and brushed past her into the office.

Mayor Cirino hastily stood to greet them. Bits of sweat clung to his graying hairline despite the air conditioning. He gestured to the worn leather chairs in front of his desk. Dayo dropped carelessly into the one closest to the door. Gered eased into the other.

Cirino shuffled papers, not quite looking at him. "Production fell a bit this week," he mumbled, fumbling for the reports.

Gered tapped fingers against his leg, waiting without a word. Dayo propped a foot up on his opposite knee. Cirino finally found the correct paper and extended it to Gered.

He took it and read over the rig reports. The oil pumped from the ground had taken another dip in the last few weeks. Usually it wasn't abnormal to see fluctuations, but Darrow had seen a steady decline over the past four months across most of its oil fields.

And when oil was the primary export Rosche sold at twice its worth to the refineries outside the territory, that was a problem.

Gered set it back on the desk. "You know how this looks?"

Cirino looked down at his clasped hands.

"The foremen have located another drilling spot. They're going to try for another four wells here soon. They think they can recoup some of the production losses."

"Drilling and setting up wells takes time."

Cirino trembled. "I know. Gered..."

Gered didn't relax the hardness of his features. He'd already bought them time. It couldn't go on for much longer.

"Can you give us a chance to try the new wells?"

Dust, the man looked close to tears. Gered didn't blame him. Rosche didn't like losses. He controlled most of the oil and gas in the lower country, and any decline in productions limited the goods and money Rosche allowed to trickle back into the towns.

Gered took the report again, tapping it against his knee. "Unit Six has already mentioned to me they've noted a decrease in transpo trucks going to Rosche's personal refineries in Treshing. Those supply our bikes and your trucks. Telling them that more is going across the border isn't going to work forever. What am I supposed to tell Rosche when they bring it up at the next meeting?"

Cirino swallowed hard. "He has to understand that wells dry up. More have to be drilled. Sometimes production has to be abandoned."

Dayo extended a hand for the paper. Gered passed it over.

"You know the last town that fell behind on production like this?" Dayo asked.

A nod from Cirino. "Please," he appealed again to Gered.

He clenched his jaw a little tighter. The town already suffered. Gered had fudged the numbers a little so the supplies distributed to Darrow hadn't been docked too much, but Rosche wasn't above cutting them off completely in punishment. Never mind the townspeople had no real control over the natural resource.

Dayo angled a look at him, already guessing what he'd do. Gered looked past the mayor to the windows. They opened onto a view of the town center. Small shops, a church that wasn't functional thanks to Rosche, and worn-out vehicles and people. The same run-down look pervaded each town on their route.

Rosche kept a tight border and nothing traded in or out without his consent. The units made sure of that. He kept a stranglehold on any goods brought in, each town earning based on their production or however Rosche felt that day. Even the highway refueling stations were regulated to exclude most townsfolk who weren't among the lucky few to have the lock combos.

A tanker truck lumbered down the road. If Darrow was lucky, they'd be able to fill up enough of the trucks from the new wells to barely satisfy quotas.

"How soon can you get the new wells up and running?" he asked.

Cirino leaned forward on his desk with a relieved gasp. "We're drilling now. We can have a production report the next time you come in."

Dayo flipped the paper back on the desk and stood with Gered.

"Last time, Cirino," Gered warned. "Get the numbers up without fudging or you know what happens."

Cirino swallowed again. "Yes. What do you want me to put on the report?"

Gered twisted the paper to look at again. He'd have to be extra careful now. Reports of Callan's execution the day before had already spread through the Barracks. "Raise them by a few numbers, not all the same. Put in two extra trucks going to the border checkpoints."

Cirino nodded furiously and grabbed the paper. "I'll do it now." He fed a new sheet of paper into his typewriter and set to work. The clack of the keys filled the office as he input new data on the blank sheet.

Dayo shot Gered a look asking if he should be doing this… again. Gered ignored it. Dayo knew the dangerous game he played. It was the only way he could screw Rosche over, but if he got caught, he'd go down in fire with the town.

But Dayo wouldn't tell and neither would Cirino. He'd let the mayor give the good news Darrow had bought themselves another chance at the wells.

"Make sure you include the date on the new wells and what you think you'll make from them."

Cirino nodded again, not taking his eyes from the paper. The typewriter dinged for the last time and he pulled the paper free, extending it to Gered. He looked over the new numbers. They were barely adequate now, but nothing for Rosche to rage at. Yet.

"Get those wells up and running," Gered warned. Dayo led the way from the office.

"Gered!" Cirino shot up from his chair. Gered paused from folding up the paper.

"Thank you."

"Last chance, Cirino." Gered refused to acknowledge the thanks. The mayor nodded and slumped back in his chair as they left.

The unit still sat on idling bikes outside the office. Gered filed the report into a leather folder in his small saddlebag and started his engine up again. They'd stop once with the head foreman on the edge of town before heading out.

The unit fell in behind him as he led the way through town.

He caught another rebellious glare from a young man wearing the dirty jeans, boots, and long-sleeved shirt of an oil field worker. It was a familiar expression in the younger people—those who hadn't seen what Rosche was capable of. Gered hoped he wouldn't have to remind them. Darrow hadn't had a demonstration in years.

Someone tugged the young man away, probably hoping the riders hadn't seen his look. But Dayo had. He slowed his bike, turning his featureless helmet at them, not looking away as he cruised slowly by. The worker lowered his gaze, cowed for the moment. Dayo revved the engine before slowly accelerating back up to Gered's right side.

Outside town, more pumpjacks moved their steady way up and down, bringing up oil from the earth. The oil fields were even dustier than normal, any grass or brush dug up to make way for the trucks and equipment. It snuck under Gered's helmet, teasing at his nose and throat with rugged persistence.

Barely paved roads spread out among the pumps. A heavy truck lumbered ahead of them. Gered slowed to follow it. The driver also slowed, leaning out of his window to wave them around.

Gered came even with him and flipped the helmet's visor open.

"Looking for the foreman," he yelled over the rumbling engines.

"Another mile down this road, take a right, and another two miles. New wells!" the driver shouted back.

Gered lifted a hand in thanks. The driver crept along the side of the road, letting the unit roar past.

The trucker's directions held true, and traffic built up in the last two miles. All of the trucks moved aside to let them pass. Activity hustled across the drilling site. Towering equipment spread over the ground. The noise of the drill droned over everything.

Men in dust- and grease-stained clothes stood on the ground, or atop equipment, protected by gloves, hardhats, and safety glasses. The unit's approach brought heads up. Most looked away just as fast, turning their attention back to the equipment. Gered knew enough about the process that even a moment's distraction could be deadly.

One man separated from the activity and strode over. His dark blue overshirt, neatly buttoned, marked him as the foreman.

Gered ground to a halt a safe distance from the site, and flipped his helmet back open.

"Gered." The foreman nodded.

"Just came from Cirino's office," Gered said.

A bit of paleness struck the man's tanned face. "We're doing what we can."

Gered flicked fingers up to halt the protests. None of the other workers were in earshot, and his unit kept back so they had a bit of privacy.

"You have until next time I come through to get production up." Gered nodded at the new well. "These are your last chance."

The foreman swallowed hard. "The surveying crew thinks the sites are good. We're about to finish up drilling here and then start on the second location."

Gered cut him off again. "Anyone else know the numbers?"

He shook his head. "They know it's not good. They see fewer trucks leaving filled with oil, but only Cirino and I know the full story."

"See it stays that way." The older rig hands knew what failure could bring them. They wouldn't snitch to Rosche. It wouldn't serve anyone. But the younger townspeople might get it in their head to do something stupid.

"And make sure you remind your younger crews what we can do." Gered propped a foot back up on the footspike. "I don't want to have to act on some of the looks I saw in town today."

The foreman nodded vigorously. "Yes, sir. I'll talk to them again."

"Two weeks!" Gered shouted over the noise of his engine revving. He accelerated in a tight circle around the foreman, leaving him in a cloud of dust, and headed back to the main roads.

CHAPTER FIFTEEN

Y ou look exactly where you're going to attack." Laramie relaxed
her stance. "It's a dead giveaway."

Axel's shoulders slumped and he groaned. "How are you supposed to attack but not look where you're going?"

Laramie allowed a faint smile. "Like this." She took him over to one of the punching bags hanging in the training room and placed him on one side.

"Watch." She took up her stance opposite him. She brought up her hands in a ready position, shifting her weight lightly between her feet. A light tap against the bag to start. *Find a spot to focus. Follow the sway of your opponent. Don't let them get too close.*

Quick jab.

Faster.

Laramie quickened the pace of her strikes, interspersing now with kicks. Always watching the same spot on the bag. One more kick finished the routine.

She reached in to steady the bag and looked to Axel.

He nodded, chewing on his lower lip. "Okay. Can I try?"

Laramie stepped back and gestured for him to start. His punches were too hesitant, but at least he kept his eyes on the bag, not on every little movement around him.

"Harder!" Laramie encouraged. "You're not dancing over there."

A faint grin swerved across Axel's face, but he started throwing more weight behind each punch.

"Aw, look. The drifter's helping toughen up the dead meat," a sneering voice cut over the sounds of punching.

Laramie's shoulders tightened up and she faced off with Saver, the older recruit who'd killed his way into the gangs.

"Just getting in some extra practice." She shrugged.

She'd met Axel in the room after dinner almost every night since she'd offered. He'd improved without Harlan shouting in his ear and the older recruits tripping him up every chance they got.

"You know you can't have boyfriends around here?" Saver kept a smirk.

"Upset you can't either?" she shot back.

He chuckled nastily and came closer. Axel ghosted up on her left side, fists hanging by his sides.

"Relax, pipsqueak," Saver sneered at Axel. "A few of the units challenged us to some races. Think they can screw us over. As much as I hate to admit it, you two are some of the best riders. Want to earn some cash?"

Laramie tilted her head to look at Axel with a raised eyebrow and still keep one eye on Saver. Eagerness lit the teen's eyes. Laramie almost didn't want to admit she felt the same confidence in her ability to go toe-to-toe with some unit riders.

If I can beat their riders, I might be able to make it out of here. And on the faster gang motorcycles, she'd have an even better chance.

"Where?" she asked.

"Track. Garage is open, so get your bikes and follow us down there." He left with a swaggering walk.

Laramie narrowed her eyes, a survival instinct of doubt creeping in for a second. "You think there's really a race and this isn't some setup against us?"

Axel shucked the wraps around his hands. "It's happened a few times before. I've never ridden, but there's no fights tonight, so the units all need something to do."

Laramie peeled off her wraps and left them on the table against the back wall. "Okay. Let's go kick some ass."

Her fears proved unfounded as they met up with the other trainees at the garage. Laramie took the gas can and topped off her tank. They'd all been given plain red helmets—blank until they earned a place in a unit and could paint it with the unit's symbol. She pulled hers off the wall and followed Axel as he pushed his motorcycle from the garage.

"Run all bets by me," Saver announced as the others joined them outside. He pulled the garage shut after getting nods from them all.

"Who died and made him leader?" Laramie muttered to Axel. The teen ducked his head to hide a smile.

"What's that, drifter?" Saver leaned in close. His breath already reeked of the cheap beer.

She lifted her chin. "We gonna stand here and chat forever, or we headed down?"

He backed off with a warning look. One of the other teens shot her a faint grin. She winked back and pulled her helmet on leaving the visor open, and slowly accelerated behind Saver as he led the way across the compound and down to the track.

The setting sun left the western sky above the mountains

awash in vibrant reds, yellows, and oranges. Darker purples lingered on the fringes, deepening the shadows of the mountain slopes into imperceptible blocks of rocks and trees.

Tall floodlights set up around the track bathed the track in bright white light. Motorcycles already grouped around the track. Dust kicked up from several riders tearing their way around.

Jeers and shouts rose up as one skidded and wiped out. The rider took a second to get up and back on his bike to try to catch up to the others.

The recruits idled to a stop in their own group. A lanky figure approached, red jacket undone and beer in hand. Moshe.

"Barns is handling the entries and races." He swept a cool glance over them. "Don't come crying when you get cleaned out by real riders."

"That why you're not riding?" Laramie smirked.

Moshe allowed a huff of a laugh. "Yeah, heard you were a cocky one, drifter."

Laramie arched an eyebrow. Who else was talking about her?

But Moshe turned his attention to the other trainees. "Most of the unit leaders are out. Could be a chance to make an impression." He left, heading back to his unit, walking with the same deceptive grace as Gered.

Laramie didn't feel a threat from him, but he could become one too easily. He was still one to watch out for.

"I'll talk to Barns about setting the next races," Saver said.

Laramie rolled her eyes at Axel again and followed the self-appointed leader to the track. They set up on a small rise, braving the scorn of the nearby units. The jibes devolved into something more friendly after the initial abuse. Laramie stayed out of it, preferring to let the other trainees rub shoulders with the units.

She didn't have anyone to impress. *Just focus on who to beat here.*

"Drifter, you're up first!" Saver waved her to the start.

Two other riders were already revving their engines at the starting line by the time she made it down.

"Three laps," Barns shouted over the noise.

She gave a thumbs up and snapped the visor closed. Barns dropped a hand and she pushed off in a roar of dust. The unit riders rode more aggressively than the trainees, forcing Laramie to a higher level of riding she wasn't used to. The travelers would often hold races like that—but less cutthroat.

She came in second, respectable enough for her first race of the night. Saver glared at her as she rode back up to the group. She flipped the visor up and returned his look with a slight curl of her lip and ignored him, turning to wish Axel luck before he headed to the starting line.

The floodlights grew brighter as the last lingering vestiges of sunlight faded from the sky. The stars appeared—cold bright spots pinpricking every available inch of the night sky. A broader band of light streaked overhead, running from one end of the horizon to the other—a deep track cut through the sky with a wake of lighter clouds and stars around it.

She pulled her helmet off to better look. Aclar legend said it was the wake from Jaan, one of the four winged messengers of God, taking the form of a mighty eagle to roam the skies between earth and heaven. She'd never seen it so clearly before as stretching above the Christan mountains.

"John's Path," Axel pulled up beside her, turning his head up to look. "It's always clearer in the summer."

John, Jaan—the difference in culture she sometimes forgot existed. Aclar, like the Itan, weren't natives of Natux. They'd come over shortly after the Rifts opened on each continent—the Itan to try to engineer bridges between the newly formed upper and lower countries, and the travelers, driven from their own home by wars between the tribes and invaders trying to harvest more magic from the barely affected Aclar. But they'd each clung to the original tenets of their culture, passing them on to subsequent generations until some bits merged across the barriers into new ways of living.

"It's beautiful," Laramie said.

"Yeah." Wistfulness covered Axel's voice. "You think there's some being up there who flies around as a giant eagle, keeping an eye on all of us for some other greater being?"

"Interesting place for an existential conversation." Laramie flicked a finger down at the track.

Axel chuckled. "Yeah."

Laramie balanced her helmet on the seat in front of her. "Travelers are pretty religious, so I was raised with the preacher and the books, and plenty of other Aclar legends." She tipped her head back to the stars. "Yeah, I think someone's up there. Doesn't seem like it sometimes though."

Axel grunted his agreement. "Churches don't really function around here, but we still talked about stuff back home. Just sometimes looking up at the sky like this, you're struck by the vastness of everything, and then look back down and see this." He jerked his chin at where a rider wiped out on a turn and took another bike with him.

"Fair point," Laramie allowed. She touched the medal still hiding underneath her shirt. Jaan was the favorite of the four messengers among the travelers, and now and then she felt guilty about leaving Matteo, or Maatu to the travelers, the winged patron of the Itan, behind. But no matter which she prayed to, sometimes the heavens returned nothing but silence to her prayers.

"Stop chatting!" Saver slammed a hand between her handlebars. "You're up again!"

"Okay!" She pulled her helmet back on and headed back down. The two riders she went up against were more cautious of the turns, and one ground his clutch. She took first easily, not even pausing at the finish line and riding directly back up to her place.

Axel exchanged a fist bump and went to claim another first place win for the trainees. One of the other teens brought a round of beers. Laramie sipped hers with a grimace of distaste. She'd prefer something darker, or even water, but the grainy beer seemed to be the preferred beverage of the entire Barracks.

Betting picked up as her group showed themselves just as capable as most of the riders in the units. Saver stopped yelling so much and gave her and Axel a few more runs than the rest of the trainees. No one complained either.

The gang motorcycle was almost addicting in its speed and power. It was becoming more and more likely it would come with her when she made her run.

Midnight loomed ever closer and the races started coming to an end. Most of the units began heading back in packs, collecting whatever winnings they'd earned. Saver paid out as soon as they got back to the garage, impressing Laramie. She'd expected him to pocket the winnings. He begrudgingly lifted his chin in a nod of almost respect. Another win for the night.

She secured the wad of bills in her jacket and walked back to Unit Four's barracks with a hand on her pistol. She also figured Saver wasn't above following her and stealing the money back. Him or another of the units. But she reached the bunker without incident.

Inside was quiet. Some of Unit Five lingered in the common room. She'd beaten at least one of them in the races. Not many had participated, most seeming content to bet and drink. *They're probably already sleeping it off.*

She punched in the code to the room and stepped inside. A breath of relief escaped at the solid click behind her and the sight of the empty room. The constant tension accumulated during the day began to ease from her muscles, and she sank down on her bed.

Bending over, she unlaced her boots and tried not to wince at the smell of sweaty boots and socks, and unshowered mess. Unit Five hadn't made any sort of move. *Should I just go shower and not worry about it?*

But the late hour and the fact Harlan wouldn't care that they'd still be tired in a few hours when they showed back up for training prompted her to stay in the room. She dug out the small notebook from her bag instead. Untucking the pencil from the spine, she started to make notes alongside the rough diagrams of the Barracks.

Another page was filled up with a sketch of Rosche's territory. Or as near as she could remember from the maps she'd looked at before foolishly heading in. Most of the upper territory and borders she remembered. South was hazy lines and uneven smudges that had refused to come clear no matter how much she tried to remember.

The Christan Mountains were a thicker line of triangles sketched in. They weren't more than an hour's ride from the Barracks, but she'd yet to decide if heading west was the best option. If she made it through the mountains, there was the unknown of the western slopes. And not much after that, if Gered was to be believed.

He's probably lying. Can't trust a Viper. But an annoying part of her did believe it, so she hadn't actively pursued the idea of heading into the mountains.

She jotted notes on the units and their riding and racing tactics from that night. She'd quiz Axel on them later. The kid was a walking encyclopedia on all the units. Part of making her move would be planning it when the least threatening units were in the barracks.

Flipping back to the map, she tapped her pencil against the paper. *North?* The desert floor heaved up into a caprock at the edges of Rosche's territory. Over the caprock's ledge came greener flatlands and smaller mountains that crept east from their parent range of the Christan Mountains.

She couldn't go too far north past that or she'd hit the Rift. There might be better places to hide among the lower hills. There were sure to be units after her when she made her run.

I wonder if I'd have time to put the booster on the gang bike? The pencil beat a new pattern on the paper as she gave it more thought. A few new parts, fiddle the wiring a bit to match with the gang bike, and it could work. Give her a needed edge on the units … But the idea vanished once she remembered the canister needed a refill before getting another good use out of it, and she hadn't seen any harnessers around the compound.

I don't think they're letting me out to find a harnesser. And still don't want anyone getting a look at it.

Setting the notebook aside with a sigh, she reached into her jacket's inside pocket and pulled out the pictures. Kayin and herself smiled up in bright pigment. She rubbed a thumb along the edge. The camera had caught the bright speckles of their knacks— blue for her, gold for him. She could almost feel his arm around her shoulders, the way she fit perfectly against his side, cheek pressed against the sun-warmed leather of his jacket.

Smiling, she flipped it over. *I love you to the sun's fading*, his scrawled script reminded her.

Love you too. And I'm trying to get back, promise.

She slid it behind the small stack, the next set of faces showing Ade half turned, a mixture of laughing exasperation as she reached toward Laramie, her husband in the background, head tossed back in merriment.

A suspicious sniff tickled her nose. She quickly flipped away. The faded faces of her first family laughed up at her. Habit sent her fingers turning it over.

Solfeggietto. Her thumb traced over the curling loops of the name. Back over to brush the familiar features. Remember scattered bits and pieces of laughter, hugs, and songs.

You're the reason I'm in this mess.

Her parents kept smiling. Her younger self kept laughing.

Yeah, I know. It's my fault. She couldn't remember a time when she wasn't impulsive. Though once she'd had a brother chasing after her and telling her to slow down.

A yawn threatened to split her face. She returned the notebook to its place at the bottom of her bag, tucking the money into her wallet and storing it safely away. She trusted Gioia enough to not go through her things when she wasn't there, and she'd come to trust the lock on the door, but it didn't hurt to keep the same level of distrust she fostered when on the road.

Still, she'd be glad to see the somewhat friendly faces of Unit Four when they came back.

CHAPTER SIXTEEN

I hate cows," Dayo muttered.

A smirk twitched at Gered's lips. Dayo said the same thing every time they stopped in town. Unit Four oversaw the most diverse area—oil fields, farms, and ranch lands. Conrow boasted dairy cows, and the more common longhorn cattle raised for their tender beef.

The land around town was greener, fewer gorges and gullies furrowed by the rare rain. The river had long ago gone underground, but an efficient system of pumps had been in place long before Rosche ever settled into the Barracks. It all made for good grazing land and a town's economy built off the animals.

The more pungent scent of manure overshadowed the sweet scent of hay and grain. When the wind was right, it carried the scent from the main stockyards built north of town housing dairy cows and the current batch of cattle ready to be loaded into trucks to be shipped off as trade.

They just needed Gered's approval on the papers and numbers so he could carry the reports back to Rosche before the trucks rolled out under the supervision of the lower level enforcers who drove the trucks.

"Just hold your breath then."

"Right." Dayo rolled his eyes. "Then you'd miss out on my lovely voice."

"Not hearing a downside here." Gered pulled off his sunglasses and opened the office door.

He swore every office was manned by a middle-aged woman with the same graying hair pulled back in a serviceable bun. *How many are there in the entire territory?*

This one—he never learned their names—nodded. She was less timid than any of the other secretaries in their route. She could probably stop a stampede just by standing in its path.

"Mayor's out. Left the reports here." She extended a sheaf of papers.

Gered exchanged a glance with Dayo. The mayor was never just "out." He took the papers. At the first brief skim, the numbers looked good.

"Where is he?"

The secretary looked up, ice in her eyes. "Headed out to the stockyards. Trucks will be here soon, won't they?"

Gered leveled a glare back and she had the decency to sniff a slight concession. "When did he leave?"

"Just a few minutes ago."

Gered nodded, folding the papers away with deliberate slowness. "Then we'll head that way."

He patted two fingers against the gun on his right thigh. Dayo nodded and tapped on his earpiece connecting to the unit's comms outside.

A warning to stay sharp. The mayor never left the office. The unit's route through the towns was more regular than Rosche raising the taxes again.

Gered rested a hand on the door, reaching the other down

to softly click the safety off his right pistol. The street was empty through the glass door, the unit sitting on idling motorcycles the only sign of life. The buildings around the mayor's office naturally sheltered the unit's current position. The best place for an attack would be just down the street on their way out of town.

He shook his head. This was going to end badly. He shifted his weight back to the secretary, who watched them with eyes sharp as a desert hawk.

"I'd stay down and stay out of this if I were you."

She swallowed hard, breaking from his gaze for the first time since he'd started coming in.

"Dust," Dayo whispered behind him, twisting his head side to side with a crack. He pulled out his gun. "Plan?"

"I'll draw them out. Scramble the unit." Gered hooked his earpiece back in and tapped his chest to make sure his armored vest was still in place under his jacket. Nervous tick.

Taking one short breath, he strode out of the office like nothing was wrong. He paused only briefly at his bike, pulling his rifle from its holster. Its comforting weight settled him a little. A piece of him coming home.

No movement on the wooden boardwalks, or atop the flat roofs. *There.* A long shadow falling from an alleyway.

He pushed on his glasses with a careless gesture.

"All set?" he asked.

Nods came from the unit. He stared a little longer at Gioia. She gave a quick thumbs up and pulled her pistol free.

Another breath. Safety off his left handgun.

Then he walked out into the middle of the street, keeping an even pace as if he hadn't a care in the world. Behind him the unit moved from bikes and began to spread out. More shadows, movements intended to be stealthy, but untrained and calling attention to the sharper eyes of a man trained by the Tlengin. He softly called out positions through the comms.

Shadows in alleyways, one on the bank roof, another on the leatherworks. He shook his head. The best the town could hope for was to claim ignorance and pin it on a group of bandits or rogues.

"You have one chance," he shouted, easing his finger toward the trigger of his rifle. "I'll be lenient if you put down whatever weapons you have and turn yourselves in."

A shadow solidified in the street ahead of him. And another up on the roof with the glint of a gun leveled at Gered's chest.

"Lenient?" the man scoffed. His voice came muffled from behind the dust scarf wrapped around his lower face. "Like Rosche has been lenient all these years? We'll take it back, just you wait."

Gered sighed. "If you manage to kill a few of us, it won't make a difference. You have ten men out there. Think that'll be enough to stop the rest of the gang when it comes to level this place?"

The shotgun in the man's hands bobbled as Gered stated the number. Correct then.

"Who put you up to this?" Gered asked.

He could just shoot, but he preferred to try to talk the men down before bullets started flying. It was less messy that way. And it was against everything the Tlengin and Rosche had tried to cut into him.

"Who do you think did? You and every rider like you." Desperation leeched from behind the dust scarf and the gun trembled again. The man on the roof held steadier.

Gered shifted his finger closer to the trigger. But not every rider was like him. He swung the rifle up, settling comfortably against his shoulder, tucking it into the space that curled just for it.

"I won't miss. Not this close." The man was a scant twenty yards away. He could make it in his sleep. "Back off and I won't even go after the men trying not to piss themselves in the alleys."

"Just me then?" The man laughed, raising his shotgun.

Dusting hells.

"You were the only one stupid enough to come out." And Gered pulled the trigger.

A scream pierced the air before the crack of his rifle had finished echoing. He pivoted to his left, clearing the chamber as he did. The trigger compressed under his finger, and the rooftop shadow fell.

A yell sounded from his right and another shadow lurched from an alleyway. Dropping the rifle, he yanked out his left handgun and spun. One shot to the chest, another to the head before the man hit the ground.

Quiet lingered for three heartbeats before the sharper cracks of pistols broke out. Glass shattered somewhere down the street. Gered reholstered the pistol and backed off into the shelter of the boardwalk, sweeping the rifle back up, searching for more threats.

"Update, Dayo?"

"Sani took a hit in his vest. He's okay. We're cleaning up now," Dayo's breathless voice sounded back.

Gered eased a breath of relief, and began to walk a little faster back toward the bikes. The panicked bellow of cows sounded from somewhere to his left.

Movement out of the corner of his eye sent him turning too late. A snap, then burning pain in his chest as an impact sent him to the ground. He twisted, shaking his hand free from the rifle straps. His lungs tried to obey his will and start breathing again.

A figure leaped on top of him, driving a blow into his face. His head snapped to the side. Coppery wetness pooled on his tongue. Weight bore down on him.

He bucked his hips, twisting and throwing his assailant off. His vision blurred from the punch, but he kicked out, connecting with the figure.

It tumbled to the ground with a surprised cry, but scrambled to its feet. Gered didn't bother standing, pushing forward to tackle it around the waist. He slammed it to the ground, delivering his own punch to its face. The dust scarf tore loose, exposing the features of a young man.

He blocked Gered's next punch, but Gered redirected, shifting to grab his wrist and twist. The man cried out, wriggling against the armbar hold as Gered kept twisting, flipping him over onto his stomach.

Knee to the back, gun in his left hand, warning trigger cock. The man stilled.

"Move again," Gered growled, spitting out blood.

"Gered!" Boots pounded and he spared a glance up to see Dayo and Gioia running toward him, guns held low and at the ready.

"I'm okay." *Pissed off, but okay.*

Dayo relaxed a fraction. Gered couldn't bring himself to look at Gioia, knowing he'd break if he saw any sort of emotion in her eyes or signs of any injury.

"Good. We got one prisoner. Rest are dead or ran off."

Gered's captive let out a despairing moan. "Hey." Gered jiggled his arm a little more. "I gave you a chance. This is on you."

The man slumped, pressing his forehead against the ground.

"What are we doing with them?" Dayo holstered his gun and grabbed the man's jacket, helping haul him to his feet. Gered kept his pistol leveled at the man.

Rules said no mercy. Which meant an immediate execution. Gered dabbed blood from the corner of his mouth. He hated that he could do it. Pull the trigger without hesitation. The loathing himself would come later.

Taking them back to Rosche meant a slight delay in pulling the trigger. The rest of the unit began to appear. Dec and Julen hauled a wounded man between them, blood dripping from a bullet wound in his leg. They shoved him to a halt in front of Gered.

"Anyone else around here going to take their chances?" Gered asked the man he'd taken.

The man shook his head as his entire body bowed in despair.

Figures and shadows had begun to appear in doorways and windows again. Coming to see the results of an ill-advised re-bellion. Disgust welled in Gered's throat. They'd been willing enough to see ten men sacrifice for some stupid cause and now came to watch the rest of their failure.

Kill them now, or delay the inevitable by radioing it back to the Barracks? The sun's heat increased tenfold.

"Gered?" Dayo asked, bringing him back.

"Get them on their knees." Gered harnessed the coldest voice he could manage, only hoping it could leach all the way down into his soul so he could get through the next minute and the one after that.

Dayo nodded and shoved the man forward, pushing him down to his knees. Dec and Julen simply let their prisoner drop to the ground. The unit began backing away. The wounded man at least had the courage to lift his face still set in resolve to meet Gered's gaze.

He moved his hand toward his jacket. Gered saw too late the bulge around his chest.

"Get back!" he screamed, raising his pistol.

The unit scrambled for cover. Gered pulled the trigger. Too late as the man struck his chest.

Another impact took Gered to the ground as an explosion shook the air.

CHAPTER SEVENTEEN

Gered blinked slowly. The deep blue of the sky and puffy clouds fuzzed overhead. Ringing warbled in his ears. Heaviness compressed his chest.

Bits of dust crept into his mouth, triggering a cough. He turned his head. The bodies of the two rebels lay torn to shreds. He lay just outside the blast radius.

He blinked hard. It should have reached further. Someone had done a dusted job setting up the charge.

No other bodies were visible, but glass had shattered in the shops across the street. He coughed again. Another thought took over.

"Gioia..." He tried to move, his hand scraping the dirt and asphalt.

The weight on top of him groaned and rolled off. "I'm fine too, thanks for asking."

Gered craned his neck around. "Dayo..."

Dayo's smile flashed through the dust coating his dark face. He tapped Gered's chest. "Couldn't let you kill yourself just yet."

Gered's boots scraped against the road as he started moving in an attempt to sit up.

Then she was there, leaning over him, hand extended.

Relief cascaded over him like a mountain stream at the sight of Gioia standing tall and unharmed. He reached up and she hauled him to his feet. He held her hand a moment longer, squeezing tight.

She squeezed back twice. She was good. He was good. They were good.

Gioia touched his shoulder as he hunched over, sudden pain blossoming in his ribs.

"Dayo!" she called in concern, not taking her eyes from Gered.

Gered unzipped his jacket, pulling it aside to expose the armored vest. He didn't need Dayo to tell him it had stopped a bullet, but bruised his ribs in the process.

"I'm okay," he said.

"Sure you are." She rolled her eyes, but stepped back. The rest of the unit gathered around. Gered straightened and accepted his rifle from Dec. It had escaped the blast unharmed. He slung it over his shoulder.

"Find the mayor," he said, and strode toward the office.

Ten minutes later he'd figured out how to breathe around the tightness compressing the left side of his ribs. He stood on the boardwalk, watching as the unit dragged the bodies out. Six total, including the men killed in the blast.

One lay off to the side. Julen hadn't moved fast enough.

"Got him," Dayo's voice sounded in his ear.

Gered adjusted the strap of his rifle around his neck, situating it so he could rest an arm on the butt end of the rifle as it hung in front of him.

Townsfolk gathered across the street on the boardwalk, walking hurriedly to duck through doors. Gered nudged his sunglasses up.

They'd escaped the blast with a crack through the right lens. Annoying, but better than squinting in the late afternoon brightness.

Dayo appeared, shoving the mayor in front of him. His pistol hung loose in his hand. Dec and another rider shepherded a second man up to where Gered waited.

Mayor Antton swallowed hard as he looked up at Gered.

"Gered…" he started, hands extended.

"Tell me you didn't have anything to do with this," Gered barked.

Antton's face blanched. "They came to me, told me to go along with it."

Gered shifted his weight and the mayor flinched back.

"Some weren't from here. They came in with the guns and said they could take down Rosche if we worked with them."

"And that went well for you, didn't it?" Gered jerked his chin up, indicating the bodies behind the mayor.

Antton hung his head. "I tried to tell them no," he whispered. "Some of them were just kids."

"Who else?"

Antton's head flew up.

"Who else was in on it?" Gered forced his voice to stay cold.

"You can't expect me to know—"

"Who else?" Gered shouted.

Antton cringed.

"Tell me now and I can hold back Rosche's full wrath from falling on this dusted town. You killed one of his riders. You know what he does to towns who do that?" Gered stood in the men's faces now.

Antton shook like grass in a dust storm.

"What are you going to do to them?" he whispered.

Gered regarded him for a long moment. Despite the situation, he couldn't muster much sympathy for the man. They knew what would happen. No one went up against Rosche or the gangs.

He leaned closer to Antton. "What do you think?"

Antton shook his head, jaw tightening in stupid refusal.

"You want me to take it out on someone else?"

He hastily shook his head again.

"You want to die for them?" Gered twitched his gun toward the other prisoner. "You don't tell me, I kill you, and work my way down the line until I get the names."

Antton clenched his fists. He licked his lips, and dared look Gered in the face. "I thought you were a little better than that. I thought you weren't really one of them."

A bit of regret chipped at the ice around Gered's heart. He spoke loud enough for only Antton to hear. "If I was truly like them, this place would be burning to the ground around corpses right now. You want to save the rest of this dusted town? Give me the names."

Antton's shoulders slumped. Defeated. He mumbled the last two names, where they might be hiding. Only one was from the town.

The rest of the townspeople seemed to realize they had nothing to gain and everything to lose. Ten minutes later, all three men knelt on the ground in front of Gered. A pile of weapons lay to the side. Gered shifted a pistol with his boot.

"Dayo." He flicked his fingers and Dayo joined him. Gered angled his head to keep his words between them.

"These are army issue."

"Dusting hells," Dayo murmured, taking in the pile with new eyes. "Closest border checkpoint around here is down in…" His eyes widened.

"Moshe's territory," Gered finished. Moshe, who had an old army issue rifle.

Dayo crossed his arms. "What do we do then?"

"Sit on this for now. I'll decide when to let Rosche know."

Dayo lifted an eyebrow in incredulity. "You are gonna tell him, right? This isn't the sort of thing you keep quiet unless you're in on it."

"You think I am?" Gered retorted.

"Even you're not that stupid." Dayo shook his head dismissively.

"Thanks." Gered flattened his mouth in a wry smile.

"What are we going to do about these?" Dayo tipped his head back at the prisoners.

"You know the kindest option." Gered's throat tightened against phantom dust.

"That I do." Dayo tapped his fingers against his bicep. "Been a while since you've enforced."

"You want me to slap them on the wrist and let them go?" Gered snapped.

Dayo rolled his eyes. "Fine. Then decide."

Gered studied the line of men again. One was barely older than a teenager. Scuffed boots and dirt-stained jeans. Cattle puncher. The town would need him.

Gered unholstered his pistol and walked over to the young man. "If someone offered you another gun and told you to go up against the gangs, would you do it?"

The young man looked up, fear in his eyes. He mutely shook his head and Gered believed him.

"Get up and get out. We have trouble in this town again and your name comes up, you know what'll happen."

He scrambled to his feet, and backed away, looking twice at the men still kneeling. One jerked his head, gesturing the boy to get as far away as he could. He obeyed, crossing the street to be pulled into the darkness of one of the buildings.

Gered turned back to the line. "You from outside the territory?" He swept a glance at each of the two remaining men.

"What's it matter?" One raised his head.

"I might be hunting down more names."

The man shifted on his knees. "Just get it over with." He lifted his chin higher.

Dayo stepped up beside Gered, gun drawn. A slight nod passed between them. He wouldn't make Gered do it all himself.

Gered raised his pistol and cocked it. If he didn't stop to question them, there was less information to pass on to Rosche. But another chance that another unit could be ambushed. A chance that one of the riders was the real traitor.

But before he did anything, he had to ask the question burning like desert winds on his tongue.

"Why did you do it?" It came out a half-whisper, closer to a plea for forgiveness.

Understanding lit the man's eyes. "One day you'll find yourself tired of living under his heel. Maybe you already are. Then you'll realize the chance for a breath of freedom is worth it."

"You can't ever be free," Gered whispered. "He always wins."

And he pulled the trigger.

CHAPTER EIGHTEEN

Dusk coaxed deep shadows in the corners of the compound. Laramie paused on the steps of the tower, rolling stiffness from her shoulders. Extra training with Axel, combined with strength training with Harlan that morning had left unfamiliar soreness in her muscles.

A few clouds skidded across the stars beginning to peek out from the blues and grays painting the sky. Laramie stepped down, mulling over the new unit who'd come in that afternoon. There were still at least five units she hadn't seen yet, and from what Axel said, newly arrived Unit Seven was not to be messed with.

By her reckoning it would take at least another week before she'd seen all thirty of the units and could possibly piece together the rotations in and out of the compound. Another week of looking over her shoulder. Another week closer to the inevitable tattoo and being trapped within the units.

Cutting it close. Harlan had even dropped a hint in the morning session that she was a step above the rest of the trainees and might be up for choosing soon.

Jaan's Wake began to peek through—faint lines dragged through the sky. A crescent moon hung low over the mountains. It always made her think of Kayin. He'd first blurted out that he loved her under a crescent moon. A flush of warmth spread over her. It might be stupid to get so sentimental over a repetitive lunar event, but out on the road it made her feel connected to him.

I'll make it back, she promised the moon.

A scuff behind her brought her guard back up too late. Hands grabbed her from behind and hustled her into an alley between two barracks buildings.

"Told you this would be easy," a breathless voice sounded in her ear. The speaker grunted in pain as she threw her head back.

A punch to her gut left her gasping and dangling in her captor's arms. She regained her feet and looked up into the scowling face of a rider she vaguely recognized from Unit Twelve.

"What do you want?" She twisted again, testing her captor's hold.

"Our money," the man in front of her snarled.

Surprise killed her struggle. "What money?"

"Little trainee upstarts like you shouldn't be riding in races. The money you won is ours."

"You shaking us all down, or just me?" She spat in his face.

"Starting with you."

She kicked the man's knee and he stumbled back with a colorful curse. The hold on her tightened, pulling her arms behind her and opening her stomach up for another punch.

"I don't have your dusting money," she wheezed. "And even if I did, I wouldn't give it to you. You both ate my dust."

Pain exploded across her temple, snapping her head to the side. A small whimper of pain escaped as she hung in the man's arms once again. Darkness edged her vision. A hand clamped around her jaw, bringing her head back up.

The man held a pistol in his other hand. He waved it in front of her nose. "You'll get that again if you don't pay up."

"You're a real hero, aren't you?" Blood dribbled down her cheek in a warm trail. *Keep calm.* She set her feet under her again, tensing her stomach, waiting for her opening.

The rider half stepped back, raising the pistol again in threat. She pushed back into the arms holding her, hitching her knees up to her chest, kicking out with her full strength into the man's chest. It threw him back into the wall. His head cracked back against the stone under the force and he crumpled to the ground.

The other rider's arms loosened a fraction. "What...?"

She dropped her full weight down, landing in a squat. The sudden dead weight, combined with the man's surprise, let her tear free. She spun on her feet, arms tucked up close to her head, but a strike never came.

The rider stood, eyes wide at the unexpected turn of events. Three quick punches to his stomach sent him reeling away from her. She pulled her pistol and aimed at him.

He slowly spread his hands wide as he recovered and caught the gleam of her gun in the moonlight. It bobbled in her hands as the alleyway listed sideways for a nauseating moment before sliding back into place.

"Laramie!"

She blinked hard to focus on the newcomer. Axel stood in the alley entrance, gun also pointed at the riders.

"'M okay." But she staggered a step to the side. She took a breath, drawing control back for a few precious seconds. Tightening her grip on the gun, she looked to the rider again, who remained in a crouched posture, arms spread wide under the double threat. His companion still hadn't moved from the ground.

"Get lost," she said. "And don't even think about coming after the rest of us."

The rider nodded and slid past Axel with a last glance at his unconscious partner before disappearing into the night.

It took two tries before Laramie holstered her pistol.

"Lare, you all right?" Axel gingerly touched her arm. "Oh, dust, you're bleeding!"

"Axel." Laramie swayed again, trying to brace herself against the wall, but it seemed too far away. "I think I'm about to pass out."

He gripped her arm before her knee buckled and the world went dark.

～

Cold pressed against her head. Too cold. She tried to move away, but something nudged her back in place.

"Hold still," a voice said.

She cracked an eye open. A face blurred in front of her eyes. Dark skin and careful hands. Her heart leaped. *Kayin?*

Her eyes focused to reveal Dayo. He dabbed at the side of her face with a cloth, then picked up a butterfly bandage.

"Okay." He looked at a point just past her. The cold moved and his deft fingers pressed the bandage against her forehead. The cold returned.

"Hey, you're awake." He looked down at her.

She blinked again. Somehow she'd gotten to Unit Four's bunker. And Unit Four was back.

"You're the medic?" her first question tumbled out.

He arched an eyebrow down at her. "You seem shocked."

She tried to adjust herself more comfortably. Something shifted underneath her and the cold remained pressed to her temple.

"Should you be? You drink all the time."

A light laugh came from above her. She turned her gaze up, flinching a little at the brightness of the light above her, to see Gioia supporting her head on her lap.

"She has a point," Gioia said.

"I don't drink much on patrol," he protested.

"We've been back five minutes, and this was going to be your second one until they stumbled in."

Laramie raised a hand to her face and felt the rounded cool of a beer can.

"I think that proves my point."

"Okay, newbie, you don't get an opinion." He jabbed a finger in her face. "And I'm waiting on ice!"

Laramie shifted again. "How'd I get here?"

"The kid brought you in." Dayo inclined his head toward her feet.

Axel stood at the foot of the couch, chewing his lip nervously. His face brightened into a smile at her look.

"Thanks," she said.

"No problem. I carried you in, very manly like, in case you were wondering." He rolled his shoulders carelessly.

"He definitely dropped you," Gioia said wryly.

Laramie looked back to Axel. Telltale redness crept up his cheeks. "You're heavy."

A laugh built in her chest. "Thanks," she tried to say as flatly as she could. But a grin quirked the corner of his mouth in response to her failed attempt.

"Look over here." Dayo tapped her cheek. He held a small light, which he shone in her eyes. She flinched away again.

"Maybe a mild concussion. You took a pretty good hit."

"The asshole pistol-whipped her," Axel spoke up, indignation in his voice.

"Figured as much." Dayo rotated her head again, moving the can to check his bandage. "You were only out for a few minutes give or take, so you'll probably be fine. We'll have ice in a second."

He disappeared for a moment before returning with a damp cloth which he used to gently dab at her cheek.

The door creaked and light footfalls approached. Gered came into her field of vision. His blue-gray eyes studied her for a moment. He extended a bundle to Gioia and took the beer in return. Dayo reached for it, but Gered opened it and drank.

Dayo scowled again and went to get his own. A sharper cold touched Laramie's head and she realized he'd brought the ice.

"What happened?" Gered asked.

Laramie squinted at the bruising along his jaw. Dayo had a small bandage on the back of his neck. *What happened to them?*

"Got caught in an alley," she said.

Gioia stiffened under her.

"Axel and I cleaned up at the races last night. They were upset about it and wanted me to give them my winnings. I told them they could shift off."

"She kicked their asses," Axel supplied.

Gioia relaxed. A faint smile hinted at Gered's mouth.

"I think they kicked mine." Laramie pressed a hand against her aching head.

"Sorry I only got there at the end. I was just coming out of the tower when I saw you get pulled into the alley," Axel said in a rush.

"'S okay. Thanks for only dropping me once on the way here."

Red suffused Axel's face as he lifted his eyes to the ceiling. A broader grin slipped through Gered's mask that he tried to hide behind a drink. Laramie felt some ridiculous triumph at having gotten him to smile.

A knock at the door sent spikes of pain between her eyes. Gered disappeared from view.

"Gered," Moshe's voice sounded.

Dayo stiffened and whipped his head around to look at the newcomer. Laramie closed her eyes, too tired to deal with more politics.

"Just heard that your drifter attacked one of my unit."

Indignation overpowered the ache and Laramie tried to sit up. Gioia tugged her back.

"Interesting." A bit of a drawl came through Gered's voice. "I was just getting a different story."

A huff of a laugh came from Moshe. "That's what I figured. Thought I'd come over and get the story before causing trouble between the units."

Laramie tried again, and this time Gioia and Dayo helped her into a sitting position. Gioia slid along the back of the couch to stay at her side and keep the ice pressed to her head. Pain speared through her stomach, sending her hunching over. *This is going to hurt for a few days.*

She managed to straighten enough to meet Moshe's appraising look where he stood, arms crossed, beside Gered.

"You look like you got the worse end of the deal," he said.

"Which one was yours?" A snap edged her words.

He arched an eyebrow. "He's got a bruise on his face, probably took a few punches to his stomach, and is nursing a wounded pride."

"You gonna shake me down for my money since he couldn't hold on to a girl?"

A laugh burst from Moshe. He tipped his head back. "This keeps getting better and better. You took down more than him?"

"There's someone else out there with a headache too."

Dayo's mouth curved down in an impressed frown.

"She's under my name here. I don't appreciate your rider stirring up trouble with her, Moshe," Gered said.

Moshe clapped him on the shoulder. Gered looked at his hand like it might bite him.

"Don't worry. This about the races?" He looked to Laramie. She nodded.

"These two outrode a lot of other riders last night." Moshe flicked a hand between Laramie and Axel. "They earned whatever they took. Put them both on the radar for some of the units."

"So you'll stand down when we have to go to Rosche tomorrow?" Gered raised an eyebrow.

Moshe nodded, the smile still lurking on his face. "I'll track down the other rider."

Gered tipped a nod.

"Now that's out of the way, what happened to you, Gered?"

Gered took another drink, a heavy pause in the air. Laramie watched in interest as Dayo shifted his weight toward Gered as if ready to fight.

"Ran into some trouble in Conrow. Some idealists had gotten a hold of guns and some explosives. We lost a rider."

Jaan's Wings! I didn't think anyone fought back here.

Moshe crossed his arms. "Sorry to hear that. You reported to Rosche yet?" His shoulders stayed relaxed, but a finger flinched against his arm.

Gered had settled back into stillness. "Was just walking back in from the tower when the kid brought her in."

Something lurked between them. Laramie fought against the pain in her head, trying to focus.

Moshe nodded again. Gered leaned a little closer, turning his head slightly away from them. "You and I need to talk later." His words came barely audible.

Moshe angled his chin down. "After we deal with this tomorrow?" His voice was careless as he jerked a thumb back at Laramie.

"Sure. Bring your rifle. We'll go to the range. Been a while since I've practiced." One of Gered's hands had fallen to his side to toy idly with his pistol.

Moshe inclined his head. "See you then."

The door clicked shut behind him. Axel was first to break the silence.

"Someone attacked you?" He sounded unreasonably excited.

"Yeah, kid. I almost got blown up. It was great." Dayo crushed his empty beer can and tossed it across the room. It ricocheted against the wall to fall to the ground beside the trash.

"You missed." The throbbing in her head had robbed her of the ability to state more than the obvious.

"You need to go sleep." Dayo pointed at her.

"I'll radio Harlan and let him know you won't be at training tomorrow," Gered said. "Where are you staying, kid?"

Axel floundered for a second. Laramie almost laughed at his panic at being addressed by his idol.

"Unit Ten's bunker," he stammered out. "Sir!"

Gered lifted an eyebrow.

Dayo snickered. "You having a stroke, kid?"

Laramie pressed her lips together, trying not to embarrass Axel further by laughing.

"Dayo, walk him back."

"He's got two feet and a gun," Dayo protested.

Gered half turned and looked at Dayo with the same raised eyebrow. Dayo groaned.

"Fine." He grabbed another beer from the cooler and waved to Axel. "Come on."

"See you later, Lare." Axel backed away and hurried after Dayo.

"Aww, I think he has a crush on you, Gered." A laugh tumbled from Gioia.

A reluctant smile broke Gered's face, crinkling up around his eyes as he looked at Gioia.

I guess it's mutual then. For some reason it relieved Laramie to see that someone could make him actually smile.

He turned to her and she froze. The blue in his eyes gleamed a little brighter with his smile and a painful flash of familiarity struck. It scored deep into her heart. Bright bits of blue lingered in her blurry memories of her family.

She remembered her father saying the song of the Itan still echoed strong in their family, showing in the bits of blue remaining in the eyes. Two lonely blotches of blue in her left iris, and one in her right compared to her parents and brother, but still more than many Itan ever since the Rifts had opened and their blue eyes faded to gray as the magic disappeared from the world.

"Lare?" He quirked an eyebrow.

She fought back from the crush of memories and found her voice. "Shut up."

He tossed his can at the trash, making it with the ease of

practice.

"What did Moshe mean about going to Rosche tomorrow?" She reached to rub at her temple. Gioia nudged her hand away.

"He likes to keep an eye on these sorts of things. Brawls between units usually go to him for a ruling. You're a recruit, but still under me, so we'll go."

"Great." Laramie twisted a wry smile. She eased forward to the edge of the couch. The distance to her room seemed more than a mile.

Gered put an arm around her, bringing her to her feet with Gioia's help. She stumbled along between them.

Gioia tapped in the code and shoved open the door. Gered helped her sit on the bed and stepped back, already shifting back into stillness, shuttering away the emotion that had leaked from him earlier. It saddened Laramie to see it go, and a bit of the same crossed Gioia's face.

"I'll come get you tomorrow when it's time." His voice had fallen back to the even cadence.

Laramie regretted her nod. He left with a gentle click of the door.

"Keep the ice on for a bit longer." Gioia handed the pack to her. She helped Laramie out of her boots and jacket and lay down. The pillow and bed suddenly seemed the most comfortable thing she'd ever laid on. Her eyes drooped closed.

"Thanks for helping," she mumbled.

The bed dipped and the ice pressed back to her temple. "No problem, drifter." Gioia's voice faded away as she fell asleep.

CHAPTER NINETEEN

Ouch. Laramie stood in front of the bathroom mirror and studied the black and purple bruising spreading from her temple down her left cheekbone, three butterfly bandages little islands of white spread-eagled across a cut at the top of the bone. Swelling pressed the corner of her left eye into a squint.

"Looking *good*, drifter." Corinne stepped past her. She turned on the water and washed her hands, splashing some across her face.

"Thanks." Laramie gently dabbed at some of the crusted blood Dayo had missed the night before.

"You stage it so you can get up close with Rosche?" Corinne leaned a hip against the sink.

"What?" Laramie stared at her. *Did* she *hit* her *head last night?*

Corinne flashed a smirk. "Get Gered to take you in so you can show off that bit of blue in your eyes and prove your worth up close and personal?"

Laramie mimicked her stance, crossing her arms across her chest. "You think I want to prove anything to that psycho?"

Corinne shrugged. "I hear you're pretty good. Could be a way to bypass fighting your way up the ranks. Knacks are rare these days and in a place like this, could be some good leverage."

"Used yours yet?" Laramie leveled a glare. A bit of copper lingered beneath Corinne's right iris—some bit of magic still clinging in her blood, refusing to die even though the world had bled out.

Corinne's smile turned ugly. "Maybe I'm happy with where I am. I'm second in a unit, get away with whatever I want, which is more than most of these dusters can say."

"Yeah, not interested." Laramie slid her feet backward. Her head still hurt, and the conversation wasn't exactly making it better.

Corinne tilted her head. "If you think you can get out, think again. You've got the look a lot of 'recruits' have had. Know what happened to them?" She raised her hand in a mimic of a gun and pointed it at Laramie's forehead.

"So I hear."

"You might as well use it to your advantage. It can get you whatever you want. Gered's an idiot not to use it more. It's the only reason Rosche has kept him around. Anyone else who's tried to run has bitten it, but not Gered. Blue eyes over there is too dusted valuable." Corinne shoved away from the sink. "Want my advice?"

"Not really." Laramie shifted to keep space between her and the rider.

"Make yourself useful and you can have a decent life here." With that she sauntered out.

Laramie stared at the swinging door before turning back to the mirror. *Make yourself useful.* Rosche had told her the same thing. *Is that why he seems interested?*

A rap at the door sent her flinching. She cracked it open, one hand on her knife.

Gered stood on the other side, jacket zipped up and guns in

place. "Time to go."

She followed him silently from the barracks building out into the morning sunlight. She squinted in the glare, wishing she'd brought her glasses along.

"Feeling okay?" Gered didn't break stride. His glasses were tucked in place, obscuring his eyes.

"Not too bad." Laramie lengthened her stride slightly to match his. "What happens when we talk to the overlord of crazy?"

"First, don't address him like that." No humor cracked Gered's voice. "Second, don't speak unless you have to."

"Third?" Laramie questioned when he fell silent.

He didn't break stride. "That's all you need to know. Moshe isn't pressing, so this should be over in a few minutes."

"What about the other rider?"

"He's in the med center. Yanis from Twelve will be there. I've already talked to him."

"And?" Laramie pressed. Dust, it was easier to wrestle a jacklion than get information from him.

"He'll stand down."

"So we've got nothing to worry about? I didn't inadvertently start some sort of turf war between all of you?"

Gered shook his head slightly as if irritated. "No. Just shut up and maybe Rosche won't notice you."

Laramie mock-saluted and jogged up the steps into the command tower behind him. Cool air hit in a welcome blast despite the early morning hour. She swallowed trepidation as Gered took the stairs up to the second floor.

Shadows lingered in the curves of the stairwell and an oppressive silence overtook the landing. She paused when she saw maps and a radio room through an open door. Gered snapped his fingers as he kept walking. She made a face at his back and moved to catch up.

"What did I tell you?" His voice came so soft she barely heard it.

"I have a mild concussion. Maybe I have memory loss."

He shook his head again and a faint flicker of annoyance broke through. But there was some resigned amusement. Laramie stifled a quick burst of triumph.

Gered pushed through into a large room. A table took up the center, maps and reports spread out over the polished surface. More maps hung on the walls—surveys, topographical outlines, and one marked with what had to be the unit routes through the territory. A large red flag and curling black viper took up the entire east wall.

Moshe and a rider Laramie dimly remembered already waited in the room. The rider glared at her. She curled her lip back, maintaining eye contact until he broke first. Another red-jacketed man lounged against a chair at the table. His lower lip pouched out and brown stained his teeth when he flashed a grin at Laramie.

She ignored him, standing beside Gered when he pointed to a spot on the floor. She studied the maps instead, desperately trying to commit something to memory.

"See something interesting, drifter?" Rosche's voice sent her turning around. He stood in the doorway, arms crossed carelessly across his chest, a smile playing across his face as he watched her.

She shrugged. He stepped forward, circling her like a hunting viper. She stiffened, hand falling to her knife. Gered shifted slightly beside her and she brought her hand away.

Rosche caught her chin and tilted her face to look at the bruising.

"Heard you were the reason for this little meeting." His thumb brushed softly against her cheek. She clenched her jaw and twisted away from his hold.

He smiled but the predatory look lingered in his eyes. He stared at her and she struggled to hold his gaze. Rosche swept a glance up and down her, assessing, weighing, before coming back to her eyes.

He's looking at the blue. Deciding what I have to offer. Her gut twisted at the thought.

Rosche stepped away, moving to the head of the table and sitting down with a soft creak of leather. He leaned elbows on the table, steepling fingers together.

"All right. Tell me what happened, Laramie."

Her stomach knotted again as her name rolled off his tongue. As far as she remembered, no one had used it in his hearing. She focused on a point just off to the side of him, out the windows framing a view of the mountains, and gave a brief report of the attack.

The other rider fumbled through a version which alternated between contradicting hers and supporting it. The unit leaders didn't move.

Rosche leaned back in his chair. "Gered?"

"Another of the trainees supports her story, sir. I'm throwing in behind her."

Rosche sniffed. "Moshe?"

Moshe shrugged one shoulder. "She proved herself the better rider at the races. I take her version of the story. I've got no quarrel with Four."

Rosche turned to the last unit leader. "Yanis?"

"Ander admitted she knocked him out. He can't ride for

sparks either. I've got no quarrel with Four." Yanis shifted the chew in his lip.

"Okay." Rosche nodded. "Then the matter is closed, and the air is clear?"

The unit leaders nodded, but the rider shot a poisonous look at Laramie.

"Now, seems like we have a contender in the drifter."

Laramie jerked her head back up to Rosche. He looked at her again with cold appraisal as if she was no more than a piece of meat.

"Still in training, but she's proven herself capable of going toe-to-toe with experienced riders and winning, so, is her choosing upon her, Gered?"

Laramie froze, trying to watch Gered's expression from the corner of her eye. A "yes" meant the tattoo and loss of the small glimpse of freedom she still saw as a trainee. She didn't know how the choosing went, but it seemed like anyone could take her and she didn't get a say in it. There was no guarantee Gered would even want her for Four.

A "no" meant she had a little more time.

"No. She could still use some work on her marksmanship. I brought her in, so I want her for Four. She's not ready to ride with us."

"Fair enough. Any of you want to stake another claim on her?" Rosche leaned back in his chair.

Laramie bristled. *Exactly like I'm a piece of meat.*

Moshe and Yanis shook their heads.

"I'll stake a claim on the young trainee who caught the fight. Axel. Local boy. He's a good rider. He'd fit well with us," Moshe said.

Rosche tapped a thumb against the table. "I hear he's struggling."

Moshe shrugged again. "I'll stake for him, make sure he passes the training. Hate to waste skills on a bike like that."

"Okay. If he doesn't make the cut, it's on you," Rosche warned.

"Understood, sir."

Rosche turned flat green eyes at Laramie again. "Then I guess we're done here. She gets two weeks to improve her marks. Then I want her in."

Gered inclined his head. "Sir."

"Dismissed."

Laramie followed Gered from the room. He didn't pause, immediately heading back outside. She jogged to catch up.

"Hey, why did you say no? You know I'm a good enough marksman."

He didn't stop.

Why would he do that? Especially if he wants me for the unit?

"You knew it would give me more time." Her feet paused and she stared at his back.

Gered kept walking.

Laramie gritted her teeth.

"Gered?" she called. He briefly paused.

"Thanks."

He half turned his head and tipped a slight nod before leaving her standing in the middle of the compound.

CHAPTER TWENTY

Why did you say no? Laramie's question dogged Gered across the rest of the compound.

You knew it would give me more time.

He tried to shake free. She needed more practice. She wasn't up to his standards.

She could outshoot and outride half the garrison.

He shook his head. He wanted her to have more time. He wanted to see if she'd make a run for it. To see if she could make it.

I'm a dusted idiot.

He flung open the bunker door, ignoring the startled glances of the riders in the rec room as he stalked by. Dayo sat up, rubbing bleary eyes as he entered their room.

"How'd it go?" Dayo dug on the ground for a shirt.

"We're square with Moshe and Yanis." Gered knelt by his bed and pulled out his rifle case from underneath.

Dayo yawned and rubbed his eyes. "You stake a claim on her?"

Gered glanced over his shoulder. Dayo shrugged.

"Figured Rosche would push for it. She in?"

"Not yet. She needs to work the range a bit more," Gered forced the lie.

Dayo scoffed. "Right."

Gered undid the clasps and propped open the lid. He lifted his rifle out and slung the strap over his shoulder.

Dayo sat more alert at the sight. "How'd your report with Rosche go last night?"

"He was pissed, but told me I handled it like I should have."

The scant praise Rosche had given had burned like hot oil, but a small, small part of him lapped it up like a man dying of thirst. He hated himself for it.

Dayo slowly nodded, a bit of understanding in his look. He knew what shooting the insurgents had done to Gered. How another bit of him died with each bullet.

"It had to be done," he said quietly.

"That help you sleep last night?" Gered spat.

Dayo didn't react. "That and the beer." His voice stayed calm.

Gered swallowed hard, tamping down his fleeting anger again. They all had their ways of coping.

Dayo nodded to the rifle. "You meeting with Moshe?"

Gered curled his hand tighter around the strap. "I want the look on his face before I go to Rosche."

"*Are* you going to go to Rosche?" Dayo's expression remained dangerously calm.

Gered swallowed again. Dayo wouldn't hesitate to tell him to screw Rosche and see what happened if more army guns found their way across the border. Except it could end up getting Dayo and more of Unit Four dead by those guns, or by Rosche.

It might not be worth it.

"I'll see what Moshe says."

"You want me to come with?"

Gered shook his head. "This stays between Moshe and me for now."

"Okay." Dayo grabbed his boots. "Good shooting, *kamé.*"

—

Moshe waited for him at the range, rifle slung over his shoulder. They acknowledged each other with a quick nod and began hiking up to higher ground in silence. The few riders out at the range watched them go, some with open admiration in their eyes. They were the only two snipers in the gangs, each with a perfect success rate.

The range they'd set up years ago was a low hill at the far end of the practice field. The targets were dark splotches in the gullies and arroyos on the far side of the range, meant only for them.

Moshe knelt first. Gered disengaged his scope as Moshe set up, adjusting his jacket underneath him. Gered tucked his glasses up on his head, and fit plugs into his ears.

"Jacklion," Moshe said, his voice muffled.

Gered raised his scope, slightly to the left, elevated for seven hundred yards, centering on a jacklion cutout. A slight breeze wafted by. Moshe paused until the air stilled.

A crack, delay, then puff of dust as the bullet struck the target.

Moshe cleared the chamber and called another target.

Another hit.

Another casing ejected from the chamber. "You got something to say to me?"

Gered waited for the next shot.

"Maybe. I collected a pile of army-issued guns from a group of insurgents down in Conrow. Closest border checkpoint is in your territory. I'm looking at an army-issued rifle. A little old, but it can't lie."

Moshe cleared another casing. "Dishonorable discharge."

"And they let you walk away with hardware like that?" Gered sighted the next target.

"Never said they let me." Moshe twisted to smirk up at him.

"Check your elevation," Gered told him.

Moshe settled back down.

"It's also a good cover if the government wanted someone in the territory."

Moshe's shoulders stilled before he pulled the trigger. Another hit. "Logical conclusion." He stood, brushing red dirt from his jacket. "Your turn."

Gered fit his scope back on and took up his position, flicking down the short supports along the barrel.

"Any truth in it?"

Moshe snorted a laugh. "If there were, you think I'd just admit to it?"

"You think I'm gonna run to Rosche with something like that?" The sun-warmed stock settled against his cheek, grounding him.

"You might. Rumor has it you've been performing recently. Maybe you want to keep your streak."

Gered eased out a breath, finger teasing the trigger. *Am I that obvious?*

The recoil rocked through his shoulder. An armadillo eight hundred yards away gained a new hole.

"And if I wanted something out of it?" He nudged the casing away, and began sighting a new target. He took another breath to calm the sudden quickening of his heart, not sure where he was going with the question.

Moshe paused for a long moment. "Like what?'

Gered tucked the rifle more securely against his shoulder. "Something to get across the border from our side." The words hung in the air. He hadn't intended to put something so heavy between them. It would be easy enough for Moshe to take that to Rosche whenever he wanted.

"That something happen to be a drifter?"

Gered cleared the casing. He shrugged.

"You've been here longer than me, Gered. We've always gotten along, and I think we know each other as well as anyone does around here."

Gered stilled, turning his head from the scope to watch Moshe from the corner of his eye. Moshe stared downrange, face pensive. He suddenly met Gered's gaze.

"We keep this between us?"

Gered tapped the barrel of his rifle. Between them and their guns, and the rifles wouldn't talk. Moshe nodded.

"I've got some contacts on the outside who are interested in what happens here."

Gered settled his cheek back against the gun.

"They trying to make a move?" *What does it mean for the gangs if the army is planning something?*

"Too timid still for a push. But more than happy to supply those restless under the viper's heel."

Gered pulled the trigger again. Eleven hundred yards down, an antelope died.

"Nine are dead in Conrow because of that."

"Didn't say I agreed with the method. But I'd have to do the same in your place. Orders are orders."

Gered climbed to his feet. "Whose?"

Moshe shrugged. "Since it seems we both have something

we'd rather Rosche not know, let's deal."

Gered slung his rifle over his shoulder.

"Anyone else figure out where those guns came from?" Moshe asked.

"I told Dayo. I doubt anyone else in my unit, or the rest of the gangs knows the difference between army issue and Callan's work we get in."

Moshe nodded. "How do you know?" Genuine curiosity filled his voice.

"Tlengin get around."

"Yeah, forgot you got around a bit before settling here. Dust, how old are you, kid?"

Gered shifted. He hadn't celebrated a birthday in sixteen years. But Moshe didn't look like he'd racked up many more years on the earth beyond him. "Not that much younger than you."

Moshe shrugged. "Fair enough. Then maybe we're both okay. Keep that quiet for now, yeah? And I'll help you out when you decide something needs a path across the border."

He dug in his pocket and took out a scrap of paper, scribbling something on it with a stub of a pencil before handing it over to Gered. "Assuming anything can make it out that far before being caught."

And that's the real trick.

Gered tapped his thumb against the rifle strap. "Fair enough."

Moshe fastened his scope back into place on his rifle. "Then we done here, or do you need some more practice?"

"I think we're all good."

Moshe flicked fingers against his forehead in a mock-salute. "See you around, Gered."

Gered waited several long minutes on the hill, watching

Moshe saunter his way back toward the Barracks. A glance at the paper showed a radio frequency. The paper crinkled in his hands before he slid it away in his jacket. He had a piece he'd missed the last time he'd tried to run.

He just had two weeks to decide whether to give it to Laramie or keep it for himself.

CHAPTER TWENTY-ONE

Hey!" Gioia knocked on the open door and leaned in. "We're going into town to blow off some steam from the last patrol. Want to come?"

Laramie gingerly swung her legs over the side of the bed to sit up. After breakfast that morning, the room had stopped spinning every time she moved her head, but the bruising on her stomach and face still throbbed.

"Sure I'm allowed to go as a trainee?"

"Yeah, I cleared it with Gered. Only if you feel up to it." A bit of hopefulness lingered in Gioia's stance as she shifted from the door to shove a hand in her back pocket. A sudden longing to see something other than the bunker walls rushed over Laramie.

"Where do you usually go?" She hooked a foot around her boots and pulled them over.

"There's a bar in town the units usually hit up. It serves more than alcohol." Gioia's face twisted in disgust.

Laramie reached for her knives, noting that Gioia still wore her blade.

"Don't bring your gun," Gioia said as she moved toward the weapon. "Bar serves stronger than cheap beer and arguments can turn trigger-happy sometimes. Unspoken rule to just bring knives along."

"Sounds like a great place."

Gioia chuckled. "Not the classiest place I've ever been, but it has whiskey, so…" She shrugged.

"Then I'm in." Laramie pushed up to her feet.

"Finally!" Dayo called when they stepped out of the bunker. He and Gered stood by a bike, several other riders with them.

"You've been waiting five minutes," Gioia retorted. "You can ride with me," she told Laramie.

Gered climbed on his bike and Dayo settled behind him. The other riders doubled up as well as Laramie swung on behind Gioia.

They headed out in a slow procession through the courtyard and out the north gate. Laramie shifted on the uncomfortable perch. The bikes weren't made for two riders.

"Relax," Gioia chided. "It's only a few minutes ride."

"Too fancy to walk?" Laramie squirmed again.

"Dayo's too important." Gioia raised her voice.

Dayo held on to Gered's shoulder as he leaned back and flipped her off. Gered tipped side to side, drawing a shouted curse from Dayo. Gered drew his shoulders up with something almost like a laugh as Dayo punched his back.

Laramie grinned. The whole unit was a bit more relaxed outside the walls. They rumbled their way slowly through town, the streets mostly clear in the pooling light of the streetlights. A tall two-storied building rose up, light and music pouring out of the open double doors. Neon signs flickered in the windows. Some trucks and more gang bikes parked outside.

Unit Four parked in a group and Gered led the way across the loose gravel scattered in front of the bar, hands inside jacket pockets. Something looked off until Laramie realized he'd left his bone-handled pistols behind. No guns, but she'd never seen a knife on him.

Then she caught it. A slight bulge in the small of his back when he pulled his jacket a little tighter. Dayo had an extra knife strapped to his thigh and walked closer to Gered as if he didn't know he was smuggling a gun in anyway.

Laramie shook her head and followed Gioia through the doors. The entire bottom floor of the building was open except for wooden columns scattered throughout. Tables stood in crooked groups, most of which were full. A sharp divide lined the room. The larger half filled with leather-jacketed unit riders, raucously drinking or flirting with girls in short skirts and plunging necklines. The rest were locals, clustered in tight groups and sending cautious looks to the riders over their drinks. A bar ran around two walls, several bartenders moving around, mixing drinks from the multiple bottles of alcohol or drawing beer on tap.

The group split, most of the riders dispersing to mingle with the other units. But Gioia stayed close to Gered and Dayo, so Laramie did too.

Gioia waved Laramie up to the counter and ordered two shots.

"Cheers." She raised her glass and Laramie returned it before they tossed back the whiskey.

"Not bad for a backwater town." Laramie rolled the glass in her hand before setting it down.

Gioia allowed a grin. "This is one of two bars Rosche allows to get something decent from over the border."

"What's the other place?" Laramie flagged the bartender down again and ordered.

"Let's just say it's the type of place Zelig likes to hang out."

Gioia scooped up her drink from the bar.

"Grimy, smoky, poor taste all around?"

Gioia clinked her glass against Laramie's. "Exactly."

Laramie laughed and followed as Gioia wound around several tables to where Gered and Dayo now sat.

"How's your head?" Gered asked as they sat.

Laramie reflexively brushed at her bruised cheekbone. "Not bad. Though this music might bring the splitting headache back. I hear it's up to the usual crappy standards around here."

Dayo laughed as he twisted in the chair, taking a proffered cigarette from another rider. "You eventually tune it out."

"Reassuring." Laramie grinned.

A flicker of amusement crossed Gered's face.

"Hey, thanks for letting me come."

"Gioia made a convincing case." He took a drink of his dark beer.

So she asked?

"Hey." Gered snapped his fingers in front of Dayo's face as the rider pulled a lighter from his chest pocket.

Dayo frowned around the cigarette as he nodded. "Okay, okay!" He stood as he lit it. "I'll be back in a few. Don't drink my beer!" He pointed at Gered.

"Then hurry up!" Gered called after him.

Dayo waved a hand as he headed outside with another rider.

Laramie leaned forward on the table. "So what happened on your patrol? Did a town really try and revolt?"

Gered's face twisted. "Yes, and everyone with a gun in their hand is dead now."

"Not everyone," Gioia's quiet voice said. Gered softened a little.

Laramie quirked an eyebrow.

"I don't kill kids," he said, throwing back the last of his beer and pushing back from the table.

"He okay?" Laramie asked Gioia as he stalked over to the bar.

"Yeah." Gioia watched him, slowly rotating her glass in her hands. "It was pretty rough."

"*You* okay?"

Gioia flashed a smile. "About the same as always."

Laramie sipped her whiskey. "I think we need a serious discussion about quality of life around here."

Gioia snorted. "Right. Have fun with that one, drifter."

But she returned Laramie's grin.

"Tell me something." Laramie flicked a glance to where Gered still leaned against the bar. "This rule about not having any sort of romantic attachments around here? What's the point?"

Fear flickered in Gioia's eyes and she hastily looked back down to her glass.

"Just curious." Laramie shrugged.

Gioia drank and met her gaze again. "According to Rosche, it weakens a rider. The strength of the unit depends on you and the rider next to you."

A derisive laugh escaped. "So he's just above the rules then?"

Gioia flashed a haunted look.

"He takes whatever he wants," Gered's voice broke in again, startling both of them. He stood by the table, drink in hand, staring down at them with his impassive look. "His rules are to keep the rest of us strong, to be able to do what's necessary."

"To kill kids?" Laramie spat.

Anger spasmed across his face, sending the blue flaring brighter. But underneath hung the same hopelessness that lurked in the corners of the Barracks and in the slope of Gioia's shoulders.

"Sorry." Laramie leaned back in the chair. "Just have a feeling I'm not going to fit in around here."

Gered took his seat again, and Gioia flashed a small smile.

"You kind of get used to it," she offered.

Laramie managed a smile, but rebellion stirred her soul again. No way was she hanging around long enough to get used to living in fear and helplessness under Rosche. Get used to the idea of killing people who dared to think they could have a better life.

"What'd I miss?" Dayo dropped back into his chair, pulling his beer back toward him.

"A deep conversation on the health concerns of cigarettes," Laramie said.

Dayo rolled his eyes. "I get enough of that from this grandma." He jerked a thumb at Gioia.

"They're disgusting," Gioia retorted.

"They're beneficial for my mental health."

"You might have a fair argument there," Laramie allowed.

Dayo grinned and reached across to bump her fist. "You can stay."

Gered shook his head, but his features had eased into something less rigid and angry.

"Is that your second? How am I behind?" Dayo downed his beer in two giant swallows.

"Spend less time outside," Gered said.

Dayo waved him off as he stood. "Anyone need anything?"

"I'll go with you." Laramie finished the last of her drink.

"You're paying, right?" Dayo backed away.

"I am pretty flush with cash right now." Laramie grinned. "You want anything?" she asked Gioia.

The rider tapped her glass. "I'll take another."

Laramie flipped a thumb up and headed after Dayo. They leaned on the bar to wait for the bartender.

"Hang on, is that *simi*?" Laramie pointed to the small green bottle.

"Looks like it," Dayo said.

"You want a shot?" She tilted a glance at him. She wasn't questioning how the bar had a bottle of the traveler alcohol, but she was getting a small taste of home while she could.

Dayo jerked a nod, suddenly quiet. The bartender poured them both a small bit of the amber liquid.

Laramie slid her glass across the counter, raising it to Dayo. "*Malidan*."

He smoothed his thumb along the glass, staring at the alcohol, before meeting her glance again. Loss and a bit of sadness filled his dark eyes.

How long has it been for him?

"*Malidan*," he said quietly, then tapped his glass against hers. They tossed the alcohol back and spicy warmth trailed down her throat.

Dayo set the tumbler down, pressing his lips together for a long moment before turning back to her.

"You're not so bad, drifter." He reached around and tapped a fist over her wrist where it rested on the bar, wrapped in her traveler bands. "Thanks."

"You're welcome," she told him in Aclar.

He smiled once, the sadness still filling his eyes before his mask fell back into place.

The bartender delivered their next round of drinks. Laramie tugged on Dayo's sleeve as he turned to head back.

"You want anything else while we're here?"

Dayo flicked a glance back at their table, seeing what she had a second before. Gered and Gioia leaning slightly closer to each other, bare suggestions of smiles showing as they talked. Sudden panic struck Laramie that Dayo would do something stupid like report what he saw.

But a bit of anger flickered in his face when he turned back to her. *He knows. And he thinks I might do something stupid.*

She lifted a shoulder. "I'm just saying, we could probably take our time heading back, right?"

He eased back into a more relaxed stance, leaning against the bar, and flicking a hand to bring the bartender back over. A brief nod of understanding and thanks passed between them.

"Another shot then?"

She smiled. "You pick. Though this'll probably be my last one. I do have to make it to training tomorrow."

"Sucks for you." He smirked.

"Though will extra alcohol help this heal better?" She pointed to her left temple.

He laughed. "Definitely."

They took the second shot, paid up, and headed back to the table. Dayo set another beer in front of Gered, who nodded.

Gioia switched out her glass with the fresh one Laramie handed over.

"Gered said he staked you for the unit," Gioia said.

"Yeah, guess we might stay roommates." Laramie dropped down into her seat. One very small positive if she didn't make it out in time.

"Shame. I was hoping to pawn you off on Corinne."

Laramie wrinkled her nose at Gioia with a grin. The rider smirked back.

"Hey, don't corrupt Gioia with your smart-ass ways." Dayo waved a finger.

"Me?" Laramie pressed a hand to her chest. "Why would you say *that*?"

A snort came from Gered as he drank. "Afraid she might beat you at it, Dayo?"

"It was a competition?" Laramie's mock-surprise dissolved into a laugh as Dayo flipped a rude traveler gesture.

She chided him back in Aclar, and he rolled his eyes.

"How'd you become a traveler?" Gioia asked her.

Laramie hid her hesitation with a sip of beer. Dayo's fingers drummed the table, and Gered shifted back to stillness.

"They picked me up after the Tlengin took out my village. Adopted me in after a few years of appreciating my sparkling personality."

Dayo's smile crept back and Gered relaxed again.

"You decide to move on?" Gioia asked.

Laramie tapped her thumbs against the table. "A few years ago, I got the itch to start drifting. Unofficially looking for more Itan, but not a bad way to see the country."

Gioia darted a quick glance at Gered who ducked his head, rubbing the side of his jaw.

"Any luck?"

"No. Think the Tlengin did a good job." But she sent a slight shrug to Gered, who tipped his head in a small nod.

Sixteen years ago, a war waged across the isthmus connecting Natux's southwestern tip with Cricea. It took too many soldiers and left the lower country even emptier and open for the Tlengin to wage their war on the Itan without any real fear of retribution from the government. They brutally struck entire towns before they disappeared back to the migratory villages their fragments of magic helped hide in seemingly thin air.

"Sorry." Gioia winced.

Laramie waved her off as she took another drink. "I might have missed the opportunity to become part of this happy little gang here, so really, a win all around."

Gered lifted an eyebrow. "How'd that make your beer taste?"

Laramie lifted the glass, a wry grin surfacing. "Pretty bad."

"Need another one?" Dayo drummed a rhythm against the edge of the table with his index fingers.

"I have to get to training tomorrow!" Laramie protested.

Gioia shook her head, sliding Laramie's nearly empty glass away. "No, I definitely think she needs another."

Laramie tossed her hands up and sat back in her chair.

"You good?" Dayo pushed back from the table and glanced down at Gered.

"Yeah. Someone has to be able to get the bikes back to the garage." Gered tapped the rim of his glass, still half full of beer.

"I'm perfectly fine!" Dayo protested, arms waving in slight uncoordination.

"You wish," Gioia snorted.

"You're up, Gee." Dayo flicked his hand, beckoning her to stand. "Let's go."

Gioia rolled her eyes, but stood. "Sure?" She pointed to Gered. He nodded, tracking her path for a few seconds as they headed to the bar.

"If I puke tomorrow, it's on them." Laramie shook her head. It had been a while since she'd drunk so much.

Gered flashed a small smile. "How do you think this normally ends?"

But not you. He'd had even less than she had. Though going up to the bar with Dayo appeared to always results in shots of some sort. She rubbed across the slow ache deepening in her bruised stomach and watched Gioia and Dayo kill another round of whiskey.

"Okay over there?" Gered caught the movement.

"Yeah." Laramie winced a little as she leaned further back in the chair. "Just feel stupid for getting jumped so easily."

"You kept your head though."

"Surprised I thought something through?" she teased gently.

He shook his head, but another smile leaked through. "I was starting to wonder."

A reply died on her lips as a rider crowded up to Gioia at the bar, hand sliding down her back. Ache forgotten, Laramie leaned forward.

"She's okay." Gered's voice halted her, but his jaw set tight as he watched. Hands fisting, Laramie decided to trust him.

Gioia thrust a hand up to collide with the man's throat. He staggered and she whipped her arm around his back, grabbing his jacket collar and slamming him into the bar. Dayo took a drink of his new beer, leaning against the bar and watching as the man pushed up, wiping blood from his nose, and glaring at Gioia.

Gioia squared her shoulders, twirling a knife in her hand. The rider backed off, arms waving as he shouted something about trying to be friendly. Laramie flattened her lips in annoyance.

Eyes narrowed, Gioia mouthed what was likely an invitation for the man to shift off. Dayo rippled fingers in a light wave as the rider backed off, anger still twisting his face. Gioia sheathed her knife and picked up two beers. Dayo stayed between her and the rider as they headed back.

Beer sloshed over the rims as Gioia slammed the glasses on the table. Gered's chair creaked as he stood and headed over to meet another red-jacketed rider. They spoke for a moment, a quick glance to where the man wiped blood from his nose. The other unit leader nodded, and they parted ways.

"All good?" Gioia asked, staring at the table as Gered took his seat again, her voice oddly light.

"All good," Gered confirmed.

Laramie leaned toward Gioia, rapping her knuckles on the table. "Nice move."

Gioia glanced up, tension shuttering away with a quick blink. "Thanks." She grabbed her glass and took a long drink. "Think this might be my last one after all." The smile she turned to Dayo and Gered came forced.

But they both nodded. Gered tossed back the last of his beer. "I'll let the others know not to do anything stupid."

"Race you." Dayo raised his glass to Gioia and Laramie.

Laramie rolled her eyes and picked up her beer, drinking half of it at a sedate pace. A warning buzz in her head cut her off. She shoved it over to Dayo.

"I really will hate myself tomorrow. Finish it off."

But Dayo stood. "Looks like I've got to rescue Gered."

Gered stood, hands in jacket pockets, face set back in his normal expressionless mask as a rider talked and gestured wildly in front of him, clearly not getting the hint.

A bit of a smile tugged Gioia's mouth. "We'll meet you outside."

As they stepped outside into the clear night air, Gioia drew a deep breath.

"Need me to drive?" Laramie slid hands into her pockets.

"No, I'm good." Gioia scuffed a boot through the loose gravel.

Her shoulders rose and fell with another deep breath.

Laramie angled her gaze up to the starry sky. "Another thing for me to look forward to?"

Gioia huffed a short laugh. "Yeah, well, you made a stronger impression your first day. Like Gered said, keep a weapon on you at all times and always be prepared to use it."

"Sounds exhausting." Laramie snuck a glance over.

Gioia mirrored her stance, hands in back pockets. "It's life around here."

Nothing stirred around them. Laramie moistened her lips.

"Ever think about getting out?"

"Every dusted day. But it's never happening." Raw acceptance filled Gioia's voice. "I've seen three failures since I've been here. I'd hate to see the next one be you."

Laramie allowed a faint smile. "Why'd you think that?"

Gioia leaned close enough to nudge her arm. "Because only an idiot would think you'd settle right in."

"Fair enough." Laramie smiled.

Dayo's voice broke behind them. "You can't say anything to him. He takes it as an open invitation to just start talking."

"I didn't," Gered protested. "He's gunning for a transfer to another unit."

"Please not Four." Gioia turned with Laramie.

Dayo had an arm draped around Gered's shoulders. Gered lifted an eyebrow. "No. Dayo already talks too much."

"Hey!" Dayo tugged Gered's shoulders down. Gered spun out easily from his hold, a smirk flickering.

"At least I have something to contribute besides oxygen."

"Do you?" Gioia crooked her head, but a real smile appeared.

Dayo glared at Gioia. "Laramie, take my side."

Laramie spread her hands wide. "I'm staying out of this."

"I take it back. You'd be a terrible fit for Four."

Gered shook his head, allowing Dayo to wrap an arm around his shoulders again as they headed to the bikes.

Laramie hung back a step, unable to accept the resignation in Gioia's voice as she repeated the belief that there was no way out of the Barracks. But it seemed she'd already given up.

Maybe when I have a solid way out, I'll ask again. She shook her head as she hurried to catch up with them. Being a trainee at the bottom of the pecking order was hard enough, she didn't want to try to make it in the units where extra battles for survival were waged every day.

They made it back to the bunker without incident and stored the bikes. Laramie headed upstairs as soon as she saw a pause in Gioia's movements. Dayo followed her up, tapping her shoulder with a fist as the door closed behind them, leaving Gered and Gioia behind for a brief moment.

Laramie nodded and headed to the room. She had boots and jacket off by the time Gioia stepped in. She seemed a little more relaxed.

"Thanks for the invite," Laramie said.

Gioia shucked her jacket. "No problem. Sure you'll be okay for tomorrow?"

Laramie rinsed the taste of beer from her mouth with water. "We'll see. You and Dayo will be first to hear about it if not."

Gioia grinned as she flipped the lights off. "Night."

Laramie lay back. "Night." She carefully rubbed her eye around the bruising. Maybe she shouldn't have gone with them. Because now, between the three of them, it seemed like she already had something she'd regret leaving behind.

CHAPTER TWENTY-TWO

The hiss and crackle of radio static jerked Gered from sleep. He half pushed up, fumbling for the handheld radio on the floor.

"Gered!" the disembodied voice snapped.

He cursed under his breath, still trying to find it and blink away the last vestiges of sleep.

"Gered!" The voice became progressively angrier. Who knew how long they'd been calling?

"Make it stop," Dayo mumbled.

"Where'd you put it?" Gered growled back.

Dayo rolled over with an annoyed grunt, dipping his hand under his bed and shoving the radio toward Gered.

"I was supposed to find it over there?" Gered fumbled with the switch. "Gered, over."

Dayo put his back to Gered and pulled his blanket over his head.

"Finally. Rosche wants you."

"When?"

"Ten minutes ago."

Gered swallowed dread and sat up. "On my way."

Dayo rolled back over with a yawn. "Get the rest of the unit up?"

Gered leaned over to the dresser and pulled a clean shirt and socks out. He checked the time. Just after eight hundred hours. "Get them up anyway. We could use some training even if Rosche doesn't send us somewhere."

He shoved feet in boots and ran a hand through his hair. Dayo grumbled as he pushed away his blankets.

"I shouldn't have asked."

His holsters settled against his legs with a comforting weight. Dayo tossed his red jacket over and Gered shrugged it on, not bothering to zip it up.

"Good luck." Dayo offered a tight smile.

Gered nodded and left. He jogged his way to the main entrance of the tower. He paused only for a moment in the atrium to zip up his jacket and slip his expressionless mask back on before taking the stairs on the right two at a time and heading to the war room.

The door hung open and Rosche stood on the other side of the polished oak table, hands clasped behind him as he stared out the wide windows.

Gered touched the gun on his right leg to further steady himself, and stepped in. Moshe and Barns waited, slouched in relaxed positions beside the table. Barns tipped his lazy smile as if finding it hilarious that Gered was late.

"Sir." He stood at attention, hands clasped behind his back.

Rosche turned. "Not like you to be late, Gered." His voice held a gentle rebuke.

"Didn't hear the radio at first, sir."

Rosche's features fell into sharper lines. "Don't let it happen again."

"Sir."

Gered tried to release the tension curling his fingers even

tighter. There was another reason Barns and Moshe were also in the war room and it wasn't to lecture him on oversleeping. Although that shouldn't have happened either.

"The tower got a call in from Zelig's unit this morning. They ran into an ambush in Springer and most were taken captive. Their radio man was the one who got out and was able to call in for help." Rosche leaned on the table, pushing a map closer to them, inviting them to step closer.

Gered followed, letting Barns and Moshe have first look as they both held higher rank. Zelig's unit ran one of the routes in the northern patch of territory housing cattle and some crops. Laramie had caught the tail end of their route when she'd ridden through. If she'd timed it a half hour better, she could have made it past them. As it was, she'd exposed a hole in the patrol patterns which Rosche had since rectified. He'd also beefed up the number of border checkpoints with the low-level enforcers.

He shoved the thought of the drifter away. A red block marked a town pressed up against a butte.

"Numbers, sir?" Moshe asked.

"About fifteen. Though you would have been able to handle that, wouldn't you, Gered?" Rosche raised an eyebrow at him.

Gered forced a swallow. "Sir." He could never bring himself to answer more than that to Rosche's pointed questions.

"Sounds as if they lost a few riders." Barns crossed his arms, rubbing a hand along his chin.

"Yes. They're down to seven riders at last count."

"What do they plan on doing from here?" Moshe asked. "Take riders captive and expect to hold the rest of us off?"

Gered shifted his arms across his chest. "The ones we ran into in Conrow seemed to think because they had guns, they were on equal footing."

Barns scoffed a laugh. "Put them straight, did you?"

Gered tightly nodded. All but one.

"Moshe and Gered, I want your units ready to ride. Barns, you have control here until we get back." Rosche pushed up from the table.

"We?" Moshe wasn't the only to raise an eyebrow. It had been some time since Rosche had left the compound on a mission.

Rosche picked up the long-barreled pistol laying on the table, running a hand thoughtfully over the engraved slide. "This is the second attack in three days. Someone is supplying these people with guns and they are attacking my men. If they want to see me, then I'll oblige."

A chill slithered through Gered. The look had returned in Rosche's eyes. The light of madness that only came from having survived the war, watching his unit massacred in front of him, and then deciding to build his own army and carve out his own territory.

It didn't appear often, but when it did, it meant trouble.

"I want the trainees you two staked to go with us." He looked between Gered and Moshe.

"Sir."

As if Laramie needed any more motivation to leave.

"We ride in thirty minutes."

Gered snapped a salute and turned to follow Moshe, but Rosche's next words stopped him.

"You'll still put a bullet in whoever I tell you to, won't you, Gered?"

Cold dread ran down his arms, freezing his fingers. "Yes, sir." But the words spilled dry from his mouth. It seemed like Rosche had remembered what he could do.

"What was that about?" Moshe asked on the stairs.

Gered pushed past him. He knew exactly what it was about. Rosche wanted to remind him he was completely and totally controlled.

"We going to find any of your friends there?" Gered snapped.

"If we do, you and I are going to do our dusted jobs, aren't we?" Moshe maintained his even pace.

You'll still put a bullet in whoever I tell you to, won't you, Gered?

"I'll send the kid your way." He took the last steps two at a time, desperate for sunlight in the dim lighting of the hall. Moshe called thanks as he stepped outside.

Gered stopped at the bunker first, leaving Dayo to muster the rest of the unit. He turned next to the training ground where Harlan had the recruits wheeling out their bikes. He jogged over to the trainer and informed him of Rosche's orders over the rumble of engines.

Harlan frowned. He didn't like it when he was overruled, even if it was by Rosche himself. But Laramie and Axel were flagged down and drove slowly over to him.

"We're headed out and Rosche wants you two along. Kid, head over to Moshe's bunker. He staked for you, so you're riding with his unit. Grab whatever weapons you have, or they'll make sure you have what you need. Drifter, you're with us."

Laramie's eyes peered out of the helmet, full of questions. He ignored them and swung on the bike behind her. She headed to the bunker, tipping a slight wave to Axel when he parted ways toward Moshe.

Once parked, Laramie pulled off her helmet. Damp bits of blonde hair stuck to her cheeks, flushed from the heat of the helmet. The bruising on her left temple had darkened overnight, but other than that, she looked no worse for the wear from the night out.

"What's happening?"

"Rebels in another town got Zelig and his unit trapped. We're headed there. With Rosche."

Her face twisted in a more solemn expression with each word.

"So you're going to kill them all?"

Gered eased his hand out of a fist. "We'll do whatever Rosche tells us to."

You'll still put a bullet in whoever I tell you to, won't you, Gered?

He shook himself slightly. "Dayo will make sure you have enough ammo for that gun. Get yourself a vest and a comm."

He left her to follow him into the bunker. The unit moved about with a vague sense of efficiency. Dayo left off strapping on his armored vest to take Laramie to the small armory in the back room.

Gered pulled his vest and rifle out from under his bed. He zipped his jacket up over the vest, feeling more settled than he had since stepping into the war room. The rifle went over his shoulder and he headed into the armory. Laramie was there, loading more magazines for her pistol. The florescent light reflected off the blades of her twin knives laying on the table.

He swallowed hard and placed his rifle on the table beside them. Pulling his personal ammo box out, he began loading up his spare mags for the rifle. They clipped onto another belt that would go across his chest. Extras for his twin pistols came next. Another check to his weapons and he was good.

A rasp sent his back teeth clenching together. Laramie ran one of her knives across a whetstone. Most of the unit had figured out not to do it in front of him, though no one really knew why.

"What's my role in all this?" she asked, blithely unaware of the effect the sound had on him.

"If Rosche doesn't step in, you're hanging back with someone so you get a feel for how the unit works. Two units should be more than enough to put down the trouble." He slung the rifle over his shoulder, trying to find the calm that came with the action.

"What, so I can be even more excited about getting a stupid tattoo?" She faked an excited expression.

A chuckle broke through before he could stop it, and tension leaked from his shoulders.

"Something like that."

She wriggled her eyebrows. "Can't wait."

He paused in the door. "I'll pair you with Gioia. She usually takes rear and you can help her on the sweeps."

Not much got past Gioia. She was good at stalking through shadows and using either gun or knife to dispel any threat.

Laramie slid her knives into the sheaths with a skin-crawling hiss of steel on leather. "Sounds good."

She reached for her green jacket to pull over her vest, but he shook his head.

"Leave that and your scarf behind. You're riding with us, so Rosche will want you to look the part."

Gered opened a locker and tossed her a dark leather jacket. "Wear the helmet."

Laramie slowly pulled the new jacket on. It hung a little loose around her chest and arms, the vest not even helping to fill up the extra fabric. She carefully folded up her dust scarf and jacket as if she was putting away parts of herself.

He looked away. She had to. He'd be lucky if he could still

convince Rosche she needed the full two weeks after they got back.

~

They assembled out in front of the main tower. Rosche rumbled around to join them, impassive in a red leather coat and a black helmet. A shotgun rested in a carrier in front of his left leg. The armored vest under his jacket lent him an additional threatening bulk.

"Ready?" His voice crackled over the comms as he flipped the visor of his helmet down.

"Yes, sir." Gered and Moshe replied.

"Moshe, take lead with me." Rosche pulled out. Gered held back, waiting for Moshe and his riders to file after Rosche before waving his hand for his unit to follow.

Out on the road, Gered checked his mirrors. Dayo to his right. Gioia to his left. And just behind Gioia, a plain red helmet. He'd placed Laramie in the middle of the pack. She could easily stay even with them, and she'd be right at Gioia's side when they got to the town.

Dayo accelerated enough to come up even with him. He tapped the left side of his helmet. Gered nodded and flipped frequency to the one only he and Dayo used.

He lifted his index and middle finger from the throttle in reply.

"Why are we coming on this little party?" Dayo asked.

"I'm assuming it's because we already put down a group like this." Gered drifted around a pothole.

"I think that means we should have another day off."

Gered found Rosche riding at the front of Moshe's unit. They'd fanned out for better angles to ride up around him in a protective pattern if it came to it, but still far enough back to give him the appearance of careless boldness.

"It's because I've finally done something useful by bringing in the drifter and then killing that rebellion. Maybe he wants to see if I can keep delivering."

Dayo grunted. "You gonna?"

Gered's left hand clenched hard around the grip. "Before I left, he asked me if I'd still put a bullet in whoever he asked."

Dayo's whistle cut shrill through the radio. "The guy's shifting crazy."

"You gonna say that to his face?"

"Unlike you, I don't have a death wish."

Gered waved his arm again signaling the upcoming exit onto the northbound highway. He couldn't deny it.

"Switch back. We've been on too long."

Dayo dropped back behind him and the channel fell dead. Gered waited an extra ten yellow strips of paint on the highway before switching over. Death wish. He'd want it so bad some days, and then wake up and find he wanted to keep living. And sometimes he hated himself for it.

He checked his left mirror. Gioia hugged the edge, but still stayed visible. She turned her head. Nothing was visible past the darkness of her visor, but she lifted two fingers and tapped twice. He breathed a little easier. They still had each other's backs.

Three hours' ride brought the emergence of the butte in the distance.

Rosche pulled over to the side of the road and waved Gered and Moshe up beside him.

"Go scout it out."

Gered left his helmet and slung his rifle over his shoulder. Moshe did the same. They killed their engines and set off at a light jog.

CHAPTER TWENTY-THREE

Five minutes' easy lope brought the town in sight.

"I'll take east," Moshe said.

Gered nodded and turned west. Another few minutes' half jog, half walk brought him closer to the outskirts. He ducked into a shallow gully and wound his way closer.

Voices paused him mid-step. He eased a glance over the embankment. Two men with shotguns stood twenty yards away on either side of the road cutting through town.

Gered backtracked, slipping out of the gully, and army-crawling his way through the scraggly bushes and rocks into the shadows of the closest house. From there he ghosted between houses and across an alley, avoiding three other similar patrols.

The towns all shared the same basic structure. Main highways leading in and whirling into a roundabout at the center where the mayor's office stood. Gered chose a two-storied house and scaled up the jagged bricks with the help of a gas pipe and window ledges.

Worming his way along the roof, he eased his rifle down beside him and raised his head above the crenellated ledge.

"Moshe, we've got a problem," he murmured into his comm.

"Yeah, I see it too," Moshe replied.

At least eighteen men and women paced in groups across the center green or on the office steps. Seven unit riders sat in the center of the green, hands cuffed, under the full glare of the sun.

"They got reinforcements." Gered nestled his rifle into his shoulder, checking through his scope. "I'm looking at pistols and shotguns. Everyone's got at least two mags on them."

Moshe grunted agreement. "So is our radio man still out there somewhere?"

"Maybe. I wasn't checking on the way in, were you?"

Moshe scoffed. "He can keep hiding for all I care. They let these people get the drop on them."

A smile tugged at Gered's mouth. Zelig wasn't exactly popular among the other unit leaders. There were more than a few opinions on his, and his unit's, overall intelligence.

"I'm up to at least twenty-five hostiles including these down here."

"I'll raise you to thirty to include the three patrols I dodged on my way up here," Moshe said.

Gered shifted for a quick scan of the rooftops. A faint wink of sunlight reflecting off something metal blinked from the roof of the courthouse. He shifted his rifle slightly, letting his catch the light to signal his place back to Moshe.

Below them, the rebels kept walking. Gered shook his head. They didn't even think to look up, secure in their position of having a few guns and a few riders cuffed on their lawns.

"Okay, I'll boost my range and make the report," Moshe said.

"Sounds good." Gered tapped his finger along the rifle's stock. "You okay with this?"

A long pause lingered over the comms. "Like I said, we'll both do our jobs, won't we?"

Gered waited just as long to reply. "Yeah."

"Good hunting."

"You too." Gered resettled the stock against his shoulder and set to scanning the square as Moshe began a report to Rosche and the units.

A few patrols came in and switched out. No concern stirred their meandering. Gered fought frustration at their inexperienced patrol patterns. At least three major gaps were evident, and most of them looked like they'd never held a gun. Though, living in Rosche's territory where he hoarded weapons along with everything else, that wasn't surprising.

"Gered, he wants you on." Moshe broke through his concentration.

He pulled a small adapter from the front pocket of his jacket and clipped it to the comm wire.

"Sir."

"Gered, thoughts on the situation?" Rosche's voice came clipped and business-like. Military.

"Looking at numbers and weapons, we're matched, but most of these people look like they'll bolt at the first sign of a motorcycle. Shouldn't be a problem."

It would be a massacre.

"I'd go for the leaders and be lenient on those who surrender," Moshe said.

Gered lifted his head in surprise.

"Oh?" Rosche asked sharply.

"Most of these look like workers. It'll take away from the fields around here. Production will fall."

Gered wouldn't have dared to say something like that, even if he thought it. But Moshe had more pull as leader of Unit Two.

Rosche grunted. "We'll see what happens when we ride in. I want two blade formations. Your units know those, don't they?"

Gered imagined Dayo rolling his eyes from the safety of his helmet. It was one of the easiest attack formations used.

"Unit Four will take east." Rosche said. "Unit Two, sweep west. We'll catch them in the middle. Moshe and Gered, stir them up once you see dust."

Gered tapped his earpiece once in acknowledgement. "Dayo, take lead. Gioia, you and the drifter cover the rear."

Two taps came back through the earpiece.

Gered settled in to wait, his world shrinking down to the scope and the rifle and his body pressed against the hot roof.

He sighted one of the rebels, crosshair on his chest. Gered's heart hammered for a split second before he eased a breath to calm it. A spasm clenched his throat. Killing. More killing.

Dust. How many people had he already killed in the last two days, and how many more would he add to the tally in the next few minutes?

He flicked the safety off and shifted his finger closer to the trigger, heart thudding down to its normal, slow rhythm. The bits of blue in his eyes that let him master the weapons shoved in his hands let him control his heartbeat with a simple breath.

The Itan were more than builders and tinkers. They were warriors, and you have that inside you. The ability to carry death with you like nothing.

Severi had told him that nearly every day since he'd taken Gered from the burning remains of his home. The Tlengin raider had carved it into him, and Rosche had been more than happy to continue.

"I got incoming," Moshe's quiet voice slipped over the comms.

Gered lifted his head from the scope long enough to see a dust cloud approaching from the west.

"Start calling them." He turned back to the crosshairs.

"They're coming!" A panicked voice cracked in a shout and a man burst into the square.

"I'll take the runner," Moshe said.

A shot rang out and the man's legs buckled beneath him like he'd had the air punched out of him.

Everyone froze in the square. Gered pulled the trigger and his target collapsed.

Pandemonium broke out. Men and women bolted in every direction, weapons shaking, and shouts overlapping. Two men waved their arms, trying to bring back order. None of them ran for cover.

Dusting idiots. Gered shook his head and shot again.

The casing clattered beside him. The incoming riders split just outside town, some making their own roads between houses or down alleys. Three rebels knelt in cover at the main road.

Gered made a quick adjustment and killed one. The lead rider—Rosche—pulled a pistol and shot a second. The last gunman dropped his weapon and dove for cover as the bikes roared closer.

Gered took one more shot before pushing to his knees and gathering up his rifle.

"Going down," he told Moshe.

"Got it covered," the sniper acknowledged.

Rifle settled over his shoulder, Gered scrambled down from his perch, scraping his hands even through his gloves. Once his boots hit ground, he pulled a pistol and started making his way forward.

"On your left," Gioia's soft voice came over the comms.

He shifted to catch a glimpse of her down the alley to his left. She held a shotgun. Laramie stood a few paces beyond her, pistol comfortable in her hands, lips pressed together in a tight line.

Gered tapped his earpiece. Gioia tapped back twice.

A faint warmth budded in his chest despite the gunfire and screams.

"Let's go." He moved forward, clearing every alleyway and corner.

The patter of feet sent his finger to the trigger. A young man rounded the corner, sweat dripping from his forehead, his fingers clenched around a bloody arm.

He skidded to a halt, eyes wide as he saw Gered.

"Please…"

Gered eased his finger away. "Get inside and stay out of sight," he growled.

The man nodded and shoved through the nearest door.

Gered kept moving forward. The next rebel wasn't so lucky. The man swung his gun up with a look of desperation. He fell without a sound. Gered stepped around him and kept moving.

He entered the town square as a few more rebels stumbled back from the alleys and side streets, ushered along by riders with raised guns.

More bodies had fallen in the square in the few minutes it had taken Gered to get there. Those still alive threw down their guns and allowed themselves to be shepherded into a group. Dayo freed the captive riders. Most had thrown themselves flat on the ground after bullets started flying. At least two had a wound which might have come from a rebel trying to get a kill in before it was too late.

Gered crossed to the crumpled body wearing a black jacket. He eased to a knee and gently turned the body over. His gut clenched as he recognized one of his own unit.

"Four, check in." He pressed a finger to his comm.

All but the one rider replied, Laramie sounding off at the very end. An odd bit of relief swept through him at hearing her voice, even though he'd kept half an eye on her and Gioia on their slow trek through the alleys.

"Get them on their knees!" Rosche bellowed.

Gered swallowed hard and went to join him.

Fifteen men and women were all that were left. Some had tears running down their faces. Some looked strangely relieved as if they'd just been waiting to be caught and executed.

Rosche paced the line. "Who was it that started this little rebellion?"

At first no one spoke. Rosche cocked his pistol and pointed it at the closest woman.

"No!" A man leaned forward out of line. "It was me. I said we could do it. Please, let them go."

"And what? Just take you?" A sneer curled Rosche's lip.

The man nodded, his face already falling.

Rosche towered over him. "Do you know who I am?" he bellowed.

Trembling, the man nodded again.

"And you still thought this was a good idea?" Rosche waved his gun around him.

The man slowly drew himself up, daring to look Rosche in the eye. "One day someone's going to challenge you, and then take you down. And then even the dust will breathe a sigh of relief."

Rosche nodded, looking around with a thoughtful purse of his lips. He turned back to the man. "Pity you won't be able to see it." He pulled the trigger and the man collapsed.

A woman stifled a screaming sob, half collapsing against the man next to her.

Gered's gut twisted as Rosche stepped over to her. She tried to pull herself up, but another glance at the dead man drew another sob.

"Pick a number between one and ten," Rosche said.

"What?" Confusion broke through her grief.

"Simple enough. It might save your life."

A bit of hope stirred in her face. Gered wanted to look away. He couldn't see Rosche's face to determine if he really meant it, or if it was another one of his games.

"Seven?" she hesitantly said.

Rosche lifted his gun to inspect it.

"Close enough. You can go."

"What?" She stared at him, incomprehension spread across her face.

He waved the gun at her as if shooing away an irritation. "Go! And I'd leave before I turn some lucky rider loose on you."

She pushed to her feet, throat bobbing as she darted wild glances around at them.

Go. Gered silently willed her. She backed away a step, then sprinted toward the nearest house. The slam of the door cracked through the stillness like another gunshot.

Rosche ignored it and turned to the next in line. "Pick a number."

At some point Moshe came to stand beside Gered. Another man fell to Rosche's game. Gered caught a glimpse of hatred directed at Rosche in the unit leader's eyes before he shuttered it away.

Five rebels were left.

"Gered." Rosche beckoned him forward.

Dread anchored him to the ground. Rosche turned to him in impatience, and Gered forced his feet forward.

"How many bullets do you have left in that mag?"

Gered didn't have to check. "Six."

"More than enough."

The nearest rebel shuddered as Rosche loomed over him like a stalking jacklion. "Pick a number."

"Five!"

"Not close enough." Rosche shook his head. "Gered."

Please don't make me do this.

Rosche turned his head to fix him with a hard stare. A look that promised consequences he couldn't take.

He stepped forward.

You're made to kill.

Raised his gun.

I don't want to.

He pulled the trigger.

Blood dusted over his jacket and face. His arm fell back to his side. Rosche moved on. He let the next three go. The last man wasn't so lucky.

"Gered."

His breath froze somewhere in his chest. The square stayed eerily silent.

He couldn't do it again.

He had to.

He was made to kill.

The man toppled to the side. The gunshot faded. A faint ripple like a sigh of relief eased through the square. Gered couldn't look away from the dead.

Rosche stooped and rubbed his hand over the bullet wound and turned to Gered.

Not this.

He braced.

Rosche smeared the man's blood across Gered's left cheek. His thumb traced across Gered's lips, covering them.

"I'm glad you're remembering your duty, Gered," he said in a kindly voice as if the action would make Gered happy. "I want to keep seeing this side of you."

He couldn't move. Couldn't breathe. The cloying scent of blood overwhelmed him.

"Sir." He forced an answer. It wasn't a yes, but it satisfied Rosche.

"Good. Be ready to ride in five minutes," Rosche called, and the units stirred back to action.

Gered took one step back.

Then another.

Holstered his gun.

The sun blazed hot and the gun's faded discharge echoed back in his ears.

Faces blurred by him, covered in fear and awe.

An alley opened to his right and he plunged down it, gasping a breath in the shadows.

A sob caught. Knives sliced his skin. Screams and burning scorched his senses. Tlengin voices howled for blood. Another hand slapped blood across his face.

He gasped again, slamming the palm of his hand against the

rough brick wall, over and over, until he stood in the alleyway, his eyes and ears clear of any sounds but the muffled rumble of bikes and units calling to each other.

He braced his hands against the wall, leaning into it to keep himself up. Another breath tore from him. Over and over, he focused on slowing the rhythm.

"Gered?" A timid voice whispered.

He lifted his head. Gioia stared at him, one arm hesitantly lifted out toward him. He brushed her fingers, and the last whirling bits settled back to earth.

Beyond her, Dayo leaned against the alley entrance, facing out to ensure privacy.

"You okay?"

No.

Never.

He nodded.

She reached again to brush at his bloody jaw. He shifted out of reach. Her hand fell back to her side.

"I'm fine." His voice came hoarse and gravelly. "Get ready to ride."

She squeezed his hand twice. He clutched her hand a long moment before releasing. She stepped away and left. Dayo tilted a questioning glance. Gered nodded again, not trusting his voice or the shaky walls he'd built back up.

"Gered!" Moshe jogged up to his side. His comm dangled from its wire down his jacket. He stared at Gered, jaw working as if to say something.

Gered pulled his comm from his ear, silencing it.

"Was it worth it?" he ground out.

Moshe half-raised his shoulders in answer.

Anger spasmed. Gered shoved a hand into Moshe's broad chest, pushing him back.

"Was it *dusting* worth it?" he hissed and whirled away.

He climbed on behind Dayo as the units began to pull out. They paused long enough for him and Moshe to reclaim their bikes on the outskirts of town.

Gered pulled his helmet on. His throat constricted as the blood remained on his cheek, filling his helmet with the scent. Each rasp of air in brought a tang of iron and salty sweet to his tongue.

He couldn't make it.

He could make it.

He would make it.

He'd make it back to the Barracks, through the debrief with Rosche, and then fall apart with no one watching.

CHAPTER TWENTY-FOUR

Relief swept through Laramie as they pulled up in front of the bunker in the dim light of evening. It looked almost home-like in the last golden light of day. Especially after what she'd seen that day. What she'd been a part of.

Gioia pulled her helmet off. "Go put your bike up and then meet up in the mess hall. We'll be celebrating." But her face twisted in a frown.

Nausea threatened Laramie's stomach. "Yeah, think I'll pass."

Gioia leaned closer. "It dusting sucks, but at least stop by. You're part of the gangs, almost a part of the unit. You'll have to get used to it." Sorrow clouded her brown eyes.

Laramie sat back on her bike seat, her gaze falling to where Gered was a lone figure heading toward the tower, his helmet dangling from a hand. He walked like the sky itself pressed down on him.

Maybe she'd go, just to make sure he was okay. *I shouldn't care that much.* But an insatiable *something* had drawn her toward him since she'd first seen his gray and blue eyes.

"Okay."

Gioia flashed a poor smile and wheeled her bike into the garage. Laramie pushed off and drove slowly toward the trainees' garage. Harlan was there, waiting on her and Axel.

The kid parked his bike in silence. Something stained his dark jacket in uneven patches. Laramie swallowed. She assumed making a kill graduated a trainee right up into a unit. Harlan clapped him on the shoulder, a nod of understanding passed on.

"Go get a drink, kid. You too, drifter."

Laramie turned away. If she said anything, she'd regret it. She forced her feet into the command tower. It was full of the units who'd stayed behind, clustering around Two and Four's tables, chattering and shouting excitedly.

A few of the riders called back just as excited. Others like Dayo and Gioia, even Moshe, sat in silence, picking over their food with clenched jaws and distant eyes.

Restless anger thrummed through her muscles, turning her away from the mess hall. She wouldn't be hungry for a long time. She stumbled down the stairs, jerking the zipper of the oversized jacket open as she headed back to the bunker.

She dumped the jacket and armored vest in the armory. She hadn't discharged her gun. She didn't need to clean it. Didn't want to even look at it.

Her fingers itched to hold a tool. To find something to build instead of threatening to destroy. Laramie jerked the door to the garage open and stepped inside.

The light was already on. She came up short at the sight of Gered sitting against the wall by the workbench. His knees were pulled up, arms draped across and hands dangling limply, a vacant look on his face as he stared at nothing. His helmet lay discarded on the ground beside him. Blood still stained his face.

Her own struggles vanished. She whispered a curse and turned back in to grab two water bottles and a towel before heading back down.

He barely stirred as she knelt in front of him.

"Hey."

He blinked, his eyes focusing on her.

"What are you doing down here?" His voice tumbled and ground like tires across rocks.

She held out a water bottle. He made no move to take it.

"Get out." Fire crept through the words.

Defiance flared. "No."

He blinked again.

"Drink some water." She forced authority into her voice.

He stared at her a long time before lifting a shaky hand for the bottle.

"Are you hurt?" she asked.

He shook his head.

Laramie took a short breath. "Can I...?" She pointed to his cheek and held up the towel and other water bottle.

He just stared at her again before slowly nodding. One leg slid down and he unscrewed the cap. He drained half the bottle as she dampened the towel.

Gingerly, she touched it to his cheek. He didn't move, and she pushed a little harder. He blinked a few more times, inhaling shakily.

"Why would be do this? It's barbaric."

His jaw worked a moment. "It's Tlengin."

Laramie's knuckles clenched white around the towel. "Like I said. Barbaric."

"It's to celebrate a good kill. To mark a warrior upholding the raider way." His eyes lost focus again.

"It's murder. He made you murder them," Laramie snapped.

"And he wanted you to be happy about it."

Gered pulled his head up, shaking it slightly. "He wanted me to keep remembering what they taught me. What he taught me."

Laramie doused the towel with more water and scraped it across his cheek.

Water dribbled down his neck under his collar. He stirred again and looked down at himself.

"Dust." He brushed a hand over his stained jacket. His movements came stilted as if he was drunk as he fumbled for the zipper, at his comm wire hanging loose, his fingers uncooperative.

She caught his hand. "Hey!"

Gered forced a breath, his grip tightening around her fingers with painful intensity.

She swallowed. When she'd wake up screaming from nightmares as a kid, Ade comforted her by speaking in Itan. Something familiar. She had no idea if it would help Gered, or send him further into whatever spiral he was in. Maybe it would be different enough to shock him out of it.

"Take it easy." She switched to the lilting cadence of Itan. "Let me help."

His head flew up, gray-blue eyes locking on to hers with painful intensity.

"Is this okay?" she asked.

He looked at her and it seemed she could see him piecing himself back together, shoring up the barricade that kept him from the world. He nodded. "*Sa.*"

Laramie offered a slight smile. "Let's get this jacket off, yeah?"

He slowly released her hand and shifted forward, fingers cooperating now on the zipper, and let her pull it off his shoulders. She laid it aside, and took the armored vest from him next. He unhooked the comm and tossed it into the pile before pulling his knees back up and leaning on them, taking a shaky breath as he rubbed a hand across his face.

Laramie dampened the cloth again. "You've still got some on your face." She held out the cloth in offering. He didn't move. "Can I do it?"

He clenched and unclenched long fingers. "*Sa.*"

She gingerly nudged his chin to turn his cheek toward her, and quickly scrubbed the last traces away.

"There." She sat back on her heels and extended the water bottle again.

He took a few sips, drew another breath, and slumped against the wall.

"Do you want me to get Dayo?" Laramie asked, then dared to add. "Or Gioia?"

Fear lurked behind the bits of blue in his eyes at the rider's name, and he gave a frantic shake of his head.

"It's okay," Laramie reassured. "I'm not telling anyone." Sadness filled her smile. She couldn't, didn't want to, imagine a life where she couldn't be with the person she loved.

Gered's jaw worked a moment. "Is it obvious?" The fear remained.

Laramie remembered Corinne's words in the showers, and half smiled. "Probably only to another woman." *And to your friend.*

He slid his legs back down and leaned his head back against the wall to stare at the ceiling. The water bottle crunched between his hands.

"You still thinking about running?"

Laramie caught her breath. Her heart hammered loud enough

for him to hear. He hadn't switched from Itan.

"*Sa.*"

Another shuddering breath from him before he looked at her. "Good. I'm coming with you."

She stared in shock. "You're...?"

"I'm dusting suffocating here. I can't—can't stay here and keep—killing. I can't." His voice began to rise and panic resurfaced.

"Hey!" She grabbed his hand again. "Okay. This saves me the trouble of trying to convince you to help me."

Tension eased from his grip. "You really are persistent."

"Some see it as a character flaw."

The corner of his mouth quirked up. "What's your grand plan then?"

Laramie settled against the wall beside him, stretching her legs out. If this was an act on his part to try to get her caught running, it was a hell of a convincing one.

"You tell me. I've only halfway got the unit numbers and routes figured out. I was able to supplement what I remember of the territory from Rosche's map I saw the other day. Still not sure on the best route out of here."

Gered hesitated a moment. "I have something that might clear us a way out by the eastern border. We just have to get there first."

His lips pressed together again, and Laramie decided against asking what it was.

"That's something, right?"

He jerked a nod. "More than I had last time."

"I was planning on going before my two weeks was up." Laramie leaned her head back.

"Smart. I think we could do it." He curled his hand in a fist and relaxed it one finger at a time, over and over. "Unit Four has to go out again in two days for another sweep. Rosche wants to ramp up our presence after … all this."

Anxiety jittered through Laramie. "How long will you be gone?"

"Three days. When we're back, I'll start taking you out for shooting lessons, or extra training, so everyone gets used to seeing us leave together. They know I've staked you, so it won't turn heads."

Laramie raised an eyebrow. "You've already put some thought into this."

He flicked a sideways glance at her. "Maybe," he reluctantly admitted.

She grinned. "Okay. So I keep training while you're gone. When do we make our move?"

He rested his head back again, lips moving silently. "Two days before your last test. The weakest units will be in. We'll need to time it right to avoid the patrols still out."

"You know all the routes?"

"Close enough. I'll look at what you've got. And," he swallowed hard. "I'm guaranteed to go back into the war room between now and then, so I'll look a little closer at the ones I'm not as familiar with."

Something squeezed Laramie's heart. What difference would it have made in his life if the travelers had picked him up?

"We get across the border, then what?" she asked.

"Part ways?" He lifted a shoulder. "Might be easier to split up anyway since we'll have someone after us."

She nodded slowly, turning her attention to her hands in her lap. "Sure you don't want to keep together? We might stay stronger together." Something didn't want to see him leave if, *when*, they made it.

A little more tension released from him, and he slumped further against the wall. He stared across the bikes. "No," he finally said. "You've got a place to go back to. I don't. And I don't think there's anywhere for me to belong."

Her heart twisted harder. "You don't know that."

He lifted an eyebrow, but still didn't look at her. "You've seen what I can do. No one wants that around."

Laramie bit back a sigh and the urge to hug him. That probably would go over as well as trying to pick up a red-scaled viper by the tail. She settled for nudging his arm with her elbow.

"Maybe we can figure it out when we hit the border."

A half smile stirred his face. "Maybe."

She rubbed at a grease spot on her trousers. They hadn't slipped from Itan once since she'd begun. "Your Itan is pretty good."

Gered rolled his neck side to side, eliciting a faint crack. "Severi saw the value in keeping me fluent."

A chill prickled her arms. Severi—a Tlengin-sounding name.

"The travelers do the same for you?"

His question caught her off guard, and she bristled at the implication before she realized he probably didn't see it any way other than a skill that provided value.

"They helped me stay fluent because they knew it was important to me. That, and my common wasn't so good when they found me, so it's what we had to communicate in for a while."

Gered stared at her a moment, then shook himself. "Easy to forget sometimes not everyone is out to use you."

She looked back at her hands to disguise the sting in her eyes. "I'm sorry."

"For what?" Confusion coated his voice.

Laramie met his gaze. "I was just thinking how different things would have been if the travelers had taken you in like me. We might not be sitting here right now."

"Yeah, well, daydreams never got anyone anywhere." His thumb pressed against each of his fingers individually, some cracking under the pressure.

"I'm sure they would have taken one look at the extra blue in my eyes and decided to make something of me as well."

Anger flared bright again and she sat up taller. "They'd never do that."

Gered raised an eyebrow. "Ask Dayo about travelers' priorities. His family sold him to Rosche for safe passage through the territory. He was the easiest to let go because he doesn't have any gold in his eyes."

Laramie's mouth hung open in shock. No wonder he'd been so hesitant at the bar. "Those … those *dangarn*!" She heaped the worst traveler curse on them she could. "My family isn't like that."

"You'll have to forgive my life experience then," Gered said wryly.

She shook her head, still incensed at the thought of a traveler family giving up one of their own. Aclar families were closer than layers of rock crushed together over millennia. And giving a member up like that would have—should have—been like the Rift splitting the land in half.

Voices, thumps, and the slam of a door jerked her attention up.

"Time to go," Gered said, but he sounded just as reluctant as she felt. "Head up first. We don't need to be seen together more than's necessary."

Laramie pushed to her feet. "When do we talk again?" Maybe then would be the time to bring up the possibility of Gioia, or Dayo, coming.

"I'll come find you," he said. "We can use Itan if we need. Dayo is the only other one who might know a little."

She nodded, then propped her hands on hips and stared down at him. "You going to be okay?"

The way his eyes widened in shock nearly drew a laugh from her. "Yeah. Get lost, drifter." But the words didn't have any weight behind them.

She smiled and headed back toward the door.

"Laramie." His soft call halted her. She pivoted.

He stood, hands fisting around his jacket. "Thanks."

"You're welcome, *kamé*."

"What's that mean?" The question came quiet, almost small. "Dayo says it sometimes."

Laramie half smiled. "Depends on how you mean it. Between us, it means friend."

Gered shifted a little, but didn't seem displeased.

"I think for Dayo, it means brother."

He stared at her a long moment then cleared his throat. He took a moment to speak, but when he did, his voice came oddly tight. "Thanks."

She tipped a nod. "See you in the morning."

CHAPTER TWENTY-FIVE

Gered stared at the door for a long moment after Laramie disappeared through it. *Friend. Brother.* The words seemed almost foreign, like a memory that had faded just out of reach. His hands tightened around his jacket, bringing him back to the musty smell of the garage.

"Want me to get Dayo? Or Gioia?" He swallowed hard. She'd been there all of two weeks and had already seen what they tried so hard to hide. But he'd believed her when she said she wouldn't tell. He'd believed everything she'd said.

That they could make it.

That they might be stronger together.

He rubbed a hand across his left cheek. She didn't know him enough to be afraid when he didn't want anyone around. Didn't know he didn't really like being touched. Maybe it was the bits of blue in her gray eyes. The blonde hair. Hearing Itan again, spoken with love and care, instead of butchered by a Tlengin accent.

Whatever it was, she'd barged her way through the first layers of his defenses. And it didn't make him mad. It almost made him relieved.

He stooped and retrieved the armored vest and comms. *Should I tell them?* Dayo and Gioia deserved to know he'd decided to run again. Maybe offer to let them come. His heart clenched. The world rocked a little under his feet. They'd say no. No one ever made it.

Gered took a deep breath. No. The fewer people who knew what he was about to do, the better. Step by step, he made it to the door, through the darted glances and whispers of his unit when they saw him, and into the armory.

The light glinted off his pistols and nausea threatened again. Habit made his fingers itch to clean them immediately, but his heart rebelled against the task. He holstered them again and went to his room.

Dayo wasn't back yet. And probably wouldn't be for several hours. He knew Dayo, and the traveler would be several beers in already. He left the door open. Last time something like this had happened, Dayo had passed out in the rec room, unable to remember the code to unlock the door.

Gered sank onto the bed. Back inside, and away from the brightness in Laramie's eyes, he'd already started to second-guess himself. Memory of the last time he'd tried to run sent a shudder down his back.

What am I doing?

Gered leaned forward on his knees, rubbing his face. Maybe this time it wouldn't end in complete failure.

He shoved to his feet, trying to banish the thoughts. The more he thought about it, the more restless he'd become. He pulled a clean shirt from the dresser and peeled off his sweat-soaked shirt.

How shall I fear that from which I am protected by Heaven's wings?

The tattoo caught his eye, and a breath eased from him, slumping his shoulders. Not that he believed the message anymore. Since the Tlengin had taken him, he hadn't once felt protected by the invisible winged forces his parents once claimed coursed the sky, interceding to the high god on their behalf.

It had been a small act of rebellion. Something etched into his skin *he* had wanted. Something that might be able to remind him of life before the Tlengin every time he looked at it. Something so different from the spotted jackal on his ribs.

"You get cleaned up?" Dayo's slurred voice sent him spinning. The traveler leaned against the door, blinking slowly at him.

Gered pulled the clean shirt on and nodded.

"You sober?" Dayo lurched into the room, knocking the door closed.

Gered nodded again.

"You want to be?"

Gered swallowed. Any other day he'd be fine with drinking himself into near oblivion, but something held him back. Maybe it was gray and blue eyes. Hearing Itan. Something had snapped him out of the terrifying spiral, and he wasn't sure he wanted to go back.

"You've got too much of a head start on me." He tried for some levity, but it had vanished from his voice.

Dayo raised an eyebrow, as surprised as Gered was at himself.

Dayo snorted and collapsed onto his bed. "I've got more than that." He pulled a slender cylinder from his jacket. "Already one down. You want in?" He fumbled for the lighter in his left breast pocket.

Gered forced a swallow. He'd never smoked one of the joints. Severi had drugged him with the smoke when he was sixteen so the jackal tattoo could be inked into his skin without resistance. It was enough to bring bile up to the back of his throat.

"No."

Dayo blinked unsteadily at the sharpness in his voice.

"You know I've told you not to smoke in here."

Dayo flapped a hand at him, laying down without bothering to take off his jacket or boots and fumbling with the lighter.

"Lighten up." He snickered at his own poor joke. "You might actually like it."

Irritation surged. Gered reached over and grabbed the joint.

"You want to do this, then go outside. I'll leave the door unlocked."

Anger creased Dayo's features. "You think you can tell me what to do?" He struggled to his feet. "Like you're not the only one fed up with this dusting place? Like you're not the only one who shifting hates having to do whatever that psycho wants us to do?" His voice rose as he listed closer to Gered.

Gered clamped a hand over Dayo's mouth, cutting off any further tirade. He had limited trust to his unit, but there might be someone more than happy to report Dayo's outburst to Rosche.

"Shut up! You want to get yourself killed?" he hissed.

Dayo clawed his mouth free of Gered's hand. "Maybe I do. Think you're the only one who has a monopoly on that too?"

Another shudder ripped through Gered as he stared at Dayo. Dayo occasionally joked about it, had called him out on it before, but had never said something like that so seriously. He tried to tell himself it was the drugs and the alcohol surrounding Dayo with a nauseating stench, but his eyes were serious.

Dayo just glared back. He held out a hand. Gered slapped the joint back in his palm.

"Fine. Just take it outside."

Dayo clenched it in his fist, turned and stumbled to the door.

He flung it open and disappeared into the hallway. Gered stared after him, heart gradually slowing. He clenched and unclenched his hands. Would a friend go after him? Make sure he was all right? Apologize?

How would I know?

Dayo would. Gered shook his head. He only knew how to cope by disappearing from everyone, hiding until he felt like he could face the world again. But he left the door propped slightly open.

Both guns went on his bed. The small sliver of light coming through the crack unsettled him. He lay down, staring at the darkness surrounding the ceiling until he fell asleep.

—

Gered woke up screaming. A darker shadow leaned over him, gripping his arm and sweaty shirt. He fought against it until Dayo's voice broke through.

"Gered! Calm down!"

A ragged breath tore from his aching throat. He stopped the frantic pushing of his hands, gripping Dayo's arm instead.

"You okay?" Dayo's voice sounded surprisingly crisp. The cloying scent of alcohol and drugs had dissipated from his clothes.

Gered sucked in another breath, his heart still hammering like an engine at ninety miles an hour.

"Yeah," he eventually said.

"Good thing you finally woke up, or else the entire garrison would have heard."

Gered flinched. It had been a while since he'd been that bad. He eased his hand open, releasing Dayo.

Dayo did the same, shifting his weight away so he sat on the bed instead of pinning Gered down.

"Want to talk about it?"

Gered rubbed a hand over his eyes. *No.* It had been a wild confusing mess of heat and dust, his gun pointing at men and women on their knees as he pulled the trigger. This time it had been Gioia, Dayo ... Laramie ... right before Rosche had appeared and sunk a knife into his skin over and over while laughing.

"Good talk." Dayo clapped his shoulder and made to stand up.

Gered caught his sleeve. "Hey ... thanks..."

He barely caught Dayo's nod in the dimness.

Swallowing against the dryness in his throat, he asked, "You good?"

The bed creaked as Dayo's weight shifted back. "Yeah. I don't know. Maybe."

Gered pushed up to a sitting position. His hands found only empty space at his side. Panic hit until he realized Dayo would have moved his guns before trying to wake him up.

That shoved the apology from his mouth. "Sorry about earlier."

Dayo tapped a fist against Gered's shoulder. "Me too. If it makes you feel better, I tossed the joint and waited until I sobered up to come back in."

Maybe it's a good thing you did. Gered cleared his throat. Dust, he didn't know how to do this. "You've always got my back. Sorry I don't always have yours."

Dayo's sigh broke the silence between them. "You do, *kamé,* more than you know."

Gered shook his head. That word again. He didn't know if he

should believe Laramie about its meaning.

"What's that word mean?"

Dayo tapped his shoulder again. "It means I've got your back no matter what."

He eased his hand in and out of a fist, fighting against the thought that no one ever did that without expecting something in return.

"Just warn me before you're about to go off on Rosche again."

A chuckle broke from Dayo. "Okay, *kamé*."

"I need you to take care of yourself. You keep me sane around here."

Dayo tapped his shoulder. "Same to you. Sure you're okay after today?"

Gered rubbed a thumb against his left cheek. Only the slick of sweat met his touch, not the thickness of blood. He latched onto the last thing that had shaken him free.

"*Sa.*"

The bed creaked again. "Never heard you use Itan before."

Something like a smile touched Gered's face. The easy way the syllable rolled off his tongue helped banish some of the darkness clinging tight around him.

"Laramie used it earlier. It helped," he admitted.

"Huh. Guess I won't mind if she sticks around then."

Just like that, Gered's heart fell again. He was leaving. He opened his mouth to tell Dayo, then closed it. If Dayo came and they failed, he'd die too. There were no second chances for anyone else. It was a raw twist of fate he'd been given more than one chance after running twice.

Dayo leaned down, faintly scuffing the ground as he picked something up. Gered touched the comforting cool of his guns where Dayo laid them on the bed.

"Thanks."

"Any time." Dayo shoved to his feet. "I'm gonna crash, so don't wake me up again." The light words carried a hint of worry underneath.

"I'll be fine."

Dayo grunted and a muffled creak announced he'd made it over to his bed. Gered eased back down, making sure his pistols were tucked safely away. He rolled on his side. Even after all that, Dayo would hate him for leaving. He'd probably be more than happy to pull the trigger if he got close enough. Gered squeezed his eyes shut.

In the end, it would still be for the best. It would keep Dayo and Gioia safe if they didn't know. They'd get along fine without him anyway. He didn't have that much to offer. No matter what they said.

CHAPTER TWENTY-SIX

Laramie stared at vague outline of the ceiling through the darkness. *In two weeks, this could be nothing but a faint, nasty-smelling memory.* A sigh escaped. Of course, in two weeks, she could also be dead by psychotic warlord if they didn't plan just right.

Joy.

The time counter rolled over, telling her she was going to be late for training. Decimating a town called for at least a morning off in her opinion. She gingerly pressed fingers against her left temple. The swelling was down, but the bruising still darkened her cheek and temple. It wasn't worth getting punched in the face again to be able to sleep in.

She rolled out of bed and to her feet, stretching enough to crack her back. Dressing in the dim lighting was easy enough and she grabbed her knife belts and gun.

"Have fun," Gioia's mumbled voice lilted with sarcasm.

"Don't sleep all day," Laramie retorted.

A muffled snort came from the mound of blankets before Laramie pushed out of the room. Her grin faltered a moment as she paused long enough to arm up. She wondered if Gioia had slept at all since they'd both woken up in the middle of the night to the sound of anguished screaming.

Gioia had told her Dayo would take care of Gered, but the rider had curled on her side and Laramie swore she'd heard a sniff or two. Not unexpected. She'd been ready to bust down a door until Gioia had spoken up.

Laramie paused in the main room. Silence reigned over the building. No one besides her had any reason to be up already. There was no way knocking on Gered's door ended well.

Dayo and Gioia will make sure he's okay.

With that forced reassurance, she headed out. The morning sky, awash in pale pinks and yellows, promised another cloudless day of heat. Warmth already pervaded the air and the sun hadn't even made an appearance.

The other recruits straggled in with her to the training barracks. Axel rubbed at bleary eyes, looking much worse for the wear. It looked like he'd taken Harlan's advice to get a drink. Or five. She sidled over to him.

"You okay?"

He flinched. "No yelling," he mumbled.

She flashed a sympathetic smile and tapped his shoulder. He managed a miserable looking nod and yawned.

Harlan stomped in. Axel flinched with every step, until the gruff trainer stopped in front of him.

"Drink this." He extended a steaming mug of something that should have stayed dead.

Axel gagged at the smell. Laramie turned away to escape the worst of the fumes.

"You wanna have a headache all day, kid?" Harlan narrowed his eyes.

Axel grabbed the cup and bravely swallowed. His brow gradually unfurrowed with each progressive sip. Harlan stomped away, satisfied.

Axel mimed another gag to a smirk from Laramie, but kept drinking.

"Grab enough for two hours at the range," Harlan yelled. Axel only minimally flinched this time. Laramie tapped the bottom of the cup as he drank again, sending the liquid sloshing over the rim.

"You better hope that works really well in the next few minutes."

He wiped his face, glaring at her. She smirked again and headed over to the gun station to fill up extra mags.

"You okay this morning?" Axel joined her, his motion slow as he pushed bullets into empty mags.

"Yeah. Still thrilled to be here." She kept her voice light.

He shook his head. "Moshe told me to get ready for my choosing." His hands fumbled a bit.

"That's good, right?" Laramie put two mags into her trouser pocket just above the knee.

"Yeah." He trailed off, staring at the table.

She nudged his shoulder. He jerked and resumed his task.

"I just … I know what the gangs are, and what they're capable of … but seeing it…" His low murmur trailed off. "Some would say I'm on the right side of it now."

Laramie darted a glance around. The other trainees had spread out across the other long tables, engaged in the same task. She kept her voice low.

"You want to be?"

His head flew up, eyes wide. "Dust, Laramie! Don't say what I think you're going to say."

She narrowed her eyes and he dropped his voice.

"No one gets out. Look." He took a shaky breath. "I chose

this because it can keep my family safe, no matter how bad a harvest gets, or if the town decides to go stupid. I *chose this*. It's my life now, and I have to get used to it."

Laramie's heart twisted as she watched Axel age years before her eyes. No seventeen-year-old should be making decisions like that.

"Well, some of us didn't have a choice, and some of us don't want to get used to living like this."

He shifted a glance at her before tucking mags away into his pocket. "You're not bad to have around, Lare. Please don't do anything stupid."

"Can't promise that. I got told once my middle name was stupid."

That drew a reluctant smile. "What is your middle name?"

She shrugged. "Wouldn't you like to know?" Travelers still believed names had power and very rarely shared their true names outside of their family.

"Fine. But when I beat you at practice, you have to tell me." He finished the last of his mags.

Laramie raised an eyebrow, placing the mags she'd finished three minutes ago into her pockets. Technically, she was supposed to still show a decline in marksmanship so Gered could help bring it back up in a few days. But how was she supposed to resist a little friendly competition?

"Right," she drawled out the word. "How are you supposed to do that with no gun?" She held up the handgun she'd lifted from his holster.

He flattened lips in exasperation and reached for it. She gave it up after two unsuccessful grabs on his part and followed him from the building.

Unfortunately, common sense won out in the morning sun and cracking echoes of gunshots. Laramie rolled her neck side to side and sighted the target. She could have made seven shots in the bullseye, even with her left eye still a little narrowed from bruising.

She planted a bullet in the third ring from center with an internal groan. Kayin would give her no end of grief for this. Another one off-center. She adjusted her stance to put herself a little off balance and not make it look too obvious she was aiming to look bad.

A grunt behind her sent her tipping a glance back. Harlan stood there, sighting her shots with binoculars.

"You've done better, drifter."

She shrugged a little, no excuse coming to mind. He shifted a glance to her feet, a scowl spreading.

"Spread your feet. Weight even. You know better."

Laramie ducked her head in a sheepish expression and adjusted her footing. "Sorry, sir. Just tired maybe."

"No excuse for losing form I know you have. I want to see five bullseyes in the next round."

She rolled her shoulders back as he left and slid a new clip in. *How about three?*

~

I hate making myself look bad. Laramie jogged up the tower steps. A grueling day of poor performance had grated on her nerves, along with suddenly being the focus of Harlan's attention.

She'd been able to deflect some of it to her bruised left eye, but he'd only bought so much of it. *I didn't think it would be this hard.*

230

A light shiver eased over her skin as she stepped into the entry. A glance up into the dim light over the top of the stairs revealed nothing. Her unease deepened as she remembered Rosche's focus on the trainees. What would happen when Harlan reported her sudden flagging this morning?

She stuck hands into her pockets and hurried to get in line. The cook shoved a tray of food at her.

If anyone asks again, I'm running because of the food. She jabbed a fork into the pile of rice and chicken and turned to see Axel sitting nervously at Moshe's table. The riders mostly ignored him, but some reached out to slap his shoulder as they sat with their own food. Already being accepted into the unit.

Though she was glad Axel had a place, something tightened in Laramie's throat. *I'm a big girl and can sit by myself.*

"Laramie!" Gioia's voice cut over the hum of conversation in the dining hall. The rider beckoned her over to Unit Four's mostly full table.

Laramie raised an eyebrow, but headed over. *Guess I'm on my way in, too. Yay.*

She slid onto the bench alongside Gioia. Dayo lifted his chin in a nod. Gered shoved food around his plate, staring at the grain of the table. The other riders gave slight nods or clipped greetings.

"How's training?" Gioia asked.

Laramie darted a glance at Gered as she sawed through the chicken.

"Harlan told me I need to improve my marks at the range."

The corner of his mouth twitched but he didn't look up. Gioia hummed in disbelief.

"Thought you were near the top of the class?"

Laramie shrugged. "Think my eye's giving me some trouble."

"Want something for it?" Dayo opened another beer.

"Not if it's a can of beer."

This time something closer to a grin touched Gered's face. Dayo rolled his eyes.

"Have some faith in my abilities, why don't you?"

But a few snickers had gone around the table.

"All you did was put butterfly tape on my head. Sorry for my lack of confidence."

Dayo chugged half the beer. "Fine. Don't come running to me the first time you get shot."

Laramie mock-saluted and tried to chew her bite of chicken into submission. "Does *anyone* know how to cook around here?"

"I've tried to get into the kitchen, believe me," Gioia said. Her eyes widened in almost shock at her admission as the riders looked up at her.

"You can cook?" Dayo asked.

A bit of red touched Gioia's cheeks. "Maybe."

"So why haven't we benefitted from this?" Dayo waved his fork.

"Because they keep the kitchen locked up tight. And besides, I think they only have three ingredients in there anyway," Gioia retorted.

"And salt isn't one of them." Laramie scooped a forkful of rice, trying to help wash it down with water.

Gioia snickered. "Eating rations is like fine dining at the capitol compared to this."

"At least sometimes they include chocolate," Laramie agreed.

Gioia tipped her head back with a slight groan. "Don't talk to me about chocolate."

The entire table stared at them now, Gered watched Gioia

like he was seeing something new. Maybe he was. Gioia didn't exactly go around talking that much.

Laramie ignored them. "Any time you want to raid the kitchen, let me know." She nudged Gioia's shoulder.

Gioia's smile faltered for a second as she glanced up at the ceiling. Rosche's territory lay right above them. But she forced her gaze back to Laramie.

"Will do."

Laramie kept a grin in place. Dust, she really didn't want to leave Gioia there. It didn't seem like Gered would be too opposed to the idea either. She'd run it by him next time they had a chance to talk in private.

CHAPTER TWENTY-SEVEN

Gered stuck his hands into his jacket pockets as he stood on the steps of the bunker, taking a short breath of the clear air. The heat of the day had waned and now brooding clouds hung low over the mountains, delivering the faint promise of rain on the breeze.

He might hate the dust and the heat, but the moments caught in the dusk, with the sky painted in deep purples and pinks, and lumbering clouds heavy with rain causing the sage nestled away in the corners of the compound and atop the gullies to perk up and display their purple flowers, had a bit of magic. Moments that hovered on the edge of a breath, promising the end of something, and the start of something new. A bit of rain would bring the desert gasping back to life and show that even the deadest plants had a bit of life stored away in them after all.

It made him able to breathe again.

The door clicked open behind him and Gioia came to lean on the wall beside him. They stood in silence for a moment under the pretense of watching the game of stickball taking place among some of the units in the open space between barracks buildings.

Dayo and Laramie were currently an unbeatable team, with sticks as well as with insults.

Gioia slid her hands into her back pockets. "You good?"

He shifted, propping a boot up against the wall. "Yeah."

Dayo hadn't said anything that morning, but Gered knew someone else had to have heard him last night. He'd been on edge all day, waiting for some attempt to manipulate his weakness.

"I hate what he did to you." Her low voice filled with vehemence.

He swallowed hard and stared down at the uneven edge of the cement. "I did what I was supposed to do."

"And that's a reward?" Her voice shook with more suppressed fury.

He shifted against the rough wall, shaking his head a little. Explaining the Tlengin way would take too long. Take too long to make someone understand the way the raiders thought and rode. The way living up on the Rift's edge only exacerbated their remnants of warrior magic. He didn't want her to hear it anyway.

Gentle pressure against his arm brought him back to earth. He tipped his head to watch her from the corner of his eye. She offered a slight smile but kept her gaze forward on the game. He stared five seconds longer than he should have.

The memory of her smiling at dinner with Laramie brought a faint smile to his face. He'd never seen her so open with someone other than him or Dayo.

Gered leaned back against the wall. Below, Laramie passed the ball to Dayo, who flicked it through the goal markers with a quick turn of his stick. They shuffled an odd dance of victory, sticks held high, heads tossed back in laughter.

"Must be a traveler thing." Gioia chuckled.

Gered smiled. It was good to see Dayo laughing like that with something other than a beer in his hand. If it was a traveler thing, he was glad to see Dayo doing it, too.

"So ... you've been to the capitol?"

Dust, he should have kept his mouth shut, but it was just the two of them, and caught in the moments in the dusk, the scent of rain getting stronger, he'd become a little braver.

She half laughed. "You caught that, huh?"

He shrugged. Didn't say anything. Wouldn't press her, but desperately hoping she'd talk so he could unearth a little more about her. Moments like those were preciously few.

"Yeah. A few times. My grandma and me..." she paused. "She's pretty much all I had. We lived up above the Rift. She insisted I go interview at some of the universities there."

Gered tilted his head to better look at her. In a previous life, his parents had talked about universities, about learning, how maybe one day, he might go to one in the upper country's more civilized eastern cities if he did well enough. But the Tlengin had different ideas about his education.

"And?"

A smile curved the side of her mouth. "I studied science at a smaller school closer to my grandmother. It still got me on the surveying crew that was mapping the caprock when..." She swallowed and looked down.

He shifted enough to push against her arm this time. She flicked a grateful look up at him.

"Sounds like you might have done well for yourself," he said.

"Yeah. I might have. But I think I'd be missing out on a few things." The look in her brown eyes stole the breath from him.

He had to look away to keep breathing. "This? Not much then."

"I'd like to be the judge of that," she said firmly. It sparked a bit of warmth in his chest. Warmth that died just as quick as it came. He was leaving.

What if she came with us? He opened his mouth to ask, then clamped it shut. Not in the open where anyone might hear. She'd fight the idea. He had to figure out the best way to ask her, convince her to come, hopefully convince her it was worth it to try. Because he worried he wouldn't be enough.

Triumphant voices broke through the sudden silence between them. Laramie and Dayo jogged up the steps, faces bright in victory.

"Behold the undisputed champions!" Dayo draped an arm around Laramie's shoulders, dragging her with him into a bow.

She jabbed his side until he straightened. "You're decent backup."

Dayo's jaw dropped in mock horror. Gioia laughed.

"Careful, you'll hurt his feelings," Gered said.

Dayo rubbed his chest. "They're already hurt. See if I ever team up with you again."

Laramie patted his shoulder. "Sorry, didn't realize you were so sensitive." She shied away from his jab with a laugh.

Her eyes brightened in her merriment, the blue glinting a little brighter. Gered blinked hard. The sight stirred at the buried memories. He hadn't seen anyone with bits of blue and laughter in their eyes since before his family was slaughtered. The only other Itan he'd seen since had been prisoners of the Tlengin and there had been no laughter there.

He shifted away from the wall, clenching his fists in the jacket pockets to shake himself out of the memories.

Laramie caught the movement, her look fading to concern immediately. "You okay?"

The lilt of Itan grounded him in a rush. "*Sa.*"

A faint twitch brought his glance to Gioia. She glanced between them, her eyes turning guarded. She turned inside with a sharp movement.

Dayo arched an eyebrow at him. Gered ignored it. He'd talk to her later.

"I'm headed in too." Laramie slid past without a backward glance.

Dayo leaned a shoulder against the wall, a quick glance around confirming they were alone.

"You look comfortable with her."

He wasn't talking about Gioia.

"Would you be if she started talking traveler?"

Dayo's mouth pulled down at the corners. "Fair enough."

Gered shifted his weight back and forth. "It's nothing ... just didn't realize how much I missed hearing it spoken correctly."

Dayo nodded. "I hear you, *kamé*. Just don't do anything stupid."

Gered tilted his head back. Strange to hear those words directed at him for once. "What do you think I'm going to do?" Despite himself, a hint of challenge surfaced.

Dayo shrugged again, a suggestion in the rise of his shoulder.

"When have I ever?" A faint sneer curled Gered's lip.

"Just don't want to see you dust anything up." Dayo pushed away from the wall and headed in.

Gered turned his face back to the clouds still lumbering their slow way over the mountains. The light had all but faded, leaving only faint bits of gold clinging to corners and roofs. The artificial lights of the compound gained courage to spread their circles wider.

Sober Dayo might be more annoying than high Dayo. He

scuffed his boot against a crack in the concrete. He knew what Dayo meant. The traveler had kept quiet, found excuses to help him and Gioia steal a moment together more than once. He hunched his shoulders against the look Gioia had flashed at the simple exchange between him and Laramie.

I'm leaving. If I make it or if I don't, I'm losing both of them either way.

He turned his face up to receive the first drop of rain on his cheek. Strange how he thought he had nothing until he stood to lose something.

CHAPTER TWENTY-EIGHT

Laramie frowned at the sputtering motorcycle. Harlan propped hands on his hips.

"Of course this decides to act up as soon as Gered leaves," he muttered.

Laramie arched an eyebrow. Seemed like Gered was the mechanic for more than Units Four and Five.

"I know my way around an engine, sir. I can take a look."

Harlan regarded her from the corner of his eye. "All right. Take the afternoon. Might as well look at the rest of these too." He gestured around at the rest of the bikes in the garage.

Laramie rubbed the back of her neck. The exhaust coloring, along with the slower acceleration she'd noticed yesterday, likely meant the piston rings were going bad. It'd take all afternoon for that bike alone. Not to mention running a maintenance check on the other six.

"Okay."

"But I want you out early at the range tomorrow." He leveled a glare at her.

Not forgiven for her continued poor performance over the last few days. Laramie ducked her head, trying for contrite.

"Yes, sir."

"All right, rest of you, let's hit the mats." Harlan waved his hand at the rest of the trainees waiting by their bikes. Kickstands went down, engines were killed, and jackets and helmets shucked.

Laramie left the helmet on the workbench along the wall and exchanged it for a box of tools. She'd prefer her own, but it was a long walk back to Unit Four's garage, and her fingers itched to start.

She dragged a stool over and went to work, acknowledging Axel's well-wishes with a half-wave, already focused on the task.

When was the last time these rings were changed? Laramie shook her head. That, combined with the continual dust and wear, surprised her the engine hadn't officially died yet. She had her work cut out for her.

Grease stained her fingers and left smears on her pants. The sight comforted her. She always felt a sense of peace and purpose with a tool in her hands. Ade had always said it was the Itan in her, faded magic still trying to make its mark in the world through her.

"You have the knack too?"

Rosche's voice sent her spinning around on the stool. She'd been so engrossed she hadn't heard any approach. Though the way his boots barely whispered over the garage's concrete floor, she hadn't been meant to hear him.

"Travelers know their way around engines. I learned." She tried to relax a fraction, but her fingers clenched tight around the wrench.

He sidled forward until he stood over her, looking down at the bike with uncomfortable interest. She stayed in place, half facing him, waiting for his next move.

But he stood there, arms crossed, gaze flicking over her. "Oh, don't let me stop you."

Her shoulders bunched tighter, but she obeyed the unspoken order and turned back to the engine. His shadow blocked some of her light, but she didn't dare tell him to move. Silence filled the next minutes so they felt like hours.

"Why aren't you on the mats?" His question came so sudden the wrench slipped.

"Harlan wanted me working on the engine now, and then looking at the others to make sure they'd stay running."

He grunted. "You spend much time in a garage?"

She swallowed, focusing on her grease-stained fingers. "There's always something to fix around a traveler camp. Sir." Some respect probably wouldn't go amiss, as much as it galled her.

"Leave much time for experimenting?"

Her heart stuttered for a moment. His questions were still too casual. What did he think he knew?

"Sometimes. I like to build things."

"Hmm."

The silence fell again. Unease crept under her skin, lingering there like dust just itching to be shaken free.

She could no longer take it. "You need something built, sir?"

A hum came from him again and she realized with a jolt that it was amusement. Like he'd been waiting for her to break.

The itch deepened.

"No, I'd hoped you'd show me something you've already made. Something you came in with."

She forced her hands to keep working. Had someone else noticed what Gered had on her bike?

"Only thing mechanical that came in with me is my bike, and it was built in a yard back east."

"Hmm." Suddenly he was inches closer. "Zelig had something interesting to say about your bike. It … piqued my interest, shall we say?"

Laramie glanced up. "Zelig didn't strike me as the type to notice much of anything." She couldn't help the retort.

A brief flicker of amusement crossed Rosche's broad face. "That's true enough. But he was insistent. No harm in checking it out, right?" He flicked his hand, beckoning her to stand up.

She did, every movement wary until she put a half step more distance between her and the warlord.

"And don't worry, I've already let Harlan know I require your services for now." His smug expression didn't falter.

He really believes Zelig. And just what did Zelig tell him?

No one had mentioned the canister, except Gered. She'd begun to hope no one else had really noticed it.

"Lead the way." He waved to the door.

Laramie gently sat the wrench back in the box, wiped her hands, and tried to maintain a normal pace back to Unit Four's garage. Rosche kept stride easily, staying within arm's reach of her.

"I also hear you're faltering a bit in marksmanship. Guess Gered was right to keep you back for another few weeks."

Laramie brushed the knife hilt on her left leg to try to maintain confidence. "Guess so."

"Hmm."

That hum had begun to grate on her nerves. It disguised what he knew and made her doubt everything she thought she did.

An irritated shout brought her head up and a faster pace to her feet. Zelig stood in front of the closed doors of the garage, gesturing angrily. Connor stood in front of him, arms crossed, a bored expression on his face.

Corinne leaned against the garage door, fingering a knife with an amused smirk. She raised an eyebrow at the sight of Laramie approaching with Rosche.

Connor stood a little straighter and snapped a salute to Rosche. Zelig swallowed his next swear and saluted.

"Sorry for the fuss, sir. Didn't realize you were coming." A perpetual drawl seemed to fill Connor's voice.

"I thought it had been made clear?" Rosche sent a look at Zelig that would have made Laramie wince if she didn't already hate the guy.

A smirk flicked across Connor's face. "No. He just showed up demanding we open the garage for him to rifle through."

Rosche flexed his fingers and jerked his chin at the doors. "Open up."

Connor saluted again and turned. Corinne punched in a code beside the door and Connor hauled it open.

"Mind if I ask what's going on, sir?"

Laramie fought the urge to gag at so many "sirs" floating around.

"Just checking in with the drifter." Rosche moved into the garage, flicking a hand at her. She led the way into the corner where her bike still stood. It looked alone without the bulk of Unit Four's motorcycles to hide behind.

"What do you want me to show you?" Laramie asked, keeping her face clear except for a venomous glare at Zelig.

The unit leader sneered back at her.

"A canister, big enough to fit here, I think." Rosche squatted and ran his fingers over the space on her engine, hovering gently over the slots where the tube fit.

She didn't think her stomach would be able to take another

punch of dread. But she shrugged.

"I don't make a habit of stripping parts on and off my bike." She made a mental note to thank Gered for taking it off in the first place.

"Really? What about Gered?" Zelig piped up as if he'd read her thoughts.

"What about him?"

Rosche hummed again and straightened.

"Open your bag."

Laramie shrugged to disguise the way her hand clenched at the order. *Did I pack it in right?* New panic gripped her. She still might have a way out if she'd had her head on straight when she'd put it at the bottom of the bag weeks ago.

She unhooked the saddlebag from the bike and handed it over to Rosche. Time to see how screwed she was.

He flipped open the top and began to pull out each item and toss it to the floor. She clenched her jaw at the sight of her toolkit carelessly tossed aside with a clatter. An extra pair of socks, three ration packs, a tin of tea bags. A prayer book in the traveler language, its pages well worn, was tossed aside with an extra flick of scorn.

Laramie eased a breath out. So far, so good. Rosche reached the bottom, his hand sweeping the weatherproofed canvas. Her heart stuttered. His hand came out empty.

Rosche turned the bag upside down and shook. Nothing fell except a hair tie she'd been sure had been lost for good. He turned and fixed Zelig with a look.

Corinne snorted behind Zelig. Connor raised an eyebrow.

"She had another bag," Zelig blustered.

Laramie shoved hands in her jacket pockets, forcing her

shoulders to relax into nonchalance. "I can get it for you if you like, sir."

Rosche narrowed his eyes. "I think I'll go with you."

Laramie looked to Connor and Corinne as if asking permission. The unit leader just stood aside with a careless shrug, but his green eyes had taken on a calculating look.

Laramie briskly jogged up the steps. She had nothing to hide in her other bag except for clothes she'd really prefer Rosche not dig through.

The few Unit Five riders in the rec room bolted to their feet as Rosche stepped through the door. Murmurs followed Laramie down the hall. New panic gripped her. *What if they see the combination? Gioia will never forgive me!*

Corinne stepped up beside her, angling her body to better hide Laramie's hand for the two seconds it took to punch in the code. She kept moving past Laramie as if it had been purely accidental she'd happened to be there.

Laramie shoved the door open, sending a prayer of thanks to Jaan that Gioia wasn't there to witness Rosche in the room and going through her things. Rosche grabbed the bag from her hands as soon as she pulled it from under the bed.

She shoved her hands back in her pockets, trying to act like she didn't care as Rosche scattered more bits of her carefully packed life all over the bed.

Corinne leaned in the doorway, keeping Zelig at bay as the rider tried to push through. Connor lounged against the wall opposite the door, face brightening in amusement with every passing second Rosche clearly didn't turn up what he was looking for.

Rosche snapped the bag shut and threw it on the bed. He

shifted a glare to Laramie.

"I'd advise you not to hide anything from me, drifter."

"Wouldn't dream of it, sir."

Her head flew to the side as his hand cracked against her left cheek. Dampness spread across her tongue. The vision in her left eye blurred for a moment before clearing. She straightened, carefully moving her tongue around the blood in her mouth.

"Anything I brought with me is in those bags." She didn't try to keep the bite from her words.

Rosche's eyes narrowed warningly.

"Search anywhere else you like, but I don't know what he thinks he saw on my bike." She directed a sneer at Zelig.

Anger suffused the rider's face, turning his swarthy skin a shade darker.

"Zelig, feel free to check in the garage again." Rosche didn't break Laramie's gaze.

The rider whirled and stomped back out to the garage. Laramie followed after another invitation from Rosche. She paused long enough to shut the door firmly behind her. Corinne and Connor again trailed after them, and she'd never felt so grateful for two slightly unhinged people.

Zelig took his invitation literally, and Laramie winced at the destruction he wreaked on Gered's orderly garage.

But the canister didn't turn up. Zelig turned redder by the second and Rosche tapped fingers against his upper arm.

"Enough!" Rosche finally said.

Zelig halted, panting slightly. "Sir, I—"

Rosche flung a hand up, cutting him off. He fixed Laramie with a glare that burned like the afternoon sun. "I'm still putting a little stock in this story. I'd advise you to think on that. And I'm going to ask Gered when he gets back in two days."

Laramie dipped her head in a nod, not trusting her voice.

"Out." Rosche growled at Zelig and they left through the open garage doors.

"Interesting, drifter," Connor drawled.

"What?" Laramie shifted, tightening her defenses.

Connor shrugged. "Not sure how you're hiding something from them, but I'd take Rosche's advice. He doesn't like to be made a fool. Neither does Zelig."

He turned back up the stairs. Corinne lingered a second more, picking under a long nail with one of her knives.

"Thanks for your help," Laramie said.

Corinne lifted a shoulder. "Not sure what you're talking about, drifter."

Laramie hid a smile. *Sure.*

"You gonna tell Gioia what happened?" Corinne kept cleaning her nails in studied disinterest.

The weight settled back in Laramie's stomach. "Yeah. I'd like her to hear it from me."

Corinne flicked a glance up at her, then sheathed her knife. "You seem to be causing quite a stir around here, drifter. You're going to be around a while, so learn to keep your head down."

"I thought you said I should make myself useful."

"There's plenty of ways to do that without bringing him around." Her green eyes lit up in loathing, the spark of copper brightening, as she cast a glance the way Rosche had gone.

"Thanks for the advice."

Corinne's lip curled in a sneer. "Might as well clean up while you're down here, then."

She whisked away, hips swinging as she headed back inside.

Laramie waited until the door closed behind Corinne. She hauled the garage door down, the clang of metal against concrete breaking the last of her façade.

She gasped a breath, leaning forward, hands on knees as she tried to breathe. *So close.* Rosche had been too close to finding the canister. She brushed trembling fingers over her still-stinging cheek. The blow hadn't done the healing bruise on her temple any favors.

He's going to ask Gered when they get back. What if I can't say anything first? What if he finds out? Dust, I've got to get out of here!

She straightened with an effort, her breath still coming in irregular gasps. She began picking up her scattered possessions and tucking them back in the bag. She cast one quick glance around before reaching into the bag and pressing against the right seam.

Her fingers closed around a long tube of hardened leather. She closed her eyes, easing a breath out. She shouldn't have doubted traveler knacks. She didn't understand their bits of magic even after spending years among it. Everything seemed to have an extra pocket, extra space, places where things appeared where they hadn't been before, all depending on what the owner wanted when they placed something inside.

She pushed the canister back into place and buckled the saddlebag onto the bike. The next few minutes were spent straightening up the garage. Rosche might be pissed at her, but she knew Gered would have some choice words if he came back to see it tossed.

She rubbed her eyes. Two days. She could make it. They'd plan and then get the hell out of there.

CHAPTER TWENTY-NINE

Laramie stared downrange at the target. *Extra practice. I'm dusting tired of this. Next time Gered is pretending to suck.*

Next time. She shook her head at herself. Hopefully there wouldn't be another instance of having to escape a warlord's gangs.

Harlan was long gone, as were the other trainees. She halfway thought of pretending to have practiced again and then just head in for lunch. She rolled her shoulders. Maybe she'd skip lunch and spend it in the garage working on the bikes. Rosche's interruption the day before meant she hadn't finished working on her bike.

Laramie risked a glance over her shoulder. For all she knew, Harlan was standing on the walls behind her, sighting her shots. She rolled her eyes. *I'm getting too paranoid here.*

She brought her pistol up, aimed, and emptied the mag, pulling four shots out of the bullseye. Sliding it free, she reloaded and did the same with the second mag.

Slightly better accuracy than the day before. It still galled her to miss that badly. She holstered her gun, her extra practice complete, and headed toward the gate.

Laramie paused between the trainees' garage and the tower. She'd have to walk past Rosche's domain. Going to dinner the night before had been bad enough after the search that afternoon. She'd snagged a nutrient bar for breakfast so she didn't have to go.

I should have thought ahead for lunch too.

But with the threat of Rosche, and the glares of Zelig, lunch had no appeal. She turned toward the trainees' garage instead.

A light breeze stirred the dust and helped wick away some of the perpetual sweat beading her brow. She left the garage door open for better light and to keep encouraging the breeze. The others would return after lunch and she'd meet back up with them. Maybe Axel would be smart enough to bring her something after she didn't show.

She shook her head and sank down onto the low stool, pulling the toolbox over. That might be an unrealistic expectation.

A shadow fell across the bike. She kept her head down, turning slightly to see who it was from the corner of her eye.

She swallowed hard.

Zelig.

Laramie forced her hands to keep working. "What do you want?"

"I want to know how you did it."

"Did what?" She eased her feet back.

"Hid that device."

A smirk she knew she'd regret quirked her lips. "What device?"

His growl put a jacklion to shame. "You made me a fool."

That's not hard.

She dropped one hand.

"You'll pay for that."

She bolted to her feet, twisting to meet him as he lunged forward. His weight knocked her backward, stumbling over the stool. She regained her balance, using her wrench as a knife and jabbing it into his ribs.

After one hit, he danced away, rage clouding his eyes. She readjusted her grip, staying in a low crouch, waiting for his next move. He stalked forward, blocking her strike and pinning her arm under his.

She followed the motion in, jamming her free fist into his stomach. His breath blew out, but he kept his hold. She punched twice more and was rewarded by a faint loosening of his grip. She spun free. He kicked out as she stumbled back and she barely blocked.

He kept up a steady barrage of kicks and punches, keeping her off balance. Her knuckles broke open under a strike she managed to put on him.

Frustration turned to concern as he drove her back, back, back, into the work bench at the wall.

She grunted as her back hit the unyielding metal. Ducking his next punch, she dropped her shoulder to drive into his stomach and push him back. His elbow crashed down on her back. She hit her knee with a breathless grunt. She kept falling, rolling onto her side and over her shoulder, intending to come up on her feet.

But another kick kept the breath from her lungs. Zelig knocked her back down to the ground, straddling her hips, hands closing around her neck. Tighter … tighter…

Reflexive panic sent her thrashing until her training set back in.

"Where is it?" he snarled, spit flying onto her cheek.

"Shift off!" Laramie rasped past his hold.

She wrapped her foot around his before pummeling the crook of his elbow with a fist. Her other hand went for his face as he pitched forward, pushing his chin up. She bucked her hips. It shifted his weight enough to allow her to knock him off.

Zelig grabbed her as she tried to roll away, yanking her back down to the ground. He picked her up by her jacket and slammed her back down. Black clouded her vision as her head cracked against the ground. His hands closed around her neck again.

"I know you have it. You don't want me as an enemy."

Laramie wheezed past his grip. She pulled her knife and jabbed it into his thigh.

He released her, curses pouring from his mouth as he grabbed his bleeding leg. Laramie rolled on her side, hacking and gasping for breath.

"Bitch!" he snarled.

She forced herself up onto hands and knees, then to her feet, holding her knife in front of her. She cursed herself for not re-loading her gun. But maybe he didn't need to know that.

Her knife traded hands and she yanked the pistol out. Zelig didn't look the least bit concerned at the weapons pointed at him.

"Kill me and Rosche will know you're hiding something." He slowly gained his feet.

Laramie fought her body's attempts to cough air and feeling back to her throat.

"You keep coming after me, I will kill you," she rasped, spit beading the corners of her mouth. "Shift off."

His lip curled in a sneer. "Don't get too cocky, drifter."

"Out." Her throat spasmed again and her gun wavered.

He limped past her, turning one more warning glare at her. "Rosche won't be kept waiting."

Zelig vanished into the bright afternoon sunlight bouncing off the concrete, leaving a spotted blood trail behind. Laramie managed to holster her gun before staggering back into the tool bench and sliding down to the ground.

A sob broke before she could stop it. Her knife trembled in her hand and she almost cut herself trying to wipe Zelig's blood off.

She closed her eyes, breathing in, out, in, out until her heart steadied.

"Laramie?" Boots thudded toward her. Her eyes flew open, ready to stab again until her brain registered Axel barreling toward her.

"What happened?" He sank to his knee beside her.

She gingerly rubbed her neck, imagining she could feel indents in the skin where Zelig's fingers had squeezed.

"I guess I really pissed Zelig off yesterday," she managed.

"That thing they think you have?" His eyes radiated concern as he looked her up and down.

She managed a nod.

"*Do* you have it?"

She trusted Axel but wasn't about to let him in on the secret. Zelig would crush the kid.

"They didn't find anything, did they?"

His lips turned down, but he eased back to allow her to shakily stand.

"What the hell?" Harlan strode in. He crossed his arms and looked her up and down. She kept her hands away from her neck.

"Little disagreement carried over from yesterday, sir." Another cough tore from her aching throat.

He shook his head. "You the reason for this blood?" He pointed a finger at the small pool and the dribbles leading outside.

Laramie patted her knife as answer. It was only the third time she'd stabbed someone with the knife, but this time she had absolutely no regret.

"Guess you do know something after all."

She bristled a little. *Not my fault I'm pretending to suck.*

Harlan softened a fraction. "You want to take the afternoon?"

She'd love nothing more than to barricade herself in the room and wait for Unit Four to get back. But she couldn't afford to show weakness. And it was a long walk back to the bunker. Someone else could be lying in wait.

"No. I'll finish out today."

A bit of respect edged Harlan's grunt. "That bike up and running yet?"

Laramie took one more breath. "Give me ten minutes."

—

Axel walked with her to Four's bunker after dinner. He'd done it without being asked, without saying anything. She probably should have refused in order to not present a façade of weakness, but her heart warmed a little more toward the kid.

Evening cast long shadows across the compound. Each darkened corner sent her heart skipping in fear. She kept one hand on her knife, trying to scold herself into calmness. But then the flash of Zelig's hands around her throat returned and sent her flinching.

"Sure you're okay?" he asked when they reached the building.

Laramie nodded, not trusting her still-raspy voice beyond a "Thanks."

He watched in silence as she punched in the code for the garage and hauled it open. She didn't much feel like running into Unit Five still camped out upstairs.

"See you tomorrow." She flashed a smile and ducked under the door.

Relief crashed through her at the dusty bikes filling the left side of the garage. Unit Four was back.

She flipped the light on and eased the door back down. Fresh gasoline and dirt mingled with the sharper scent of grease. Familiar. Calming.

Laramie wove through the motorcycles to her bike, strange compulsion taking her to make sure her things hadn't been searched again. The bulky motorcycle stood untouched against the wall. Her breath of relief caught in her throat as something scuffed behind her.

She whirled, knife drawn.

CHAPTER THIRTY

Laramie halted the knife a fraction from Gered's throat. He spread his hands, edging back a step, his eyes flicking down to the knife before meeting hers again.

"You okay?" His quiet voice eased the tension from her muscles.

She lowered the knife and stepped away. "Sorry."

His shoulders relaxed a fraction as her knife disappeared into the sheath.

"Connor said I should check on you before seeing Rosche. Guess he was right." His eyes swept up and down her and locked on her throat.

She stiffened and inhaled sharply as he reached toward her neck.

"Hey, let me see." Itan further gentled his voice.

She blinked away the sudden moisture beading the corners of her eyes, trying to cover it with a smile.

"Using my own trick on me?"

A half-smile appeared. "It works, doesn't it?"

She raised her chin, clenching her hands tight as his fingers gently touched her neck. A brief glance in the visor of her helmet earlier had reassured her bruising had set in.

"What happened?" His thumb gently pressed around her collarbone.

She winced at the sharp twinge. "I think Zelig's trying to save some face. He told Rosche about the canister."

He froze. "Did they find it?"

Laramie shook her head, sore muscles protesting the movement. "It's still hidden, but Rosche searched the place yesterday. It made Zelig look like more of an idiot and he didn't take kindly to that today."

Gered's face hardened with each word.

"Don't worry. I stabbed him in the leg."

He cracked a faint smile. "Rosche still believed him?"

"Yeah. He said he's going to ask you when you got back."

"Good thing I haven't been to report yet."

"What are you going to tell him?" Sudden doubt she hated filled Laramie. It would be an easy way for Gered to curry favor with Rosche. It didn't take a genius to see staying on the warlord's good side made life easier for everyone.

Gered crossed his arms, biting his lip pensively. Her heart stammered beat after beat.

"I have an idea. You probably won't like it."

Laramie twisted the traveler bands around her wrist. "I don't like anything here."

Gered allowed a brief smile with a tilt of his head. "We tell Rosche we have it."

Outrage filled Laramie despite his warning. "You said—"

He held up a hand. "I took it. I've been trying to replicate it. You're helping. We were going to tell Rosche when we had a working prototype. We need more parts…"

Laramie quirked an eyebrow. "Parts we might need to go get?"

Gered inclined his head.

She took a breath in, out, in, out. If Rosche bit, it gave them a sanctioned excuse and maybe a head start on running. But every bit of her rebelled at the thought of even showing it to Rosche.

Gered waited patiently.

"Okay," she finally said.

"Okay. Grab it and come with me to report. He's going to question me on it anyway. Might as well cut down on time."

She caught the flicker of nervousness in his eyes.

"He's not going to like that we were keeping secrets, is he?"

"Probably not. But it's on me, so don't worry." He turned back to the stairs.

Too late for that.

Laramie pulled the canister from the saddlebag, again blessing travelers and all their saints for keeping it hidden, and followed Gered up the stairs.

Gioia's greeting died at the sight of her neck. She dashed forward.

"What happened?"

Laramie eased away before the rider could try to touch her. Dayo appeared at her side, dark eyes assessing the bruising.

Laramie forced a smile. "Nothing a cold beer wouldn't fix."

Dayo snorted in exasperation.

"Laramie, let's go." Gered's even voice beckoned her toward the door. Dayo and Gioia glanced between them in confusion.

Laramie reached out and squeezed Gioia's arm. "I've got something to tell you later."

Gioia nodded, concern still edging every angle of her face. Laramie forced her feet to follow Gered from the building.

A few other riders walked back and forth between barracks,

snatches of conversation drifting in the breeze.

"If he bites, what about Gioia and Dayo?" Laramie switched back to Itan.

Gered's stride didn't falter. "What about them?"

"If we needed some extra help on a shopping expedition, would they want to come?"

Gered didn't speak for a long moment. "I don't know. There's a reason people don't run."

Laramie jerked a hand to her knife as a rider emerged from the alley between two bunkers and turned up into a stairwell. The man didn't spare them a glance and she hurried to keep up with Gered.

"You should ask," she said.

He didn't look at her, but his shoulders slumped under an invisible weight. They stepped up the stairs into the main tower.

Sweat began to form in her palms, making the leather of the canister stick to her hand.

"Any chance the same rules still apply this time?" Her voice bobbled in nervousness.

"Yeah. Let me do the talking." He jogged up the steps. She took a breath before following.

"Gered," Rosche's soft growl halted them at the top of the stairs.

He prowled from the shadows. Laramie stood tall against the urge to shrink back behind Gered.

What's gotten into me? Any semblance of self-control seemed to have vanished with her breath under Zelig's hands.

Rosche turned flat eyes on her, taking in every bruise before lighting on the canister gripped in her hand. A spark of triumph was replaced with anger.

"War room." He stalked past them.

Gered followed without a pause. Laramie took an extra second to force her legs to work.

The harsh lights of the war room chased away the shadows lurking in the upper hallways. A faint bit of sunlight lingered over the mountains as a swatch of lighter blue under the press of night.

"Report," Rosche growled, taking his place on the opposite side of the table.

Gered tucked his hands behind his back. From her place slightly behind him, Laramie caught the quick whiteness in his knuckles.

"Didn't run into any trouble. We did pick up a load of weapons from Teague. Someone heard about the uprising and decided they wanted to do the honest thing. Guns are in the transpo truck in the main garage. Harlan said he'd doc them in."

Rosche sidled forward. "Good. Now." He fixed an unblinking glare on Laramie. "Since she's here, I'm assuming you're caught up, Gered. Care to explain that?" He pointed to the canister.

"Sir." Gered's fingers flexed behind his back. "I saw it when she first came in. Didn't take much to figure out it's an engine booster. I wanted to try and replicate it before turning it over."

Rosche took another step forward. Gered's chin dipped toward the floor. Laramie swallowed hard.

"I need a better reason."

"I wanted to make sure we had some more information on replication—"

Rosche's fist cracked across his face. "You don't get to think like that!" he snarled. A punch to Gered's stomach sent him back a step.

Laramie stood frozen. Gered made no move to fight back.

His expression stayed blank as he absorbed another strike like a punching bag.

Rosche shoved him against the wall. "You know the rules. It all comes to me."

"Sir." Gered kept his chin down.

A sick feeling spread over Laramie. Like a dog submitting to an alpha.

Rosche released him and turned to her. Gered straightened against the wall, tugging his jacket back in place without a change in expression.

"Now, I'm curious why you didn't say anything about this yesterday?"

Laramie dampened her mouth with a swallow. "I'd been told to keep my mouth shut on it until we had something."

She took an automatic step back as he kept coming.

"Just following orders then?"

She nodded mutely. She couldn't block in time to prevent his hand swallowing her neck. He didn't squeeze, just let it stay there in silent threat. A flicker of amusement crossed his face as her throat bobbed against his touch.

He reached down and took a knife from her side, and not the canister as she expected. He whirled back to Gered, who froze as it hovered above his chest.

This time something stirred in his eyes, making the blue shine a little brighter. Fear.

Rosche leaned his forearm across Gered's chest, keeping him pinned. Rosche touched the tip of the knife under Gered's collarbone.

"You're lucky this is something I want. Remember, I know how to keep you in your place." His soft words dripped warning.

"Sir," Gered's voice wavered over the word, his eyes locked on the weapon.

Rosche scoffed and released him. He extended the knife, hilt first, back to Laramie. She snatched it and resheathed it.

"Now, let me see it." He gave them both space to breathe.

Laramie fumbled the canister open and dumped the tube out into her hand. Small threads of electricity still flickered inside. She'd used up a big boost trying to outrun the units before she'd been caught.

Rosche took it, cradling it gently in his big hands. "How does it work?"

Laramie risked a quick glance to Gered who still leaned against the wall, the dangerously distant look flitting over his face.

"It runs on lightning drawn from a harnesser. Whatever makes the harnessers work is what actually converts the lightning strike into useable power. I can hook it up to my bike and it gives me a little more speed." She didn't add the last part. Speed without burning fuel. Rosche didn't need to know that bit just yet.

"Where does it come from?"

She tapped the side of her head.

Rosche raised an eyebrow. "You made it?"

Some of her attitude came back at the faint incredulity in his voice, like he hadn't thought her capable of something like that.

"Yes. Sir."

His eyes flattened at the last word. "Have you been able to replicate it yet?"

Gered made no move. Laramie forced height into her spine.

"Not yet. I've got some of the wiring put together. But there's not a good way for me to put the tube together here." She didn't have to force the frown. That's what had given her the most trouble to begin with. She'd had several prototypes explode in her face when siphoning small bits of current in.

Rosche turned it in his hands. "What do you need?"

Something to get me out of here. Laramie extended her hand. He passed it back with a glimmer of irritation.

She ignored it and tapped the container with a nail. "It's a hybrid of glass and plastin."

"The refinery can probably make something like that and deliver it here." Rosche nodded.

Panic struck. They had to have a reason to get out. "I also need some other parts."

"What parts?"

She didn't look at Gered, forcing a little smile. "I'm not ready to give out the entire blueprint for this."

Rosche's features relaxed into a bit of amusement. "I suppose I can respect the craftsman's code. There's a supply depot in Mance City. Gered can take you." He cast a quick glance at them. "But if they don't have it, I'll send outside the territory for it."

The meaning came clear. She wouldn't be allowed outside the territory.

"Now." He grabbed some paper and a pen. "What's the recipe for the canister?"

Kayin had been the one to fiddle out the exact ratios. She tried to shake the feeling of complete betrayal as she wrote down his formula as close as she remembered.

"I don't remember exact numbers," she said. "They might need to be tweaked a little."

Rosche picked up the paper, glancing it over as if he understood it. Sudden panic struck her that he might. But he nodded.

"I'll send it out in the morning. Until then." He extended his hand for the canister.

Laramie clutched it tight. "I need it to guide me through building another one. I don't keep the blueprints memorized."

For a second, she thought he was going to snatch it from her anyway.

"Fine. You have tomorrow from training to go find these parts. Then half days until you have one built. I still expect your marks to get up by your choosing."

Laramie slid the tube back into the canister, swallowing her sigh of relief. "Yes, sir."

"Gered."

"Sir." Gered stood tall again, hands still behind his back.

"If she can't produce one in a week, you're the first responsibility, understand?"

Gered inclined his head. "Sir."

"Dismissed."

Silence dogged their steps back to the bunker. Laramie clutched the canister against her chest the entire way. She couldn't even feel triumphant they'd managed to secure a way out.

"Wait," she said in Itan, halting at the base of the steps, the scent of smoke drawing her gaze up to a Unit Four rider leaning against the wall, the glowing ember of a cigarette in his hand. "Tomorrow?"

He paused on the bottom step. "Yes. The supply depot is centrally located in the territory. We'll start heading that way, then swing east."

"Your way out?" she guessed.

He nodded. "Take only what you need. It's supposed to be a day trip. We can't pack out like we're going somewhere else."

"Got it." She'd already begun to inventory what she did and

didn't need from her packs.

"Have Dayo look at your neck. I'll see you tomorrow." He jogged up the steps.

"All good, boss?" The rider shifted to open the door for him.

Gered nodded and pushed inside without another word.

Good night to you too.

Laramie rebuked herself instantly. He was fighting off another tailspin, she could see it in his eyes. Rosche had some sort of power over him that left him a shadow of himself and she hated seeing it.

Tomorrow. Tomorrow and it'll all be over.

CHAPTER THIRTY-ONE

Gered pushed through the rec room, ignoring the press of riders still lounging around. Laramie commandeered Dayo's attention, leaving him free to retreat to the room for a moment of peace.

He sank onto the bed, and leaned forward on his knees, hands clasped behind his head. It hadn't been bad. Until Rosche pulled the knife. Squeezing his eyes shut, he breathed in and out.

"I'm afraid of what that means."

He lifted his head to see Gioia leaning against the door, hands in her pockets.

Tomorrow. I have to tell her.

Gered pulled his hands away to press against his mouth. He nodded at the door. She raised an eyebrow, but reached out and swung the door closed.

He didn't speak, a tumult raging inside—fear and dangerous hope competing for dominance. *Tomorrow.*

Concern shadowed her face.

"What's going on, Gered?" She shoved away from the wall, taking a step forward.

He tore his gaze away from her figure, ducking his chin to drag a hand through his dark hair. He shook his head. He barely remembered what he looked like without the dye. *Tomorrow.*

"You planning on running?" she asked.

He jerked his head up to meet her stare.

She shook her head with a scoff. "It's not that hard to figure you out. You going with *her*?" A bit of pain lingered over the last word.

"It's not like that, Gioia, and you know it."

"Sure." She shoved her hands into her back pockets and retreated a step. "Because what's not to like about her? She's pretty, smart, skilled. And me? I was Rosche's whore."

He pushed to his feet. "That's not it."

She waited for him to continue, her shoulders squared defensively.

"It's ... she believes she can make it. I don't know ... maybe she's got me thinking the same thing."

"Why?"

"I can't stay here!" He slammed a hand against the wall. She didn't flinch. "I can't. Not anymore. Rosche wants her to build something. We're going on a supply run tomorrow." *And hopefully not coming back.* "Come with us. We ... you and me ... maybe we can figure out a life out there." He almost hated the pleading in his voice.

She softened, but shook her head. "I can't."

"Why?" He desperately wanted to take her into his arms, show her how much he wanted—needed—her.

She tilted her chin up. "I don't have a death wish."

He half scoffed and stepped away.

"It's suicide, Gered. You know that. You've tried before." She leaned close, eyes begging him to remember. "You think he won't send someone out when you don't come back? And when he catches you, there won't be any more chances for you. I don't want to watch that."

"Maybe this time I'll make it." He tried to hold on to the vanishing hope.

She ducked her head, scuffing the stone floor with her boot. "Maybe."

"Don't tell me you want to stay here." He tried one last time.

"Dust no. It's no life, but at least I'm alive." She raised her head. "And if I go with you? Maybe we'd make it to the border. Maybe not. And once they catch us, and Rosche and whoever else wants to is done with me, maybe they'll bury us in the same grave. That's the only way we'll be together, and you know it."

"Gioia."

"Don't." She shook her head, and he caught glimpses of tears in her eyes. The sight tore at him worse than any knife ever had. She sniffed and glanced back up. "At least you don't have to worry about me anymore. No one's tried to jump me in an alley in years."

"That's not funny."

She squared her shoulders. "I know. I just mean you made me take care of myself. I wouldn't have gotten this far without you. Would I like to see if there's a life out there for us? Yeah. More than anything. But there's not. There's only this. And I guess I'm just too selfish to risk it on a suicide mission."

They regarded each other in silence for a long moment.

"Will you make the report?"

"Of course not. Do you even know me, Gered?" She mustered a slight smile. "And I hope you make it. I really do. Just think of me once in a while after you and Laramie start a new life together."

"Maybe I'll come back for you," he said impulsively.

She sniffed again. "That's nice. Romantic."

He reached out and brushed her hand. She closed her fingers around his in a tight grip. He squeezed. She didn't squeeze back.

"Goodbye, Gered." She pulled away and pushed out the door.

He stared after her, feeling another crack in his already splintered foundation widening. She wouldn't come. He'd known deep down she wouldn't. Rosche's hold was still too strong. But it still stung.

He needed to do something. He pulled his rifle case from under the bed and removed the cleaning kit. Taking his pistols apart, he started on them first, forcing his hands to slow over the familiar movements.

"We leave for a few days and something big goes down." Dayo sauntered back in the room, kicking the door shut and flopping down on the bed. "Spill."

Gered replied with everything Laramie had given him. Dayo sat up, eyebrows inching higher with every part.

"And you didn't tell me about this thing?" he asked.

Gered reassembled one of the guns. "Didn't seem important."

"Right." Dayo drew out the word.

Tomorrow.

He swallowed hard. "Rosche is sending Laramie and me on a supply run tomorrow. We'll be gone all day."

"And?" Dayo leaned forward, suspicion lacing his voice.

Gered looked up. "And this is something I don't really want Rosche getting his hands on."

Dayo leaned back. "You're gonna help her run?" he whispered.

Gered jerked a nod, fingers fumbling with the second gun.

"You are gonna come back, right?" Hardness crept into Dayo's question. "Gered…" He tilted his head in warning.

He won't come. Dayo knew what happened to runaways the

same as anyone. He'd been the one to patch Gered up after his last attempt.

Gered forced a smile. "Yeah. How stupid do you think I am?"

"I'm beginning to wonder." Dayo frowned, but relief softened the hard lines around his eyes.

Gered replaced the cleaning kit in the case. Anything he had, anything he wanted to take with him, was already packed in his saddlebag. He just wouldn't unpack tonight.

"We'll hit the road early. If anything happens while we're gone, you're in charge."

Dayo groaned. "I hate it when you leave me in charge. It stresses me out."

A quick smile broke from Gered before he could stop it. "You'll survive."

Dayo sobered just as quick. "I hope she makes it, but she would have been decent to have around. She told me she fought Zelig off, and stabbed him in the leg for his troubles. I told her she should have aimed higher and a little more central."

"Yeah, but there's been a load of trouble since she came in." Trouble that had burrowed its way under his skin and found some way to settle a foot more firmly on the ground for the first time in years.

Dayo snorted. "True. It might be nice to go back to the same boring routine."

Gered set his pistols on the bed and tossed his jacket aside. One more day of wearing it.

"I'll try not to wake you in the morning."

Dayo saluted and said nothing more, letting him wash and turn into bed in peace. He faced the wall. He'd make the call to Moshe once they were out on the road. Then they'd ride like hell.

CHAPTER THIRTY-TWO

Gered barely slept. The time counter crept slowly toward six hundred hours. Finally, he sat up, rubbed grit from his eyes, and dressed.

His heart hammered odd patterns in his chest as he tucked spare bits of his life away. Every movement hovered with the tantalizing feeling of last, last, last.

Easing open the rifle case, he lifted out his gun. He wasn't leaving it behind. He'd built it himself. He'd find a new case.

Dayo's sleepy voice halted him at the door. "Ride safe, *kamé.*"

He swallowed hard. *Brother.* He didn't know how to be that.

"See you later." The words tasted like ash in his mouth. But he didn't look back as he stepped out.

Laramie was already in the garage, sifting through items in her saddlebags. He raised an eyebrow at the pile she was packing into her spare saddlebag and tossed her a nutrient bar.

"That's not all going to fit," he cautioned in a whisper.

She smirked a little. "Watch and see."

To his continued amazement, clothes, dust scarf, a book, ration packs, her toolkit, and finally the canister all disappeared into the saddlebag. By all rights it should be bursting at the seams.

"Traveler knacks." She patted the leather. "Anyone else coming?"

The pang struck his heart again. He glanced back at the door, halfway hoping Gioia would come through.

"No." The word barely made it out.

She flashed a sympathetic smile, and he was surprised to see a little disappointment in her eyes.

He opened the garage as she reattached one bag to her drifter bike. She kissed her fingers and pressed it to the seat.

"Sorry, babe," she whispered.

Gered pushed his bike out into the cool morning and started it up. She swung on behind him, arms settled loosely around his waist as he headed to the trainees' garage.

To keep up appearances, she'd have to take one of the bikes. Five minutes later, her bag was clipped on behind the seat and she'd pulled on the dusky red helmet. Gered donned his, keeping the visor up as they drove slowly toward the main gates.

The guard tipped a nod. "Rosche said you were coming through. Good ride."

Gered waved his hand in a salute, flipped his visor closed, and drove forward.

"Check in," the words automatically came from him.

"Hear you loud and clear, *kamé.*" Her cheerful words sent another spear through his heart.

"Okay. We'll head south for now like we're headed to the depot, then cut off."

"You know where we're going?" She eased up beside him, completely at ease on the bike.

He returned his gaze to the road. "Mostly. Once we hit the cutoff, I'll make a call to see what our path's like."

"Got it." She rode in silence for a few minutes. "How long will we have before someone comes after us?"

He stared at the flashing lines. Someone could be following them now. Someone might report in when they didn't show at the depot in three hours. He had no way of knowing what information Rosche had passed on.

"I'm not sure."

"Jaan's wings. This should be fun."

How shall I fear that from which I am protected by Heaven's wings?

Gered swallowed. He wished there was some way he could believe it.

"We need to stay off the comms as much as possible. Sometimes the tower scans the frequencies to check up on us."

"Brilliant."

She lapsed back into silence. He caught himself checking the corner of his left mirror. Empty. It would be empty from then on.

She made her choice. So did Dayo. But it felt like he was leaving some bit of himself back in the compound.

Fifteen minutes of riding brought them to a highway junction. Dust skittered across the blacktop as they stopped. A tumbleweed rattled in the breeze. Gered checked the sun already rising above the horizon. East from there, straight into the light.

Laramie waited in silence as he pulled the amplifier from his jacket pocket and clipped it onto the comm wire. He shifted the frequency to the one Moshe's unit used.

"Unit two. Unit two."

It took several tries before Unit Two's radio tech answered.

"This is Gered with Four. Moshe there?"

"Yeah, we're riding now. He'll take it from here," the tech said.

"Gered," Moshe's voice crackled over the radio. "Trouble?"

Gered tightened his fists around the handles. Did he dare?

"Calling for some advice on a problem."

A pause. "I got you, brother. Switch over for me." Gered acknowledged and changed channels to the frequency Moshe had given him the day out on the range.

"You there?" Moshe asked.

"Got you clear."

"This what I think it is?" Moshe questioned.

"Yeah."

"When?"

Gered checked his time counter on the bike dash. "About three hours, give or take."

"We're actually headed back now. Should be good to go."

His heart eased from its unsteady pattern for a moment. "Thanks."

"Good luck. Out." Silence fell on the comm. Gered switched back and lifted his visor.

Laramie did the same, her gray-blue eyes peering out at him through the narrow opening.

"We should be mostly clear. We'll take a detour from some of the main roads."

She flipped a thumb up. He pushed his sunglasses on and clacked the visor back down.

His hand froze on the throttle. The road stretched wide and empty before him and behind him.

Did he dare?

Laramie waited, her engine rumbling with the same anticipation as his. He shoved forward, accelerating, and tucking his foot back up onto the peg. The speedometer climbed and climbed. Laramie matched his speed, leaning into the wind. Her braid escaped from under her helmet, streaming like a flag behind her until she reached back and pulled it into place under her jacket collar.

Ten miles, twenty, thirty.

He moved them off the main highway onto a smaller road, worn with dust and ferocious rainstorms that left potholes in its surface.

Five miles more around Unit Seven's main stomping grounds.

Then back onto the main highway.

An hour more.

Each glance in his mirrors showed empty road. Every scan of the horizon showed mesquite and lonely mesas and empty roads.

One quick stop to top off tanks at a refuel station before the next big push.

Three miles.

The next glance in his mirror showed a smudge. He frantically looked ahead.

Empty.

The smudge grew to a small cloud.

"Dust." Laramie had seen it too.

Unspoken, they coaxed more speed from their bikes.

"How far?" Breathlessness filled Laramie's voice as if she was the one pushed nearly to her limits.

"Too far," Gered replied grimly, checking the dust cloud.

They still had over an hour's hard ride to make it to the border. Whoever was after them had probably stayed on the main highway, avoiding the time spent detouring other units.

"I don't know about you, but I'm gonna try my best to make it." Determination practically radiated from her.

Despite himself, a sort of smile tugged at his lips. That's what he liked about her.

Another gear shift, more speed, lines blurring as he hunched toward his handlebars. Thankfully the roads had been laid out in straight lines, no curves to watch out for.

The pursuit didn't have any hesitation about matching their pace. For a few minutes the dust cloud didn't grow, didn't fade.

"Gered!" Laramie's panicked voice cut through.

Dust in front of them.

"Dusting hells! We'll go around." He leaned to the right, taking his bike off the shoulder and across the rough terrain.

Laramie followed behind him, visible in his left mirror through his dust wake.

He didn't have focus to spare on the pursuit, watching instead for the devious dips and rises hidden by brush that could easily turn a wheel.

Laramie's front tire jerked to the side, but she recovered without falling, revving to make up for the lost second.

Closer and closer came the oncoming cloud.

Gered cut further right, toward the smooth streak shimmering in the morning sun. Gophers darted for cover as he tore around a mesquite bush. He leaned left this time, tires skidding on the transition from earth to asphalt. The smell of rubber burned his nose as the tires stalled and squealed before catching and pushing him forward.

Laramie managed the transition with more grace. She rode like she was a part of the motorcycle, and nothing could knock her free.

The way was clear before them again, but dust raised to their left as the oncoming unit turned and followed.

Sweat trickled down his back. His hands ached around the

handles.

A few buildings flashed by and vanished in the rearview. He hadn't even been able to see if there were people among them.

"Gered!"

"I see it."

The dust had begun solidifying into shapes. Light glinted off helmets and bits of motorcycle.

Was this how Laramie had felt all those weeks ago?

Riders emerged on their left, keeping pace on the rough terrain, then falling behind as tires hit awry on a gully. A checkered pattern on the right side of helmets—Unit Seventeen, outside their normal route.

Someone had known they were coming.

Closer and closer in the rearview. Close enough to see the single black stripe on the front runner's helmet. His heart dropped. There was only one unit with a stripe like that.

Unit Four.

His own unit had been sent after them.

And only one rider who rode loose and careless enough to outstrip the unit.

Dayo.

He didn't want to imagine the anger on the traveler's face behind the dark visor.

A few more skilled riders from Seventeen began to level with them, then finally creeping up to skid onto the pavement.

Brake lights flashed. Gered drifted side to side, but they matched his movement, preventing him and Laramie from making a bid to pass on the asphalt.

He jammed the brakes as the rider in front of him did the same. A lean to the right sent him to the shoulder, but it gave him enough space to clear the rider. A spurt of dust announced Laramie had just gone around.

A crack echoed behind him and something sparked on the pavement.

Laramie swerved wildly beside him. Regained her balance. Bullets peppered the pavement around them as their pursuers tried for their tires.

But shooting at high speed wasn't easy. Too late he saw the looming figure in his mirror.

Something caught his back wheel for a grinding moment before releasing him. It slowed him enough for more of Seventeen's riders to cut in front, forcing another deceleration. Laramie tried to edge around again, but two riders hemmed her in.

"Gered, look out!"

A rider loomed to his right, gun raised. But not at him. A shot hit his front wheel, the impact throwing it sideways. He barely corrected in time, the wheel still slipping dangerously.

Gered slammed the brakes, tires shrieking and smoking against the pavement. Another bullet skimmed off the road in a spray of sparks. The front tire slipped further. His world tipped and he couldn't do anything to stop it.

He hit the asphalt, dragged along with his right leg trapped under the bike until it skidded away, wheels still spinning.

Shock wrapped tight bands around his chest.

Pain exploded in his right side, his arm, his leg.

His helmet melded around his head, suffocating him.

He feebly dragged a hand up to fumble at the strap. It unlatched and he shoved it off his head, taking the glasses with it.

Heat from the road seared his face, barely keeping him conscious.

Breathe.

Breathe.

Breathe!

His body jerked as it finally overcame the shock and forced air back into his lungs.

Boots thudded toward him through the shimmering heat waves. Halted. Zelig crouched down to look at him.

The rumbling of engines vibrated through the ground into his chest. *No way out. There's no getting away.*

"Well, well, what do we have here?" Zelig's leering voice cut across the rumble. "I think I found some roadkill, boys."

Gered tried to pull himself forward or up, any position but the helpless one he lay in.

"No, you don't." Zelig's foot pressed against his injured side, pushing him down. A scream locked in his throat.

A boot drove into his stomach, driving the precious air from his chest again. A hand gripped his jacket and pulled him up. He couldn't force his limbs to cooperate, to block, to do anything as Zelig pummeled his face, over and over, until he fell back to the hot pavement.

"I think I like you better like this," he leaned down and whispered.

Gered turned his head and tried to push blood from his mouth. "Because you can't take me when I'm on my feet?"

Zelig kicked him again.

He curled in on himself, unable to stop a moan. Cursing himself for showing weakness, for letting them know that they'd hurt him. That whatever they did would hurt him more.

Zelig laughed. "Get this piece of trash up. Rosche wants him back. Although." He crouched enough to jerk Gered's head up.

"He didn't say in what condition."

Gered managed to spit again, leaving a puddle of blood and saliva on the road. Zelig scoffed and walked away. Hands grabbed him and brought him up to his knees. Another soft cry pushed its way up. Red, lacerated skin along the length of his thigh lay exposed under the shredded layer of his trousers. The same pain pounded at his right forearm and the right side of his chest where the road had torn through his jacket.

Each breath, each movement sent stabs through him, like knives. The thought sent another shudder through him. He couldn't bear the thought of knives cutting into him again. But that would be the least of what he faced when they got back to the compound.

"Cuff them both. Radio for a transpo truck," Zelig ordered.

Cuffs cut into his wrists seconds before more fists and boots thudded into him.

"Stop!" Laramie's voice cut through the haze of pain. "Gered!"

They got her too. No way out.

"Gered!" Zelig mocked in a high-pitched voice.

But the assault stopped, and he was dragged to the side of the road to kneel in the sand. Laramie caught his elbow with her cuffed hands, steadying him.

A shadow fell at his knees and Gered managed to lift his head. Gioia stood there, his own pain reflected in her face before she shuttered it away with a shake of her head and moved away. Already giving him up. Already accepting the inevitable. He wished he'd never let himself care.

Dayo stood by his bike. Anger and betrayal plain in his face as he glared at Gered.

Gered looked away. He'd lost everything.

"Dust, this looks bad."

He hissed a breath as Laramie tried to peel shredded cloth from his leg. His holster was destroyed, his gun lost somewhere on the road.

"Leave it." His voice came hoarse with dust and regret. He was out of chances. He was finally going to die.

CHAPTER THIRTY-THREE

Laramie yanked her hands against the cuffs. Still as solid as the moment they'd tightened around her wrists. She and Gered lay in the back of the transpo truck, jolting and rattling with every uneven bump in the road.

Gered lay on his back, staring at the canvas roof. He hadn't said a word since he'd refused her help with his awful looking injuries. He had to be in immense pain, from the road and from the beatings, but his already bruising face was expressionless as he lay in silence.

Not expressionless. His eyes burned bright with anguish and pain.

Dayo had taken control of them as former members of Unit Four. Zelig hadn't been happy, but as leader of only a skeleton unit and a lower rank, he'd had to submit. A shiver cut down Laramie's back at the memory of the look of pure anger Dayo had given Gered.

No matter what happened, it didn't seem like things would ever be the same between them.

They'd waited nearly an hour for the trucks to arrive from the nearest town. They'd been loaded into one, their bikes into another, and slowly began the journey back.

"What's going to happen?" she whispered, unable to bear the rattle of the truck any longer.

"Nobody makes it out," he finally said through clenched jaw.

"Why'd they take us alive?" she pressed, searching for some sort of hope.

He turned to look at her. "You're still useful. I'm an example." He returned his gaze back to the swaying, jittering tarp over them, his bound hands resting on his waist.

She hauled herself up into a sitting position. Useful. She knew what that meant.

There has *to be some way out of this. I've got to be able to do something.*

"How are you feeling?"

"It won't matter in a few hours."

Acceptance filled every line of his battered body. She shook her head. No. She refused to believe that.

Drifting had taught her to rely on herself. And right now, her one ally was down for the count. No matter what Unit Four might have thought of her, they couldn't help now. She was on her own.

A muffled groan came from Gered as they hit yet another hole. He tried to curl in on himself, but even that seemed painful. Her gut wrenched. She'd pushed him into this. She needed to get him out. There was something connecting them. Something she couldn't shake. Maybe it was the gray eyes or the script on his arm. Those meant Itan. And Itan meant blood. It could mean family.

Now what the hell am I going to do about it?

Brakes squeaked as they began to slow. Laramie peeked through the slit in the back of the truck. A gate stared back. Back at the Barracks, back on the wrong side of the walls.

The truck ground to a halt and the engine died. The rumbles of motorcycle engines cut off one by one. Zelig and another Unit Four rider came around. They pulled Gered out, shoving him onto his feet and pushing him around the truck.

Dayo swatted open the tarp next and gestured sharply at her. The anger in his eyes for Gered was there for her as well.

"You did this to him. I hope you enjoy what you're about to see," he hissed in her ear and shoved her around the truck.

They'd parked close to the command tower. Rosche already stood there, arms crossed. Connor stood beside him, flat eyes taking Gered and Laramie in with a dispassionate look. Moshe gave her a brief pitying glance. His jacket and clothes were stained in dust. They must have just gotten back.

Zelig jerked Gered to an unsteady halt. Rosche flicked a hand across his chin as if thinking.

"Know why I let you two go off together?"

Gered didn't answer. He kept his head down, weight bobbling on his injured leg.

Rosche stalked forward. "I thought you might run. Someone heard you two talking in Itan last night. No one does that unless they have something to hide."

Panic edged in Laramie as Rosche stepped again and Gered stayed submissive. Already giving up.

"I had Connor put a tracker on your bike."

Her breath caught. They hadn't stood a chance. This time Gered moved a little. Connor stared back, stance still uncaring.

Why would *he care?*

Rosche's fist crashed into Gered's stomach.

Gered crumpled forward with a gasp. Zelig and the other

rider let him fall.

"And you really should have stayed off comms."

Laramie pulled against Dayo's hold as Rosche kept pummel-ing and kicking Gered. Dayo held her tight. Gioia stared at her boots, fists clenched tight and flinching with every pained sound from Gered.

Finally Rosche stopped. Gered shuddered, a broken sort of moan coming from him as Rosche turned him over. The warlord pulled a knife, setting it against Gered's cheek under his eye.

"Three chances, Gered. You knew what would happen if you tried again. Three times you threw my generosity in my face." Anger rose in Rosche's voice. He pressed harder on the knife. "I should let every man here take a cut out of you with this knife."

Laramie wanted to scream and fight her way over at the sight of the wide-eyed fear on Gered's face.

"But I won't. Yet. You haven't finished understanding what you've done." Rosche stood and sheathed the knife.

Two men hauled Gered back up from the ground. He slumped between them, breath coming in wheezing gasps. Lara-mie wrenched her gaze away as Rosche stepped closer.

"As for you, you're still going to build those canisters for me," he said. "But right now take her to my room. It's been a while since I had someone with a little fight in them."

Laramie's stomach twisted.

"Or maybe," he cast a glance at Gered, "maybe I'll just do it here so he can watch."

Gered's head tilted up, loathing and hatred seeping through his battered features. Rosche only laughed and pressed his mouth against hers. Laramie froze in fear and horror for a second.

Surprise him.

Instead of fighting, she grabbed his shirt in cuffed hands and kissed him back, though every fiber of her being screamed for her to run. He withdrew, his not the only surprised expression.

"I have a better idea," she murmured, forcing a smile.

"And what's that?" Rosche asked, his hands sliding around her hips and daring to dip lower. She fought a shudder of revulsion.

What is my idea?

"The only thing he likes better than women and whiskey is a fight."

I can't beat him hand-to-hand. But maybe...

"No one's stupid enough to..."

I've got nothing left.

"A challenge."

"A what?" His voice caught in surprise and some amusement.

"A race. You and me, motorcycles and some supplies. Whoever gets back here first wins."

His eyes narrowed. "And what's the prize?"

Laramie straightened her shoulders. "If I win, I get a truck, supplies, and him." She jerked her head toward Gered. "If you win..." She shrugged. "I think we all know what you want."

Rosche's smile tightened as murmurs of interest and speculation rippled around them.

Good. Plenty of people heard.

"I'm intrigued, but why should I accept?"

Forcing down bile and praying for a miracle, she grabbed him again and kissed him. She pulled away and smiled up for a second before smashing her head into his. Rosche stumbled back in surprise, only to catch her follow-up kick to his stomach.

"Because I challenge you!" she shouted. "And I think I can win."

Murder shone in his eyes as he wiped blood from his nose.

"A race through the mountains. You make it back alive, or not at all." He turned to Gered. "String him up."

He looked at Laramie. "If he survives the heat, he's got an appointment with the firing squad when I get back."

Laramie kept her eyes locked on Rosche's as she answered. "When do we start?"

CHAPTER THIRTY-FOUR

Rosche swiped blood from his face. "Fuel a bike for her, and give her back her weapons." He turned an ugly smile at her. "I like a challenge."

Laramie held his sneer for a moment, tensing her jaw in her own challenge, before turning back to Dayo. She held out her cuffed wrists.

His glare didn't fade as he unlocked the cuffs. Her motorcycle was unloaded from the truck and a rider ran for a fuel can. She pulled open the saddlebag. If she was racing, she wasn't doing it in the Barrack's colors. She was doing it as a drifter.

Pulling off the baggy leather jacket, she tossed it into the dust. Her green jacket slid about her shoulders, fitting snug, like a second skin. The dust scarf went next, and she kept her braid tucked under its folds.

"Laramie." Gioia's quiet voice turned her.

The rider stood behind her, face still pale and drawn. She extended Laramie's knives and pistol. Laramie holstered them, confidence returning with every piece of herself she replaced.

"He'll kill you," Gioia whispered.

Laramie flicked a glance at where Rosche inspected his bike.

"Guess I'll just have to ride better."

Gioia shook her head, pressing her lips tight. "Don't…"

"Sorry if I'm not ready to just give up and spread my legs," Laramie snapped and instantly regretted it at the way Gioia flinched.

"Sorry."

A trembling smile broke across Gioia's face. "He said you thought you could make it. What about this?" A sort of desperate belief shone through.

Laramie reached for the red helmet Gioia carried in her other hand.

"I got him into this, Gioia. I'm going to do my best to get us both out."

A tear trembled dangerously on the rider's eyelash. "Be careful. And if you get the chance," her face hardened to stone, and she released her hold on the helmet, "kill that son of a bitch."

Laramie allowed a smile. "You got it."

"Drifter!" Moshe called.

She went to join him and Rosche. The unit leader held a map. He straightened the folds to better show a red line hastily marked across the surface.

Laramie tilted her head to see it, still staying a good pace away from both him and Rosche. It was a close-up of the mountains, topography drawn in wavy lines. A small square marked the Barracks at the foothills. The line traced sixty miles from the Barracks up into the mountains, wriggled its way south at least twice that distance until the elevation dipped, and then angling back to the starting line.

"Follow the markers for highway eight and keep south at the first turnoff up in the mountains," Moshe instructed. "You'll hit most of the rough terrain here." He pointed to a spot halfway through the route. "If the road's blocked, find a way around." He glanced to Laramie. "It hasn't been maintained, so there will be some patches where you'll have to get creative."

Laramie offered a careless shrug, and kept staring at the map, memorizing it.

"How am I getting back?" she asked.

"Maybe I'll just leave your body for the crows," Rosche taunted.

She coolly glared back and lifted a middle finger. He smirked.

"You'll hit a junction for highway eight and route eighty-seven. Take eighty-seven all the way back in." Moshe answered as if he hadn't heard their exchange. "Your tank should last you all the way back. Five minutes until start if you had any other business."

Laramie darted a look at him. His face stayed blank, but he gave the slightest of nods.

She turned her back on Rosche and strode back to her bike. Her steps faltered halfway there.

Gered had been cuffed to the posts in the middle of the yard, his arms stretched out to either side and slightly above his head. His head hung forward, weight shifted awkwardly off his injured leg. He looked small and vulnerable without the red jacket.

Any other business. She altered her path and went to him.

His ragged breathing hitched as she came to stand in front of him.

"Why?" He lifted his head, displaying the bloody mess Rosche had left.

"I'm not giving up, Gered."

He weakly shook his head. "He'll kill you."

Laramie crossed her arms. "So I've heard. Guess it's a good thing I don't actually suck at marksmanship then."

He didn't answer, just lowered his head again.

"I'm not giving up, Gered. Please don't give up either," she whispered fiercely.

His body jolted as he tried to shift his weight again. "It's too late for that."

"Don't. I'll be back, *kamé.*"

His breath hitched again at the word.

"I'll be back." She repeated the promise, as much for herself as for him. She pressed a hand to her jacket and the pictures crinkled in response. She had to make it back.

She turned on her heel and headed to the bike. She swung a leg over the seat and settled in. The engine thrummed to life, eagerly roaring under her touch as if it had already forgotten the miles she'd pushed it that day.

The units began to gather in silent groups. The trainees stood together. Axel offered a tentative smile, but there was no hope in his eyes for her.

Rosche saluted her as he pulled his helmet on.

She did the same. The world faded to gray under the tinted visor and compressed to a narrow scope. Moshe tossed chalk onto the ground in a straight line. Laramie kept one foot down as she slowly pulled up to the line. Rosche rolled up beside her.

He looked at her again, features hidden behind the helmet. She stared back, waiting. Moshe came to stand in front of the line, drawing their attention back to him with a wave.

Laramie revved her engine, palms already sticky in her gloves.

Moshe had no words, no caution to ride safe or fair. It would have been a massive joke if he had.

She coaxed another rumble from the bike. No glances behind. Focused on the road ahead. Highway eight to eighty-seven. Then back around.

She could do it. For Gered. For Gioia. For herself.

Moshe dropped his arm. She pushed off, twisting the throttle, and tucking her foot up as the world dissolved into dust and the road and the race.

CHAPTER THIRTY-FIVE

Rosche stayed even with her as they roared from the Barracks and onto the road. She leaned forward into the wind, her body absorbing the rhythm of the bike on the road. The early afternoon sun left puddles of mirages ahead of them, scattering as they roared through, only to reform again and again.

He matched her speed with every shift, keeping a bare arm's length away. A slight curve appeared in the road and they tracked the straightest path through, barely shifting their weight.

The mountains loomed closer with every mile. Foothills rose around them, scrub brush growing taller and perching on ledges where earth had fallen away to reveal the red dirt underneath. Curves came more often, forcing them to slow incrementally.

Still Rosche made no move.

The road rose higher with every bend. Laramie caught her breath as Rosche edged a little closer around a turn, bringing her arm dangerously close to the jagged rocks rising along the edge of the road.

Higher and higher, until pressure nagged at her ears, dulling the roar of the engines. Pines began to cluster and toss long spikes of shade across the road. A taller incline brought a whine from her engine before a quick shift calmed it.

A sign flashed to her right, warning the junction was only a bare mile away.

Laramie began to slow. Rosche didn't share any of the same caution. Whispering a curse, Laramie kept her speed down. She had no idea what the junction was going to look like.

Closer and closer.

Rosche slammed on his brakes, leaning left, his rear tire squealing and smoking as he took the turn. He stayed upright and Laramie leaned into her own turn three seconds later. She accelerated halfway through and her bike leaped to catch up.

The road narrowed, pine and boulders tumbled from the mountainsides scattered about the sides.

In the shifting shadows ahead, a rock lay in the road, leaving room for only one bike. Throwing caution to the winds, she gunned the engine, barely pulling ahead of Rosche as he got the same idea. He leaned in closer.

She screamed into her helmet as she accelerated again, gaining a few inches on him and whizzing by the rock, a shudder from the narrow brush rocking her boot.

A check in her rearview showed him creeping back up on her. He'd promised to leave her in the mountains.

Too soon to make my move?

He began to match her speed again, creeping up on her left side. His right hand released the handle and grasped his pistol.

Her heart rate spiked until it nearly jumped from her chest. She leaned left, drifting closer to him. A short breath, then she kicked at his bike as hard as she could, making contact just in front of his knee.

He grabbed the handle again, swerving and braking to avoid falling.

She peeled ahead. Sparks flew off the pavement ahead of her. Hunching lower over the handles, she checked the mirrors. Rosche raised his handgun again.

Shifting her weight, she wove side to side, narrowly missing another shot over her shoulder. The road straightened ahead, shadows draping across the road. She grabbed her gun from the holster, clicking the safety off. Wrapping her arm across her body, she used the left side mirror to keep Rosche in view as she snapped off three shots.

He swerved again. She jammed the handgun back into place, grabbing the handlebar again to take another curve.

A fallen tree sprawled across the road ahead. She slowed as she approached, finding the point to pull her weight up onto the foot spikes and bounced. A quick blip to the throttle and tug up on the handlebars lifted the motorcycle up and over the tree.

But her look in the mirror as she flew over sent her into a wobbled landing. She swerved, trying to course correct her stupid mistake. Jamming a foot down in time with a tug of the brakes, she managed to keep herself from tipping over.

The heavy whine of an engine cut through. Rosche jumped the tree and whizzed past her without a second look. Cursing, she straightened out and pushed off, accelerating.

A quick glance down at the odometer confirmed her fear. Not even halfway to the second turnoff. Over fifty miles still to go.

The road curved around another bulge in the mountain. A pit yawned in her stomach at the sight awaiting her on the other side.

Rosche, turned across the road, gun pointed directly at her.

Yanking out her gun again, she scattered shots at him. He flinched away from one sparking off his bike, the others going too wide.

The slide locked back, exposing the empty chamber. *DUST!*

She jammed it back in the holster. He raised his gun again. A shot tore through her jacket sleeve as she swerved, heat from its passing searing her skin. Another pinged off the road, the ricochet narrowly missing her knee.

Closer, closer. There was a way around. He'd left a few feet of space between him and the edge of the cliff.

Staring down the barrel again, she changed gears, leaning precariously left toward the road's edge and risking overcorrection back into the pavement as she whisked around his front tire.

A moment of vertigo gripped her as the back tire skidded on loose gravel, trying to draw her closer to the cliff's edge.

The tire caught, and she lurched forward, pressing as low as she could against the bars to avoid a bullet.

Another whizzed by overhead. The mirror showed Rosche wrenching his bike around to return to the chase.

Recklessly pushing faster, she took a curve with a lean so hard her knee almost brushed the asphalt. But he remained a small spot in her rearview.

What do I do? What do I do? The questions screamed in her head.

The road curved again, taking her up another notch in elevation. One side of the road tumbled off into a gorge, the other blocked by a towering rock wall.

A glance in her mirror showed no sign of him. The spot between her shoulder blades began to prickle. He didn't have a rifle, but he only had to get close enough to use the handgun again.

Another turn sent her slamming on the brakes. A rock fall had blocked the road four hundred yards ahead.

She skidded, tires smoking and raging against the abuse.

Still too fast.

Too fast.

At the last second, she twisted the handlebars, tipping sideways and freeing her foot to scramble free.

Her ankle wrenched beneath her but held long enough to allow her to dodge away and catch herself on the rocks. Pain throbbed through her wrists under the impact. The bike lay on its side, wheels spinning madly as the engine died.

Laramie ripped the helmet off. *Guess I'm making a stand here.*

The roar of Rosche's bike bounced off the gorge walls. She left the bike where it lay and shoved at a few small boulders until they rolled over the side of the gorge, bouncing and cracking their way to the bottom, leaving a convincing cloud of dust. She hobbled her way behind the rocks and squatted out of sight. Her fingers shook as she pulled out her pistol, fumbling in her pocket for a new mag and finding … nothing.

Panic spiked as she rifled through every pocket, replaced with horror as she came up empty. They'd taken all her weapons and ammo earlier that day, and Gioia didn't have any extra mags when she'd handed them back.

Dust.

She peered over the rocks. There was a spare in her bag. But the sound of Rosche's bike echoed off the rock walls.

Laramie ducked back down as he rumbled to a stop. She loosened a knife in the sheath, trying to bring her breath under control.

Dust. There was nowhere else to go. Time to take a stand.

A small gap in the tumbled boulders allowed her to see Rosche step away from his motorcycle and stalk his way forward, pulling off his helmet as he came to look at her fallen bike.

A little closer, little closer.

He leaned toward the edge of the gorge, peering over as dust still rose in faint bursts.

Laramie eased to her feet, tightening her grip on the knife. Rosche didn't move, inching a little closer to look.

One more breath for courage. She placed a hand on the smooth rock surface and vaulted over. He whirled at the movement. Not quick enough to block her kick.

A gun gleamed in his hand as he recovered. She charged in close, and thrust a hand out, redirecting the gun as he whipped it up. The discharge reverberated off the mountainside. A slash down toward his wrist forced him to drop the gun.

He caught her wrist as she jabbed at his chest. She dropped the knife into her left hand and stabbed again.

He released her and stumbled back. Her knife stuck oddly as she pulled it free.

He's wearing a vest!

Rosche pulled his own knife.

"This how you want to play it, drifter?"

"I'd prefer less talking," she snarled, feinting forward.

He swiped down and she backed away, passing her knife back to her right hand. *The point of this was to avoid a fight.* She cursed herself.

They circled, Laramie careful not to let her steps stray to the edge. Confidence lurked in his grin.

He charged forward, swiping at her. She jumped backward, fending him off with quick parries and strikes. Loose gravel betrayed her feet and he bulled forward as she slid. A slash tore through the sleeve on her upper arm. He grabbed her wrist. She twisted with the motion, stabbing at his stomach, trying to make it under the vest.

It hit the armor again, but Rosche released her. Both breathing hard, they faced off in a crouch, knives held ready.

"I'm almost sorry I have to leave you here, drifter," he sneered.

She moved first, following up a knife strike with a kick at his knee. A barrage of punches, kicks, and knife parries sent her stumbling back, mouth bleeding and ribs aching from his fist. But a streak of blood darkened his forearm from her knife.

She allowed her foot to bobble as she slid backward.

His next move came eager and she backed faster, until she hit the rock.

She swung her knife at Rosche, and he grabbed her wrist almost carelessly and pinned it to the rock. He raised his knife, faltering for a brief second at her sudden smirk.

He'd forgotten her left hand.

She stabbed her second knife up into his unprotected upper arm.

A roar of pain and anger broke from him. He still tried to stab, but she pushed back against the hilt of her knife still buried in his arm, her own furious scream matching his as they struggled against each other.

Then he gave way, his face turning a shade paler as blood streamed from the wound to cover her glove. She freed her right arm from his grip and shoved into his chest, throwing her weight into him and driving him back.

He grunted and twisted, trying to throw his left shoulder into her. She mirrored his move, twisting with him, pivoting in a strange almost dance.

Laramie yanked the knife from his arm and darted away.

He swayed dangerously, reflexively bringing his arm to his

chest. A glazed look coated his eyes. She tightened her grip on the slippery handle. He lurched forward. She spun into a kick, connecting with his stomach and sending him back, back, back.

Rosche's foot caught the edge of the ledge. He teetered for a moment, then fell.

Laramie dashed forward, arm outstretched as if for one brief moment she'd try to catch him.

He tumbled down the incline, coming to rest in a sprawled heap at the bottom of the gorge. One leg crooked out at an awkward angle. Blood seeped into the dust.

But he moved. A faint groan edged its way up to her.

She gasped, air filling her lungs. She leaned forward onto her knees, trying to ignore the blood covering her knives and gloves, and staining the green leather. Another breath closer to a sob broke.

I did it. Her knees threatened to give way, but she mustered control with another forceful breath.

Rosche groaned again. He grabbed at his arm, pressing it close to his body. He tried to move, then went still. She backed away, fighting the small piece of herself that dared suggest she go help him.

He was going to leave me dead on the side of the road. He's hurt countless people. Condemned Gered to die. It's no more than he deserves.

But she hated herself a little as she walked away. Wiping her knives clean on her trousers, she contemplated his bike still running where he'd left it. She righted her bike. It hadn't taken any damage other than a few scrapes from the road.

Thank you, Jaan.

She kicked the stand down and rummaged through the

saddlebag, pulling out a bandage roll from a first aid kit and wrapped it around the cut on her arm. Grabbing the spare mag packed next to her toolkit, she changed it out and reholstered her pistol as she went back to Rosche's bike. She killed the engine and tossed the keys away. Then, purely out of spite for the idea of the gangs and what he'd forced Gered and Gioia to do, and Axel to become, she slashed the tires.

Now what? She settled onto her bike, scrubbing blood from her lips as she pulled the helmet back on. If she came from any direction other than the end of the course, the units wouldn't honor her deal.

Assuming they would to begin with. Even a small part of herself hadn't expected to make it back. She carefully maneuvered the bike through the small gap in the rock fall. Her ankle ached as she propped it back onto the foot spike and drove off.

She rode as fast as she dared on the road, wary of more rock-falls. But nothing blocked the way. And nothing appeared in her mirrors as she compulsively checked them.

Eventually the road began to wind lower and lower, the pines receding back and giving way to the scrub brush in the lower hills. The sun had shifted to late afternoon when she made the turnoff.

She accelerated again, pushing the bike to the limits. Hours had passed. Hours for Gered left in the heat of the day with his injuries. It wasn't likely anyone was giving him water or shade either.

What if he's not even alive when I get back? What if they just shoot us both when they see Rosche didn't make it?

Her bike cast long shadows to her right, the sun hanging low over the mountains as the Barracks came into view.

CHAPTER THIRTY-SIX

The gates were open. She drove slowly through. Exhaustion pressed around her chest and her cuts and scrapes stung. Riders stared at her as she pulled into the center of the courtyard and parked.

She left the engine running and pulled her helmet off as Moshe came forward.

Disbelief covered his face and he stared at her. Zelig and a newly returned Barns joined him.

"Where's Rosche?" Moshe asked.

"I left him in the mountains." Laramie lifted her chin. Her voice rasped over the words. She hadn't stopped for water, desperate to make it back in time.

"Is he alive?" Moshe's voice quieted, but something lurked underneath the question. A cautious hope.

Laramie shrugged. "Does it matter? I made it back. I won, and I want my winnings."

Zelig whipped a pistol free and trained it at her head. "You don't get anything, drifter!"

Laramie glared at him. Her tank hovered at empty. This was it. She spread her hands wide, gesturing down to the blood staining her clothes.

"I took him down!" she shouted. "Honor the deal we made, and I might just tell you where I left him."

Moshe held out a hand, stopping Zelig as he pushed forward.

A frown covered Barns's face. Murmurs ran through the assembled riders. Laramie could almost taste the uncertainty in the air.

She wasn't supposed to have come back. No one had prepared for this. She'd just shattered the belief that Rosche was invincible.

Moshe and Barns conferred a moment. Barns narrowed his eyes, but Moshe crossed his arms, head jutting forward a little as he appeared to argue. Finally, Barns jerked a nod.

"Get a truck. Supplies. Get him down," Moshe ordered.

Shock rippled through the riders. Zelig turned to him in rage. "You can't—!"

Moshe grabbed his jacket and shoved him back a step. "I have the rank here," he snarled. "You want to test me?"

Zelig glared, but held his tongue.

Movement broke and Laramie recognized Unit Four riders heading out to follow orders.

She dared finally turn to look at Gered. His leg had given way beneath him and he hung awkwardly from his wrists. His head lolled to the side. Blood crusted his clothes and stained the front of his shirt where it had dripped from his face.

She swallowed hard.

"Is he even alive?" she whispered as Moshe approached.

"Barely. He's been like that for the last hour at least."

"Dust." The word hissed between her teeth.

The low rumble of a transpo truck broke the air and Dec hopped from the driver's seat. Two other riders arrived, pushing Gered's bike and her drifter bike with them. Dec lowered a ramp from the back of the truck and Laramie watched as they loaded the bikes in. She unlatched her bag and forced her feet to move around the truck to where Axel worked with Dayo to unlock the cuffs on Gered.

The traveler looped an arm underneath Gered, grunting as he took his full weight. The last cuff came free and Axel barely caught Gered's limp arm, his wrist a bloody mess. Fighting nausea, she opened the passenger side door and stood aside as they wrestled him in.

Axel hopped into the truck and pulled the belt across him. Gered didn't move, breath barely trembling through cracked lips.

Dayo walked away without a backward glance, but his shoulders hunched and hands twitched as if he wanted to turn.

Laramie bit back the urge to call after him.

"There's a med kit under the seat." Axel hopped down, staring at her with wide eyes.

"Thanks."

He nodded and hurried away as if scared to be caught helping. She closed the door and rounded the front of the truck. Gioia was there, Gered's rifle balanced in her arms. Laramie took it and set it on the floorboards. The bone-handled pistols came next.

"We got the tracker off his bike."

Laramie breathed a sigh of relief. She'd forgotten about it.

Gioia glanced from her to Gered's slumped form.

"Take care of him." She nodded once, her jaw tightening.

Laramie rested a hand on her shoulder. "Come with us. Look after him yourself."

Gioia looked at her with longing so deep it threatened to split Laramie's heart.

"Your deal was only for you two. If I go, it'll be like I'm

running. No one runs."

"What if Rosche is dead?" Laramie pressed.

"Is he? Until we know that, whoever is here still has to follow his rules. Barns will make sure of it."

Laramie glanced to see Unit One's leader watching them. His hand strayed toward a knife as Gioia leaned toward Laramie, eyes fixed on Gered again, as if about to throw caution to the wind and join them.

"No." Gioia shook her head and backed a step away. "Get out of here. Get yourselves somewhere safe. Don't look back."

Barns kept his hand on his knife, still watchful.

"Gioia," Laramie called. The rider paused again, her hands in back pockets. "Take care of yourself."

Gioia nodded. "You too, drifter."

Then she was gone, and Moshe approached.

"Where is he?"

Laramie held onto a breath. What if she didn't tell them, just said he was dead? Could she leave him to die slowly, alone, even if that's what he'd intended to do to her?

I hate being a decent person sometimes.

"About sixty miles past the first turnoff, there's a rockfall. You'll see his bike. I left him in the gorge. Busted leg and knife wound in his arm. It was bleeding bad. You might not find a pulse when you get there."

Moshe's little frown said he might not be too upset by that.

"Head northeast. There's some close border towns there. I've radioed the units that way to stay clear. Drive and don't look back." He turned on his heel and walked away, already calling orders for another truck and a unit to head out.

Laramie hopped up into the driver's seat. The gates stood

open and no one moved to block her. But Barns stood like a silent sentinel in the side mirror. She put the truck in gear and pulled out.

The bikes in the back rattled as she turned up onto the highway and headed east. A golden haze had begun to cover the world, shadows stretching out before them like guiding fingers pointing the way.

After two miles, she eased to a halt. No dust in the rearview.

Laramie undid her belt and leaned over to Gered. His skin was hot and dry to the touch. The back of his hands and neck were bright, angry red, already blistering. Grit and dirt clung to his road-inflicted injuries. His chest rose and fell in short wheezing gasps. He'd yet to open his eyes.

She reached back, pulling the med kit out from under the passenger seat. Dropping it into her lap, she opened it with one hand while adjusting the dials to bring cold air from the vents.

She grabbed the cold packs, cracked them, and waited until the cold began to leach into her hands before reaching across to tuck them on either side of Gered's neck, under his armpits, and at his groin. Fiddling with all the vents, she managed to point them all at him.

Another rummage through the kit turned up hydration tubes. Bottles of water rolled on the floorboards by the bikes. She grabbed one, cracked the lid and dumped the powder from the tube inside. Capping it again and shaking it, she nudged Gered's shoulder.

He stirred, eyelids trying to open. Laramie took a wipe from the kit and gently dabbed at his face, clearing away clotted and dried blood around his eyes and nose. He flinched and managed to open his eyes.

Confusion filled his stare. His lips moved, but no sound came. She cupped a hand behind his head and brought the bottle to his mouth.

"Drink."

His lips reflexively parted and she poured some of the mixture in. He coughed and she shifted her grip to grab the cool packs and keep them in place.

She kept giving him small sips until a quarter of the liquid was gone. She settled his head back against the seat. No change to his breathing.

Laramie gulped a few sips of the water, before capping it and throwing the truck back into gear.

She floored the gas pedal, the truck climbing frustratingly slow to near its max speed. She clutched the wheel in both hands, leaning forward as if that would make it go faster.

Every ten minutes, she pulled to a stop and repeated the process of pouring small sips of treated water into Gered's mouth, making sure he swallowed, and recracking the cold packs.

Finally, on the fourth time, his eyes showed recognition when they opened.

"Laramie...?" he mumbled.

"Yeah, it's me." She smiled in relief.

"What...?"

She gently hushed him and made him drink more. "We're getting out of here."

He tried to move, and pain contorted his face. She pressed a hand to his shoulder. A soft sob caught in his chest.

"Don't move. We're headed for a med center as fast as we can."

When she was satisfied that he'd settled back down, she started driving again.

Following Moshe's advice, she headed northeast on the first road turning that direction, praying to all the saints that she was going the right way.

At the hour's turn, she flipped on the headlights. The flatness had gradually begun giving way to hills and deeper gullies, more brush coating the hills.

Gered's breathing had barely changed. Tension locked in her joints as she drove, listening to each rasp in and out.

She didn't know if she'd done enough to break him out of the initial heatstroke. He could be shutting down from the inside and she wouldn't know it. Each stop made her less and less confident. Sometimes he'd try to talk, others he'd just stare uncomprehendingly at her. The road stretched on forever, the headlights reaching out into the deepening gloom.

Fatigue began its battle to take over her body. She'd fought and raced for her life a few too many times over the last two days. She almost missed the sign at first. It winked again in the headlights, jerking her out of the auto-drive she'd been in for the last two miles.

Arrow, fifteen miles.

She sat straighter. Arrow. She'd been thinking about heading there before trying to cross Rosche's territory. It seemed like years ago.

We're out of the territory! The elation quickly plummeted as she realized it had been well over ten minutes since she'd last treated Gered.

She slowed and grabbed another bottle. A search of the kit turned up empty for another hydration tube. A soft sigh escaped. Uncapping the water, she reached over to Gered again.

He gasped awake. In the dim glow of the interior light, he

looked even worse.

"Just a little bit longer, Gered," she said. "Fifteen miles."

He turned his head away from the water bottle. She nudged him back.

"You have to keep drinking," she urged.

He shook his head a little. His lips moved a few times before the words came. "Bury … bury me somewhere green…"

"What?" The water bottle bobbled in her hand.

"My … my name on the gravestone." He formed the words with a little more determination this time.

Swallowing hard, she nodded. "Okay, Gered. What's your last name?"

His face twisted again, back arching as he tried to move. "No … my *real* name." He tilted his head to look at her straight on. "Marcus … Antonio … Solfeggietto."

The water bottle clattered to the floor, the contents gurgling out. Laramie didn't notice. She stared at Gered, heart stuttering in shock.

"What did you say?"

But his eyes slid closed again.

"No. No!" She shook his shoulder, but he didn't respond. Frantically she found his pulse. Still too fast, but beating.

She slumped back into her seat, staring at his profile. *Solfeggietto.*

He was only a few years older than she was. The Tlengin stole him from his town after destroying it. He'd never said what town it was. She'd just assumed…

I was the only survivor. She pressed a hand to her mouth. *That the travelers found. The raiders were long gone by the time they got there.*

"Dust," she whispered.

His chest rose and fell a few more times. She turned back to the wheel, wrenched the truck into gear, and gunned the motor.

Hold on, kamé. We'll make it to the med center and then you and I are talking.

CHAPTER THIRTY-SEVEN

Laramie almost started crying when the glittering lights of Arrow appeared over a rise. She gulped a breath and kept driving. They roared past the town limits sign. Thirty-thousand people. It would have a bigger med center than the wide spots on the road she'd passed through weeks ago.

She slowed to accommodate the few other trucks and cars on the road. A few figures walked under the streetlights. Laramie kept an eye on the right side of the road, watching for the med center signs.

Finally a small blue sign with a winged bull—the emblem of Luca, the Messenger patron of healing—pointed them to the right. She took the turn a little too fast, bracing herself in the seat to keep upright.

Laramie pulled into the drive in front of the med center's doors. She rested her forehead on the wheel for a long moment, trying to gather herself, thanking the saints again for getting them there.

She laid on the horn until two nurses ran out of the doors. Laramie tried to hop down from the truck. Her right foot gave way beneath her and she clung to the frame.

One of the nurses ran around to her.

"What's wrong?" he asked.

She pointed inside to Gered. "Help him," she babbled. "He's hurt bad. Please."

The nurse vanished and she hobbled after him. He opened the door, took one look at Gered slumped in the seat, and sent the other nurse running back in.

She returned in a moment with two other attendants and a wheeled stretcher. Laramie propped herself against the hood, watching as they maneuvered Gered from the truck and laid him on the stretcher.

Every time she looked, his injuries seemed worse. The nurses swept around him, rushing the stretcher back inside. Laramie hurried after them, but her limbs felt like they were wading through mud.

By the time she made it into the bright fluorescent lights of the lobby, they were already disappearing through another set of double doors. She caught snatches of their words before the doors shut.

"Multiple contusions … abrasions … possible heat stroke…"

She kept moving toward the doors until another nurse stopped her.

"Only staff and patients allowed…" she trailed off. "Are you okay?"

Laramie turned a slow glance down at herself. Dust, grit, and blood covered her from head to toe.

"I'm fine. Is he—?"

"Sit down." The nurse guided her to a seat. "I'm going to have a look at you real quick. They'll take care of him, don't worry." Her smile brought some reassurance to Laramie.

"Okay." Laramie peeled off the gloves and reached for her

dust scarf, managing to unwind it halfway before her body rebelled at any further movement and she passed out.

She woke to a crick in her neck. A quick glance around confirmed she was still in the med center lobby. Her knives and gun met her frantic touch and she relaxed a fraction. Someone had adjusted her in the seat to be a little more comfortable, but the chairs were definitely not made to sleep in.

She sat up, stretching arms overhead, grimacing as her shoulders and back popped.

One other couple sat in the lobby with her, giving her a wide berth. She didn't blame them. She didn't even want to know how bad she looked.

"You're awake!" A cheery voice announced the nurse from before.

Laramie took the proffered water bottle and drained half of it. "Sorry I fell asleep on you."

The nurse grinned, putting Laramie more at ease. "I've had worse experiences with patients in this lobby, believe it or not."

Laramie smiled and drank again, rinsing a little more of the grimy, stale feeling from her mouth.

"The guy I brought in." She couldn't bring herself to say a name. "How is he?"

In the pause before the nurse spoke, Laramie imagined the worst.

"They're still working on him," she said carefully. "He's in pretty bad shape."

"But they think he'll be okay?" Laramie pressed.

"They'll know more in a bit," the nurse promised. "And speaking of him." She hesitated again before waving over her shoulder.

Laramie stiffened at the sight of the officer coming toward her.

"What is this?" she growled, ready for another fight. No one was taking Gered, or her, anywhere.

"I'm Sergeant Rollins. Just want to talk." The officer spread his hands peaceably. "Your friend in there has some tattoos the staff thought I might be interested in."

He smoothed the front of his dark green uniform. "You have any information you'd be willing to share?"

Laramie swallowed hard. "On what?"

"On where you came from, for starters."

The nurse dropped a nod to the officer and left. He drew up a chair in front of her. Laramie placed her hands on the arms and pushed herself a little taller.

"No one's taking anyone anywhere." Rollins leaned back to give her more space. "Just trying to decide what's going on here. Haven't seen a snake tattoo like that outside the territory on anyone but escorts for supply truckers down in River Bend."

"He's part of the gangs. I was a 'recruit.' We both got out, but had a little trouble on the way."

He arched an eyebrow. "Pardon me for thinking that's a bit of an understatement."

Laramie allowed a faint smile. "We decided to try and make a run for it this morning. We thought we had an out, and we didn't. Rosche was set to kill him, but I challenged him and won. Then we—"

"Hold on." Rollins held up a hand. "You challenged *Rosche*? The warlord? The man who's kept this territory locked up tight for near ten years?"

"I did only meet one psychotic guy named Rosche during my lovely stay there."

Rollins huffed a disbelieving laugh. "You've got some stones, girl. Looks like you had a time of it." He gestured to her throat.

She touched the bruising a little self-consciously. "You could say that."

"So you challenged Rosche?"

She nodded. "Motorcycle race. I managed to come out in front. My prize was my ... friend, a truck, and a path out."

Rollins's eyebrow raised higher. "And he let you do that?"

Laramie shifted in the seat, the memory of Rosche's broken form at the bottom of the gorge not drawing any triumph. "Let's just say he wasn't in a position to stop me."

"Dead?" Rollins leaned forward.

Laramie shrugged. "I didn't stick around to see."

"Hmm." Rollins rubbed his chin.

"Look, Gered's not any trouble. Neither am I. If ... when he gets back on his feet, we're out of here. I've got people to get back to." Now she leaned forward, trying to not sound so desperate.

"Anyone coming after you?"

"I don't know." She shrugged helplessly. Moshe had said the challenge would be honored. But someone might get it into their heads to do something different.

"Okay." Rollins pushed to his feet. "This is something I need to pass on up the chain. Stick close around here for the time being. I might need to talk to you again."

Laramie barely had the strength to nod again. The officer left and she slumped back in the chair. Safe again. She finished off the water bottle she'd crumpled in her hands during the conversation with Rollins.

The nurse came back with bandages. Laramie squirmed as the nurse dabbed antiseptic and got the worst cuts taken care of. Then back to sitting, glancing around the waiting room, and staring at the doors leading further into the med center.

After an eternity of waiting, a male nurse pushed through the double doors and headed straight for her. She shot to her feet, ignoring the twinge in her ankle.

"He's stable."

She closed her eyes against the wave of relief those two words brought. When she opened them again, the nurse waited in patient understanding.

"Can I see him?"

He ushered her through the doors. Her boots squeaked against the spotless tiled floor. She held her arms close, the quiet and sterile smell prompting slight unease. They turned into a hallway set with multiple doors. The patient wing.

The nurse took the lead, finally stopping four doors down on the right. He entered with her.

Gered lay on the bed, still unconscious. He wore a clean gray hospital shirt, and they'd washed the dirt and blood away. Another nurse was spreading blankets over him. Bandages covered his right upper arm and both wrists. Lines ran from his arm to a machine.

"Fluids and medication," the nurse explained.

"When will he wake up?" Laramie couldn't bring herself to move closer. *Solfeggietto.* It was like the name had thrown up a barrier between them.

"I don't know. We'll let him wake up on his own. He's pretty sedated right now."

Laramie traced the lines between his arm and the machine. She had to know. Had to.

"You can test genetics through blood, right?"

The nurse gave her a curious look. "Yes."

Laramie stared down at her hands. "Can you test my blood against his? I think ... I think we might be related."

CHAPTER THIRTY-EIGHT

Gered slowly peeled his eyes open. His dry lips cracked as they parted in an exhale, his mouth working to bring some moisture back. Unfamiliar ceiling tiles stretched above him. He blinked slowly, a steady beeping encroaching on his awareness. Something pulled along the back of his neck as he turned to look. Blocky medical equipment stood next to the bed. He followed the trailing lines back to where they lodged in the crook of his right elbow.

Both wrists were bandaged and resting on a woven blanket drawn up over his chest. Another thick bandage covered most of his upper right arm.

Where am I?

The plaster walls were painted in a comforting pale blue. Not the Barracks. Several faded photographs adorned the walls—one a black and white of a mountain highway, and the other a forest.

And, curled in the armchair at the foot of the bed—Laramie, asleep, her jacket tucked up around her shoulders.

Definitely not the Barracks.

He shifted his elbow to try to push himself up. A hissing breath escaped as pain ricocheted across his chest. He settled back down.

Laramie stirred and blinked slowly awake.

"Hey!" She pushed her jacket away and came to sit on the side of his bed, rubbing her eyes, still careful of the bruising staining her left temple.

"Where are we?" He flinched a little as the hoarse words grated from his throat.

"Arrow."

"Arrow?" he repeated in confusion. That was outside the territory. What were they doing there, unless...

"You won?"

She nodded, though a sort of haunted look filled her face instead of triumph like he'd expected. "Got a truck, our bikes, and you, and hightailed it out of there."

There was no way Rosche just let her—let him—go.

"Is he dead?"

She didn't say anything.

"Did you kill him?" He tried to sit up again, needing to know.

She shrugged. "I don't know if he's alive or not. I left him in the bottom of a ravine with a knife wound and what might've been a broken leg. When I got back to the Barracks, I told them to hold up the deal and I'd tell them where he was."

"They went for that?"

"Moshe made sure they did. But Barns didn't look too happy about it."

He sank back into the pillows. Barns would be more than happy to take over from Rosche if given the chance.

"How are you feeling?" She leaned a little closer.

Dusted awful. Still better than the last time he remembered being conscious, which had been sometime after being cuffed to the posts. He lifted a shaky hand to his chest. The thin hospital clothes rubbed soft against his skin.

"Alive."

A grin touched her mouth, skewed a little by swelling in the corner. "Good. For a bit, I didn't think I was going to be able to get you here."

He swallowed the faint moisture that had begun to come back to his mouth.

"Thanks."

She nodded again, her jaw tightening.

He shifted, able to make it further toward sitting before having to give up because of his chest. The rough outlines of bandages poked up through the shirt across the right side of his ribs. A bone-deep ache lingered across his body from plenty of hits he remembered all too clearly.

"Wait." She reached past him and something beeped. The bed adjusted itself so he came more into a sitting position. From there, he maneuvered himself upright.

"What's this for?" He indicated the clear line, glad he hadn't been conscious for that. He hated seeing anything sliding into his skin.

"You were severely dehydrated when we got here last night. They've been pumping fluids in like crazy. And some medication. They said the injuries from your crash were already getting infected."

"Can't believe you got us out." He shook his head.

"Me either," she admitted. "I tried to get Gioia to come, but she said no. I'm sorry." Sympathy tightened the corner of her mouth.

His fingers pilled around the blanket. He didn't want to admit how much he'd hoped she would have walked through the door. Alive. Out of the gangs.

"It's okay." He forced the words.

She briefly touched his hand, then pulled back to knot her fingers together. "Hey, when we were driving here … you told me that if you died, to bury you somewhere green. Somewhere with your name on the gravestone."

He shifted. That sounded somewhat familiar.

She swallowed hard and reached over to her jacket. She slid something out of the inside pocket.

"You also said a name … not Gered … but a name that I know."

His heart stuttered. He'd given up his name?

She extended something in a hesitant hand. His breath caught as he stared at nearly forgotten faces. He remembered the day the picture was taken. It had faded to colors and sounds and impressions. The sweet smell of the trailing roses. The warmth from the morning sun almost hot enough to be uncomfortable. The arms wrapped around him, holding him tight and tickling him to make him smile.

His fingers trembled as they took the picture.

"Where did you get this?" The words came out a whisper clogged with emotion.

"It's mine. It was the only thing left in my house besides me after the Tlengin raiders swept through and the travelers found me." She scooted a little closer, eyes bright. "I had parents, and an older brother named Marcus."

A breath edged from his cracked lips.

"My name's not really Laramie. It's Melodie. Melodie Arabella Solfeggietto."

He squeezed his eyes shut against the sudden sting. When

he opened them, he saw the similarities between the woman in the picture and the woman sitting on the bed in front of him. He remembered playing with a puppy in the green grass, giggles following him as a yellow-haired baby sister with a mischievous smile tumbled after him.

Now that he dared to look closer at her, to actually care, he saw the things he'd nearly forgotten. The same touch of blue in her left iris like his mother. The way her mouth quirked at the corner when she'd been especially smart-ass like his dad.

"I had them test some of your blood against mine. It's a perfect match. I'm sorry, I should have waited until you were awake to ask, but I just couldn't," she babbled, eyes widening as if afraid he'd be mad.

He couldn't be. Not when there was a name pushing up from his suffocated memories. He held it in his mouth for a moment, remembering the soft edges of the nickname.

"Dee?"

She pressed a hand against her mouth. A tear trembled on her lashes as she nodded. "Yeah." She reached out to touch his arm again, eyes wide as if afraid he'd vanish. "Saints, I can't believe it's you." Her lips tightened and she blinked rapidly as if holding back tears.

Something damp trickled down his cheek. *Am I crying?* The picture blurred in front of him.

"Sorry." He smudged his cheeks with fingers. Don't apologize. Don't show weakness. Cut it out.

Then arms were around him, and Laramie pulled him close. He slowly wrapped his arms around her, not even sure when the last time he'd been hugged was. Probably when the picture had been taken.

His shirt soaked up her tears as she pressed her face into his shoulder. Something seemed to finally break inside him, and he leaned on her, not even trying to stop the tears as they pushed from his eyes. With each one that fell, more and more tension released inside. From all the years of hell. From thinking his entire family was dead. From not trying harder to escape the raiders, and then the vipers. From leaving Gioia and Dayo behind.

Eventually his shoulders stopped shaking. He shuddered another breath, feeling even more drained and exhausted. She rubbed his shoulder.

"It's okay," she whispered in Itan. "It's okay."

He mustered the strength to lift himself out of her arms, dabbing at his cheeks again. She sniffed and scrubbed her sleeve across her nose.

"How did you survive?" He stared at her, feeling as though somehow she'd become something strange.

She threaded her fingers together again. "When the attack started, Mom grabbed me and shoved me into a cabinet in the kitchen. She told me to stay there until they came to get me. Then she went to go look for you."

"I was outside in the garden," Gered remembered. "Smoke and screaming everywhere..."

Laramie's lips pressed tight together. She hated remembering as much as he did.

"But no one came. I remember climbing out of the cabinet when she didn't come back. I thought I needed to help find you..." She rubbed her nose, and turned her head to look at the uninteresting machine. "Our door had been shot up. Raiders were everywhere in the streets. Bodies. Smoke. Fire."

His heart hammered in his chest.

"A raider started coming toward the door. I ran and hid in the cabinet again and didn't come out. Not even when smoke crept under the door and the screaming stopped." She rubbed her arms, more tears streaking down her face.

"I don't know how long it was until the travelers came through. The noise they made scared me so much that I must have made some sort of sound that led them right to me. They couldn't get me to talk for months after that."

"Dust," he whispered.

"They told me later that everyone was dead. No survivors. Maybe they found another body and assumed it was you, or…"

"They did the right thing telling you that," he interrupted.

She jutted her jaw like she wanted to argue.

"They took more prisoners than just me." He seemed unable to bring his voice past a whisper. "You don't want to know what happened to them. Or to any other Itan they took on their massacre runs."

Laramie's eyes widened and she placed a gentle hand on his forearm. He touched her warm hand, anchoring himself back to earth.

"I only survived because of the amount of blue in my eyes." Apparently even holy wars made excuses for someone who might have a use. "Mom tried to get me back inside, but…" He'd buried the memory so deep it didn't want to come out.

Laramie closed her eyes, tears leaking from under her lashes.

Finally she opened her eyes and mustered a smile. "I feel a little stupid. I should have recognized you. I've stared at that picture enough."

Gered looked back at it still held tight in his hand. "It's been years. We both knew our family was dead. And I'm…" He froze.

She already knew what he was. There was no hiding it. She'd just have to get good at hiding her disappointment in him.

"Hey." She nudged his arm. "I know a little bit about you, and I'm not scared or disappointed."

He could barely meet her gaze. "Maybe not yet."

"Don't say that!" Her eyes glinted dangerously. "Never."

He swallowed fear. She would be, eventually.

A knock at the door sent them both wiping their eyes again. Laramie offered a smile and went to answer it. Even though he knew they were in a med center, knew they were safe, Gered still tensed as she opened it.

A nurse in plain gray scrubs was on the other side. He carried a tray of bandages and medicine.

"Hey, you're awake!"

Gered blinked at his cheerful tone. He'd never met someone so upbeat in a med center.

"Just needed to change out those bandages for you and check your levels." The nurse set the tray on the table and grabbed a clipboard from the base of the bed. He tapped a few buttons on the machines and jotted notes.

He turned to Gered, who stiffened, wariness returning.

"How you feeling?"

"Fine," Gered cautiously replied. Fine meant he could be left alone.

The nurse pursed his lips and raised an eyebrow. "Let me know if that changes while we switch these out."

"I'll wait outside," Laramie said.

Gered edged away from where the nurse hovered closer, pulling on sterile gloves. He glanced to her. He wouldn't be able to do anything to defend himself if the nurse pulled something.

Instantly, he shook his head at himself. *I'm being too paranoid.*

"Unless you want me to hang around?" Laramie asked.

He jerked a quick nod, almost hating himself for the bit of weakness. She perched on the edge of the chair, watching the nurse almost as sharply as he did. It helped him relax a fraction.

The nurse reached for the ties lacing up the side of the hospital shirt. Once undone, he moved it aside to expose the bandages. Bruising covered his chest and stomach around the bandages. A few brown spots stained the white gauze. Gered swallowed hard, nervous to see what lay underneath.

All he remembered was the pain that had erupted after he crashed.

He bunched the blanket in his hands, breath escaping in sharp hisses as the nurse tugged the bandages free with murmured apology.

Underneath was a mess of raw and scraped skin.

"Hope you weren't too attached to that tattoo." The nurse pointed at his side.

The head and shoulders of the spotted jackal still snarled across his ribs, but the rest lay mangled and torn under the wound. He caught Laramie staring at it, her eyes distant for a moment before she turned to him and offered a slight smile.

"Not really," he said.

The nurse dabbed something cool and pain-relieving over the injury before taping more bandages over it. He retied the shirt and moved on to Gered's arm and then wrists.

Under his instruction, Gered gingerly tried to move his fingers against the sun-scorched tightness of his blistered skin.

"Keep working on it. Gently."

Gered nodded obedience, focused instead on the raw wound

that wrapped his wrist, severing the snake's head from its body. He quickly turned his right arm up. The Itan script was intact. Relief sent his eyes closed for a moment. He didn't mind the wounds so much if they'd broken the detested markings on his skin. But he would have hated to see the Itan ruined.

Their parents had kept the quote framed above the doorframe between the kitchen and cozy dining room.

"This one is gonna hurt." The nurse folded the blanket back and undid the ties on the loose pants. "Let me know if you want an extra dose of pain meds."

Gered nodded. His skin already felt raw from the treatment so far.

The nurse picked up a syringe from the tray and injected it through a small port on the main lines. Gered gingerly eased back down, his ribs and chest aching from the amount of time spent upright.

"Here we go." The warning wasn't enough for the tearing sensation in his leg.

Laramie was at his side in a second, pushing him down into the bed. He gripped her arm as well as his bandaged hand would allow until the meds kicked in.

"And that's done!" the nurse announced, gathering up the dirty bandages.

Laramie tapped his shoulder and helped pull the blankets back up over him.

"I'll be back in a bit with a food tray." The nurse checked the machine one more time.

Gered nodded, even though eating was the last thing he felt like doing. "How long do I have to stay here?"

The nurse peeled his gloves off. "A few days at least. You were in pretty bad shape when you came in. Those wounds will need consistent monitoring for now. Doc'll let you know."

A few days. Gered already itched to put more distance between them and the border. But exhaustion pressed his body into the bed.

The thin mattress dipped as Laramie sat. "I'm ready to leave too."

He tilted a glance at her. She'd been able to read him almost immediately.

"You pull some of the same expressions I see in the mirror," she admitted almost sheepishly.

He half smiled.

"Hey," she paused. "I know we hadn't really talked about what we were doing after we got out. And now it happened."

He rubbed the blankets between his fingers. Was this where she changed her mind?

"I'm headed back to my traveler family. You want to come with?"

He stared at her, still shocked even though he'd known deep down she'd offer.

"You sure you want me along?" he asked.

She rolled her eyes. "You think I'm just leaving you here after everything? Besides, I'd like to keep my brother around for a bit."

His eyes stung again. *Brother.* He still didn't know how to be that. But maybe he could figure it out.

"Okay."

Her grin put the sun to shame. She pushed to her feet.

"They'll be heading into the fall route, which means we'll have about a two day ride to get there. I'll start getting the stuff we'll need, and make sure the bikes can make it."

He frowned. "Bikes?"

"Yeah. Unit Four put our bikes in the back of the truck along with our stuff. I've got your guns as well."

He turned his gaze up to the ceiling, focusing on the one uneven tile right above him. "How was Dayo?"

Laramie paused long enough that he almost looked at her again.

"He got you in the truck, but still looked pretty pissed. I'm sorry."

He nodded. She didn't need to apologize. It was his fault. And he might never have a chance to change it.

"I'll be back later." She tapped his shoulder again. "Get some rest."

CHAPTER THIRTY-NINE

Gered rested for five days. The morning of the sixth, Laramie strode through the double doors of the med center, an extra spring in her step. Her grin grew at the bundle under her arm.

She ran over her checklist. Bikes were ready and waiting outside. She'd picked up enough jobs over the last few days to get Gered new supplies and his present and not worry about depleting the cash in her wallet. They had rations, an extra tarp, bed roll, and full tanks.

All she needed was the med supplies they'd send with Gered for keeping up with the healing injuries. The doc had reluctantly released him the night before.

"Laramie!"

Her cheer faded as Sergeant Rollins jogged over to her.

"Heard you were leaving today."

She nodded. "You heard right. Need anything else before we leave?"

She, and a reluctant Gered, had given the officer some more information on Rosche's territory. Gered had seemed to know something else, but hadn't shared. But she wondered if it had anything to do with the call to Moshe and the way the unit leader had argued to let them go.

"No, just wanted to wish you luck. We'll be keeping a closer eye on the border. Any idea where you're headed in case we need something?"

Laramie tightened her fingers around the bundle. She really didn't want to give him any personal information about herself.

"East. Going to meet up with some travelers up by the Rift."

He tipped a nod. "All right. Ride safe."

She flicked a salute that made him grin and hurried away. The nurses and staff she passed greeted her by name and called well-wishes for their journey. She'd been in the hospital every spare minute.

She and Gered had shared a few more memories of their parents, and she'd shared some of her upbringing with the travelers, but he hadn't spoken much of his own past.

Don't push, she'd constantly reminded herself. He wouldn't have shared back at the Barracks and there was no reason for him to start even with the discovered connection.

She knocked on his door and entered at his call. He sat on the edge of the bed, lacing up his new boots. He'd dressed in the spare set of clothes from his saddlebag. The bruising on his face had faded to yellows and streaks of black. Light gauze replaced the heavy bandages on his hands to protect the peeling skin from the gloves she handed him.

He carefully flexed his bandaged wrists. He'd insisted he was good to ride. She was eager enough to be gone that she hadn't argued too much.

"Got you something." She bounced on the balls of her feet and extended the bundle.

He lifted an eyebrow and cautiously took it, shaking out a jacket of dark blue leather.

"Hope blue is still your favorite color," she said shyly. She'd wracked her memories for details about him as a kid, and that was one thing that'd come back.

Gered stared at it a long moment, rubbing a thumb over the smooth leather. "Yeah." His voice caught a little, and he kept his chin down as he shrugged into the coat. He stood, tugging it into place.

It fit almost perfectly, long enough to cover his wrists. "Thanks." The blue in his eyes shone a little brighter.

She quirked a grin and held out the next part—a gray dust scarf.

"You're a drifter now. Gotta look the part."

His smiles were coming a little faster and more genuine with every passing day. He let her step close and wrap it around his neck, showing him the folds and the knot which would keep it in place and still allow for it to be pulled up around his face if needed.

"Last thing." She extended a new pair of sunglasses.

He slipped them into the jacket pocket. "Where'd you get all this stuff?"

"Worked, made a few deals." She shrugged. That was life as a drifter. She smiled again. "Good thing you're back up on your feet so you can start pulling your weight on the trip."

He huffed a laugh, and picked up his remaining thigh holster, buckling it around his left leg. The hospital forbade weapons, so she'd stashed theirs safely in her bags or in the truck.

"Ready?" she asked.

He nodded. She picked up the bag of med supplies and led the way back into the bright sunlight. Overnight the air had cooled, hints of orange and red tingeing the trees planted throughout the town. Fall had arrived. They'd have a good ride east.

She grabbed his rifle from the truck, and tossed the keys to the hospital guard. She'd traded the truck in exchange for most of Gered's care, using her winnings from the races to cover the rest.

Gered slid the rifle into the bike holster, but still stared at it.

Laramie swung her leg over the seat of her bike. "They got the tracker off before we left. I double-checked everything to make sure."

He nodded, stooping slightly to brush his hand along the engine panel she'd replaced the road-torn metal with. Finally, he settled onto the seat, pulling his gloves on carefully over his hands, and tucking the sunglasses into place.

Their motorcycles roared to life. *Time to go home.*

Laramie glanced at where Gered rode beside her. Though, this time, it felt like she was bringing a little bit of home back with her. She grinned, and shifted gears, leaning into the wind.

She was ready to leave the dust and desert behind. She was ready to be home.

EPILOGUE

Beeping. Murmured voices. Spikes of pain as he tried to move. He'd kill her. He'd pull her apart piece by piece.

Rosche opened his eyes.

The patchwork ceiling of his med center stared back. The beeping continued, but the voices fell still. He lifted his head from the pillow.

Moshe and Barns inched closer to his bed.

"Sir." Moshe dipped his head.

Rosche had to work his mouth a moment before sound came out. "How long?" he rasped.

"A week, sir."

A breath hissed between his teeth.

"Where are they?"

Barns and Moshe exchanged a glance. Rage filled Rosche.

"Gone, sir. We felt the terms of the challenge had to be up-held," Moshe said. "And the drifter only gave us your location after we did."

Little bitch. Rosche tried to lift his left arm. Pain ended the attempt. But relief he hadn't expected crashed through him at the sight of his fingers still able to move.

The relief faded as he felt a strip of numbness lurking along his arm.

"How bad?"

"The doc was able to stitch up your arm, but some of the nerves were severed too bad. You needed massive blood transfusions. And a busted knee." Barns gave the report.

Rosche frowned. The injuries meant weeks down. He managed to lever himself up.

"Gered still alive?"

Moshe jerked another nod. "He was when they pulled out of here. But he didn't look good."

The boy was a survivor. He was still alive. Rosche felt it in his bones. The drifter would pay for what she'd done to him. He'd pull her apart piece by piece and make Gered watch before doing the same to him.

"Track them down. And when I'm ready to ride, we'll go after them. No one runs. No one."

ACKNOWLEDGEMENTS

I've been so excited to write these ever since I started writing the first draft of TCAD and knew it was going to be a wild and fun ride.

Always much love to my parents and siblings for their support and love. Even though, Mom, you said you haven't been able to read it yet because the first few pages made you think of too many small towns around our west Texas home. Thanks for confirming that I'd gotten the descriptions and setting vibes just right.

Thanks to Paige for being the best friend I could have ever asked for. Your constant support and friendship and daily debriefs to keep us sane during lockdowns and pandemic have meant the world to me. I could not have made it without you.

To my beta readers—Kate, Selina, Jenni, and Jessica: thanks for all the fangirling and DMs and feedback to help me make this book into something special. Andy, thanks for the feedback and mechanic tips to help me sound like I knew what I was talking about. Y'all are all seriously amazing, and I've been so blessed by friendship and your excitement for this book!

Thanks to the Inkwell for support and chats and encouragement! Love you ladies!

Probably should also thank the Starbucks by the house and my work computer for getting me through lots of hours and word counts to churn out a first draft in record time. Lots of salted caramel mochas were consumed in the drafting of this book and this is what got me hooked on coffee. No regrets.

When I wrote this book, I had a hope for it, and that came true with the contract with Uncommon Universes Press being willing to help me genre jump a little and bring you this action packed duology.

I'm feeling a little uncharacteristically emotional as I'm writing this. The Drifter series is a book that taught me how to fall in love with writing and wild stories again. They carry bits of myself in them, like all my stories do, but this one is more me than anything, I think, filled with action and tropes and characters I have fallen in love with. I hope you do too. Thanks, reader, for sticking with me on this journey, and if you're new to my stories with this one, welcome.

ABOUT THE AUTHOR

C. M. Banschbach is a native Texan and would make an excellent Hobbit if she weren't so tall. She's a pizza addict, a multi-faceted fangirl, and a firm believer in being authentic—even if it means acting like a dork sometimes! When not writing fantasy stories packed full of adventure and snark, she works as a pediatric physical therapist where she happily embraces the fact that she never actually has to grow up.

Connect with her on social media:
Facebook @cmbanschbach
Instagram @cmbanschbach
Twitter @cmbanschbach

CPSIA information can be obtained
at www.ICGtesting.com
Printed in the USA
LVHW070814180623
750037LV00002B/116